Pestilence's Judgment

Pestilence's Judgment
Arrival of the Four Horsemen book two

This book is a work of fiction. Unless otherwise indicated, any and all of the names, characters, businesses, places, events, and incidents in this book are either the product of the author's imagination or used in a fictitious manner. Any resemblance to a real location, persons living or dead, or actual events is purely coincidental.

Contact information: marcellevalentine.com/

Published in the United States of America by Medusa Publishing.

Medusa Publishing is a registered trade name of Medusa Publishing, LLC.

First Edition 2023

Never lose who you are because you are beautiful!

Pestilence's Judgment

Arrival of the Four Horsemen Series

Marcelle Valentine

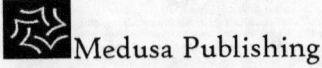

Medusa Publishing

Table of Contents

Chapter One: And So It Begins

> ***And I will bring a sword against you that will execute the vengeance of the covenant; when you are gathered together within your cities, I will send pestilence among you, and you shall be delivered into the hand of the enemy. Leviticus 26:25***

~ *Death Before The First Seal is Broke* ~

AFTER MONTHS OF WAITING, OUR CREATOR has finally granted me passage to give my recommendations. His refusal to see me over these long months is my punishment for rejecting his call. Do I regret it? No. Would I do it again if it meant I could spend more time with Avalon? Absolutely.

"This is your counsel?"

"Yes, I believe humanity is worth saving. It is my wish for you to leave my brothers asleep." I thought I had failed him, but now, seeing the grin covering his face, I suppose this was the outcome he had always hoped for. Could that be possible? Was it all nothing more than a test for one of his riders?

"It pleases me to hear you say this."

"Surely we are not just to take the word of one rider." Michael may be talking to our creator, but his glaring eyes are focused on me. We have never been friends; however, this is the first time I sensed outright disdain from him. Michael, the archangel many mortals view as their protector from all the evils in their world, would prefer they be removed from our father's grace.

"This is precisely what we will do; after all, it was the mission I sent him on. Who better to judge them than the being who carries their souls to their higher existence?"

Michael bowed his head respectfully as he replied, "Of course, Father."

With this matter now decided, our father turns his attention back to me and asks, "So tell me, what did you find most appealing about humanity?"

Avalon's smiling face flashes through my thoughts as she lies beneath me. The light in her eyes, her lips against mine. I ache to be with her once again, to ride across the countryside, for her to show me the world as she sees it, but this is not to be. For the first time in my long existence, I lie to my father when I say, "Many things, although I found their capacity to care about their fellow humans the most appealing."

The smile he wore before grows, and his eyes shine with approval. It would appear this is also what he finds truly endearing. He asks questions for the next several hours, and I answer them as best as possible. I do not mention Avalon for fear of what others may do if they realize she is the one who convinced me of these things, not humanity as a whole. One soul, one perfect being who has become extremely important to me.

On the other hand, Michael seems unimpressed and causes our father to laugh when he snorts as I explain some of their customs. His smile certainly seems to imply my father's delight regarding my council. One second, I am describing what a pear tastes like, and the next, our creator is leaping to his feet. The smile he wore falls away as his eyes slip closed, and I experience a tearing sensation within my chest.

"It cannot be," he mutters.

"Father?"

"Son, I fear the circumstances have changed. I apologize, but you must return to your previous post."

"I don't understand," I say, pressing my hand against my chest to ease the pressure building.

"The first of the four seals is no more."

"That's not possible. I don't understand. How could this happen?"

"The seal is broken, and the time for my riders has arrived." Shit, the pain was one of my brothers waking. The pull is our first sign our time grows near. The time for the horsemen has come. He created us for one purpose: spreading disease, waging wars, destroying their resources, and reaping their souls as an ultimate insult.

"Why would you do this?"

"I was not the one who had the lamb break it."

"Who? Who so carelessly broke it, and who is the one that encouraged it," I snap, furious Avalon's life is in danger because of their actions.

"The great Earl of hell disguised as a mortal. It was Raum who deceived the lamb."

"How?"

"He told the lamb it was the only way."

"Why would this lamb," I spit out the moniker, furious their actions may lead to her end. "...believe such folly?"

"To save someone."

"But of course they did. Permit me a guess. Was it a lover or a child?" My father's only answer is shaking his head as he gives me a sad smile.

"In the hope it would save a friend the lamb thought of as family."

"They unleash our wrath upon the world to save one mortal. Forgoing all others?"

"I imagine it is because the lamb had already lost the only other being she loved. You." My eyes snap to my father, confused by what he just revealed.

"I'm sorry to tell you this, my son, but the lamb who woke your brother is Avalon." He knows about Avalon. I should have known I could not hide her from him.

"No."

"A task she acquired only because of your affinity for her. She alone will now decide the destiny of her world, the one who controls the fate of humanity. Something Raum realized all too quickly. He tricked her into believing the seal held the magic to save a friend. And now your brother Pestilence has been summoned. His extermination will begin."

"So you see Thanatos," Michael sneers. "The only one to blame for her misfortune is you."

"Send me back," I beg, stepping closer to him.

"No."

"No?"

"It is too late. You will only return when the lamb calls you there. When the final seal is broken, and when you will reap their souls."

"NO!" I cannot restrain my fury. Our creator stands. A sad certainty settles across his face before turning his back on me as he retreats to his sanctuary.

"Father, you cannot ask me to do this." He does not acknowledge me or my supplications.

"Father." My pleading holds no sway and does not deter him from leaving me to deal with the emotions coursing through me. I realize his inclination is to allow this atrocity to continue, but I will not permit it to stand. As I move closer to him, his archangel Michael blocks my path.

"I will not do what you ask." This, at last, halts his retreat. His divine creations do not rebuff his commands.

"You have no choice in this matter, rider. You will do your duty; what he created you for," my father's trusted advisor snaps.

"If I have only learned one thing from my time in the mortal world, it's this, Michael.... There is always a choice."

"Not in this. The world will fall to darkness; humanity will all pay for your mortal's mistakes. She will watch as the world falls around her. Crumbles because of the choices she made. And when you are called forth, her soul will be the last you reap so the lamb can witness the end, knowing she is the one who caused this."

Bringing my eyes up, I lock them on Michael. He may be the leader of the warriors in heaven, but he does not command me. My unyielding gaze informs him of his mistake, making him wisely retreat as I advance.

"I will not," I calmly declare. I know this is one order I have no intention of following. Spinning, I storm away from them.

"Thanatos, you will return immediately; your creator has not yet released you." Michael can bellow all he wishes because I will not stand by and merely watch as Avalon suffers.

"Thanatos!"

I need to find a way back to her, but until I do, Avalon will need my brothers to protect her. She may be humanity's last hope of surviving this.

Chapter Two: The White Rider… Bringer of Scourge and Disease

> *Now I saw when the Lamb opened one of the seals, and I heard one of the four living creatures saying with a voice like thunder, "Come and see." And I looked, and behold, a white horse. He who sat on it had a bow, and a crown was given to him, and he went out conquering and to conquer. Revelation 6:1-2.*

~ Pestilence Early Winter 2024~

I ALWAYS KNEW THE DAY WOULD come when my father's judgment would prompt the little lamb to break the seal. The day when my long slumber would end. The day I would be called forward to carry out my assigned task.

A mortal who is more shepherd than lamb was always charged to be the one who would decide when our time was here. They alone hold a responsibility many would be incapable of seeing through. After all, they are the souls who will begin it all. Our father may be the one who calls upon the mortal who is tasked with this heavy burden, yet it is by their actions alone that the end of days begins. When the little lamb cracks our seal, breaking the chains that hold us, it releases us from our long slumber, and humanity's extermination begins.

For most of my existence, I have observed them from afar. Their crimes, their atrocities, their fall from grace. But I have also witnessed their successes, their fortitude, and their capacity to love. It is the last of these traits I am most intrigued by. To watch as one soul finds another and they forge a bond few can tear apart. The saddest part is that the ones who do the tearing are often the very souls who declare their love to another. Promising forever, only to toss it all away at the first opportunity of something they covet more.

It is the act of a few who spoil the many, and once the rot has set in, my brothers and I are not far behind. As I prepare to descend to carry out our creator's judgment, the only one of us never permitted to rest, my brother Thanatos, appears before me.

"Pestilence."

"Thanatos? What are you doing here, brother? Shouldn't you be waiting for the next soul to ascend?"

"Don't go."

"What? You know this is not our way. The seal has been broken, the lamb—"

"Was tricked. She believed what she was doing would save her friend. She didn't know it would bring the riders to her world."

"Brother, you know this is not possible. The lamb can only locate the seal when the time to call us forth is decided."

"She didn't find it."

"Then who?"

"Raum... and he will pay dearly for his interference."

"If this were true, why has our father not called me back to my long slumber?"

"I don't know."

"I'm sorry there is no choice to be had, brother. He created us for this task, one I must see through."

Thanatos grabs my arm, his wings flaring behind him. "Then I beseech you to stay your bow. Call back your disease, if only for a time. See for yourself. Judge them firsthand and allow her a chance to show you what she has shown me."

"Which is?"

"They are worthy."

"Who is this lamb to you, brother?"

"She is the one who swayed him from his task. With a swish of her hips—"

"Michael, if you value your existence, I suggest you still the wag of your tongue," Thanatos snaps as he steps towards him.

"Or you will pass judgment on me?" He asks as his wings extend behind him. When Thanatos refuses to back down, Michael reaches for the sword strapped to his back. Thanatos has no fear of the angel he is facing. Or any other creature, for that matter. Our father created him with one purpose in mind.... Death. He is a means to an end, and none of us, even my father's most trusted warrior, is a match for my brother.

Taking Thanatos by the arm, I give him the only oath my existence permits. "I will not halt my task because, as you are already aware, once the lamb breaks the seal, there is no turning back."

Michael's gloating smile releases a burst of fury within me. He celebrates too soon. Surely he must understand that I will do as my brother has asked if there is any way to honor his request without ignoring my reason for existing. It is also in seeing my brother's face upon hearing my decree that I deliver the rest. "And should I find the little lamb, I will stay my hand to allow her the opportunity to show me what she shared with you."

For the briefest of seconds, I find something I never expected to see: pain twisting my brother's features. My decree pains him. I do not understand why. Is this not what he wanted me to say? Is this not the promise he had asked for? Just as I prepare to query him about it, the expression is gone as he nods his head. I do not miss his eyes falling away from mine.

"You cannot do that," Michael hisses as he advances toward me.

"And you do not have the power to stop me. I suggest you fly away to the safety of our father before I release my brother, or you may discover what it means to meet our judgment."

"If you do this, horseman, I will make it my mission to see you live to regret it." He does not wait for my response, fading away as I continue assessing my brother.

"Thanatos, is there something I should know?"

"Ava — the lamb, she is someone I.... I mean, she is.... Never mind, I have made my request, and you have given me your word. I will trouble you no further, brother."

His powerful wings launch him into the sky, carrying him far from the question I am certain he knew I would ask. I watch until he vanishes from view. After sighing a frustrated groan, I turn my attention back to the reason the lamb woke me.

With no one left to stop me, I place my bow across my shoulder, click my tongue to call forth my horse, and prepare to travel to the realm where the sons of Adam and daughters of Eve await the first of four riders.

*****

The sound of thunder and the wind whipping through the trees marked my arrival. When my brother first arrived here, the souls of this realm fought against him. When our creator called him home, they believed they had beaten him, doing the impossible. What the souls of this realm do not know is that once our seal has been broken, the day the lamb releases us, they cannot defeat us. Unlike when our father sent my brother here the first time when he is called forth by the lamb, he will arrive with the full use of his powers. He will be unstoppable.

I made Thanatos a promise, one I will honor, but until the lamb reveals who they are, I have a purpose and cannot return until the task is complete.

It has been centuries since I last roamed this realm. The last time I was here, the world moved slower. The mortals still praised their creator, regardless of what name they called him. Things were different back then, and with all the advances they made during my long sleep, they forgot what they should have valued most; people, not the things surrounding them. Yet they learned their advanced technology meant little when Thanatos removed it with only a fourth of his powers and a simple snap of his fingers. Imagine what will happen when he returns at full strength.

This is not to say they should not fear me or what I am capable of. I have two ways to take their lives... by bow or plague. For the ones who are cursed to meet their end by my black death, they quickly realize that dying by my bow is a mercy.

I stayed in an abandoned farmhouse for weeks as I slowly adjusted to this new form, with the smell of musty furniture and old wood permeating the air around me. While we sleep, we are more spirit than form, unconfined by the restraints of our wakened appearance. It is not until I sense my brother's distress that I mount my horse to begin my journey. It seems he urgently wants me to seek out the lamb.

Unfortunately, it appears humanity learned nothing from my brother's time here since several are now blocking my path forward.

"Get off the horse, asshole."

"No."

"Listen, fucker, we can do this the easy way, or we can do this the hard way," each of the men behind him nocks an arrow and levels their bow at me.

"Last chance. Get off the horse. Toss the bow over to me. Drop to your knees and put your hands behind your head."

"I do not kneel to any but our father."

"Well, that's not going to work for me, pansy-ass daddy's boy. So what's it going to be?"

Looking from one man to the next, I see the fear in their eyes, the sweat beading on their brow, and the slight tremor of their hands. I am vaguely aware the one leading this group is still talking, but when he moves toward me, I calmly declare, "And so it begins."

Chapter Three: Is This What I'm Trying To Save

And there shall be signs in the sun, and in the moon, and in the stars; and upon the earth distress of nations, with perplexity; the sea and the waves roaring. Men's hearts failing them for fear, and for looking after those things which are coming on the earth: for the powers of heaven shall be shaken. Luke 21:25-26.

~ *Avalon Early Winter 2024* ~

THE SECOND THE RAVEN FLEW AWAY, the sky turned gray, and the wind whipped around me viciously; I knew the mistake I had just made. Hell, calling this a mistake is like equating a nuclear missile launch as nothing more than a thumb slip. I just sentenced all of humanity to extermination.

How could I be so dumb? Dumb doesn't even begin to cover what I am.

"No, no-no-no-no. Oh God, please tell me I didn't do what I think I just did." It can't be. There is no way this was one of those damn seals holding the horsemen at bay. When Death said seal, I imagined a metal door welded shut with yellow caution tape around it. Not a fucking drop of wax on an old piece of paper. How in the hell didn't this thing crack open a long time ago?

It is similar to Pandora's Box when every sign screams don't open it; you just know some asshole has to take a peek. The problem is that I'm the asshole in this scenario, and I have no damn idea if I just released one or all of them.

Dropping my eyes to the parchment to study the word, I can no longer deny what this means. My every fear is realized the instant I say the word out loud because it erases all doubts about the mistake I just made.

"*Pestilentia.*"

The word doesn't look English but bottoms to dollars; it says Pestilence. Damn it. I didn't even crack the right one. How could I be so stupid?

"FUCK!"

How could I let this jackass talk me into this? Talk me into releasing one of the riders I was trying so hard to prevent from being released against humanity. Jesus Christ, Avalon, you know better. You have, or should I say had, better sense than this.

Lightning cracks, and if the thundering boom is anything to go by, I would say the world is about to meet another horseman. But this time, it's not to determine if we are worthy of forgiveness. The decision has been made, and he is here to pass judgment.

*****

I have been traveling for weeks with no idea where Suki is. If I have any hope in hell of stopping what I started, I will need help, and it has to be from people I trust. Lord knows, as of late, my judge of character has been lacking.

On the upside, I haven't heard any news about another horseman wreaking havoc on the world. So either he hasn't been sent, my horseman somehow managed to stop it, or he hasn't made it this far north yet. Regardless, I need to know for sure, and no matter how much I call out for him or pray for him to return, he hasn't since the day he told me to find Suki. I realize most people would have thrown their hands up in the air long ago. Declare this task beyond impossible. Mourn the loss of someone they loved. But in case you haven't figured this out yet, I am not like other people. I don't have it in me to quit, and I certainly cannot fail humanity since I am the entire reason they now face another horseman.

So I journey both night and day until I can walk no more and collapse on the side of the road. My only protection is the dagger gripped against my chest as I let sleep carry me away.

And this is how it continues until the weather has turned frosty, and I fear I may never find her. Worse yet, if a storm hits now, I know I won't have a horseman to shelter me from the cold until I find suitable accommodations.

It was not until this morning, when I woke up with frost covering me, that I realized I either need to find her or give up, at least until winter is behind me. As disturbed as I am by the shift in temperature, I almost piss my pants when I look up and discover a raven watching me. Without delay, I throw the blade, and it instantly finds its mark killing the bird.

Not some prick who tricked me, not a god or a demon, just some poor random-ass bird who was in the wrong place at the wrong time.

"That's just great, Avalon. In addition to killing off all of humanity, now you have decided to take out the entire populace of our feathered friends as well. For Christ's sake, get it together. Not every damn bird is the asshole who betrayed me," I mutter as I lay there panting, hoping to reign in my racing heart. Knowing the creature I just killed is lying not fifteen feet from me with my dagger buried in his chest, I can't help but feel like I'm failing everyone.

"Tsk, tsk, what do we have here?" the unexpected voice startles me enough to get me moving. My joints don't move as fast as I would like since they are still trying to shake off the cold that has settled deep into my bones, which allows this guy the opportunity to get too close for comfort.

My eyes immediately shoot toward the raven, still impaled with my dagger. The only damn one I have. Unfortunately, the new arrival shifts his gaze to where my eyes are also focused, and he does not hesitate to block me from my goal.

"Ahh-ah-ah. Now don't go and do anything foolish."

"As opposed to waiting around for you to do something stupid?" I hear him snort as I roll to grab the blade. My fingers land on the hilt the same instant I feel his hands twist in my coat. He yanks me away before I can get a grip on it.

Shit! Without a weapon, I don't have a snowball's chance in hell of fending him off. He's a foot taller and outweighs me by eighty pounds. Rolling to my back, I kick my foot out, smashing it into my mark, which causes him to cry out as he bends over to cradle his throbbing man bits. The more pressing issue is that it threw him off balance, and when he leans over, he tumbles straight on top of me. Okay, this wasn't how I envisioned this whole thing playing out.

Hurling my hand toward the direction I believe the dagger-impaled raven might be, I came up with a whole lot of nothing. Not a rock, not a branch, not even a damn feather. If I don't find it soon, I know his retaliation will come swiftly, and his retribution will be slow.

Flailing my arm around, it lands in the thick puddle of what I can only imagine is blood from my first victim. I say first because once the horseman arrives, everyone who falls by his hand will be as much my victim as his.

I realize my time is up when his hand wraps around my throat, but when his fist impacts my jaw, he removes all the remaining fight I had in me.

*****

Bound, blindfolded, and tied to his horse, I stumble along, praying the horse doesn't take offense and kick out his hind legs because if he does, there's no way I'll be getting up from something like that any too quick. If at all.

"Where are you taking me?" I demand.

"You'll find out soon enough."

"Fuck that; tell me now."

"You know you're lucky to be alive after the shit you pulled. If you want to stay that way, I recommend you shut your fucking mouth, bitch."

Despite my best efforts to keep him talking, he remains silent, and with the blindfold securely tied around my head, I can't tell what direction we are traveling in, making it impossible to figure out where he plans to take me. It's not until I hear the sounds of cheers followed by cries I know we have arrived wherever our destination was.

The asshole on the horse spurs, jolting the poor creature forward and causing me to stumble. My knees slam painfully against the ground. I try to get my feet under me, but I only end up falling again. If the feel of air passing by my face was anything to go by, I would have to say my head came dangerously close to meeting the hooves of the horse now dragging me behind it. All the while, the asshole in the saddle laughs at my predicament.

By the time the horse stops, I'm choking on the dust he kicked up. The flesh on my wrist is red and raw from the ropes, and I can feel blood coating the knees of my jeans. Not willing to allow any of the hooting idiots surrounding us the pleasure of seeing me like this, I struggle to my feet, wipe the dirt caked to my face with the back of my hand, and wait for whatever comes next.

"I see you brought us some new entertainment." I feel fingers swipe along my arm, making me jerk away from the unwanted contact. My reaction is swift as I slam my head in the direction I hope the jackass is standing. His laugh tells me he's moved off somewhere to my right.

"Feisty."

"Yeah, the bitch tried to kill me."

"Hell, that's nothing new. We've all considered doing it on more than one occasion."

"Shut up, fat ass." This begins a heated argument among them, allowing me the slimmest of chances to get these damn restraints off. The problem is, no matter how much I twist, turn, or pull, I cannot break loose from them.

The fat ass shoves the dipshit who started all this, escalating this entire situation. Frustrated by the whole interaction, I throw my head back, murmuring, "If you are coming, now would be a good time to do it."

"What the fuck are you saying over there?"

Even with my blindfold, I know they are directing the question to me. Not willing to let these bastards think they intimidate me, I square my shoulders before turning in the direction of the one who made the inquiry. "The horseman. I said if he was going to come, now would be a good time to make his appearance. Actually, a great fucking time because listening to you idiots is worse than anything he can do."

"You really are stupid, aren't you? The fucking horseman has been gone for months. So if you were hoping he would come in and save your sorry ass, you're dumberer than I thought."

"Dumberer? Are you fucking serious right now? The word you're looking for is dumber, not dumberer. And I'm not talking about Thanatos, dumbass; I'm talking about Pestilence."

"Who the fuck is Thanatos?"

"And you call me dumb. Thanatos is Death, who happens to be the horseman you have been referring to."

"Then who the hell is Pestilence?"

"Do you know what a bible is?" I snap before replying, "Pestilence is the first horseman of the apocalypse."

"Shows how much you know since the first horseman was already here and got his ass kicked back to his own world. By one guy. A badass motherfucker and someone I would love to shake hands with."

If I was not so damn irritated by the conversation, I might actually laugh before telling him how friggin wrong he is. Unfortunately, the best I can manage is a snort followed by my single-worded question. "Really?"

"Yes, little girl.... Really!"

"This just proves how fucking dumb you are since Pestilence—Not Thanatos—is the first horseman released. Thanatos, more commonly known as Death, was here to measure our value, not judge us. Which I can guarantee is not what Pestilence is coming to do. Fuckin' idiots."

"And you know this how?" This voice is unfamiliar, and when I refuse to respond, he rips the blindfold off, snarling, "How. Do. You. Fucking. Know this?"

Blinking against the fading sunlight, I tell him the truth, "Because I called him here."

The guy's jaw twitches before he pulls his arm back. I have just enough time to brace myself before he hits me.

*****

The feel of lips skimming along my cheeks causes my eyes to flutter. My heart flips in my chest when I force my eyes to focus on the man hovering over me.

"Thanatos?" he pulls back just enough to smile down at me before my lips are back on his. I kiss him as if my very life depended on it. His hand roams over my breast, along my stomach to the button of my jeans.

The soft whimper he draws out of me comes down to one thing... the fact I've missed him more than he will ever understand. Missed his touch, his lips, missed the deep baritone of his husky voice. The day he left, he took everything I had just started to like about this life... but now he's here, his fingers are skimming along my skin, and his kiss is stealing the very breath I breathe.

Shifting to give him better access, he dips his hand into my pants, flicking my clit painfully. Jerking away from his unyielding touch, he yanks my shirt up as he bites down on the stiff peak of my erect nipple.

His touch is not the same as I remember from our time together. It's more aggressive; his hands don't feel right, his mouth on my breast is all wrong, and when I open my eyes, this time Thanatos is standing in the distance. I can see rage covering his face, and his mouth is moving, but I cannot make out any of the words he's saying. Blinking to clear the confusion when I open them again, Thanatos has moved closer and has a man gripped by his throat.

Another painful bite to my breast as his exploration of me is anything but tender. This doesn't seem right. Thanatos wouldn't hurt me the way this man is.

"Stop! This isn't like you. Why are you doing this to me?" I groan as I squirm to get out from under him. As my panic begins to escalate, I feel a shift. The oppressive weight he used to hold me down is gone, along with the pain. The sudden change forces me to focus. When I glance up this time, I find the beautiful tender eyes of the man I love looking back, and this time when he speaks, I have no problem hearing him, "Avalon, wake up."

"What?"

"You need to open your eyes," he tells me as he sweeps a lock of hair from my face. "Open your eyes and see the truth, Apple."

When pain accompanies the bite this time, I snap my eyes open to find that the man I thought was my horseman is anything but. I slam my fist against his head, but the action does not deliver the result I had hoped for since my thoughts still feel fuzzy from the previous assault.

The asshole on top of me laughs as he pins my hands painfully over my head.

"Don't pretend like you weren't getting off on it too. Because the whole fucking camp heard you. So why don't you go back to moaning and grinding against me until I finish up here?" He returns his attention to my exposed breast without waiting for a response. I continue to struggle under him and find an opportunity to stop him when he releases my arms to pull down his pants. The ground rumbles, and for a fleeting second, I wonder if the first horseman has arrived. The asshole on top of me must have felt it too, because he lifts his head to inspect our surroundings.

The voice of my horseman carries to me as a whisper in the wind, but his words are enough to spur me into action.

"Above you, Apple, your salvation lies within your reach...."

Flinging my arm over my head, a wave of relief washes through me when my hand lands on a log large enough for me to use as a weapon. Bucking my hips to knock him off me as much as disorient him, I don't waste the precious seconds this action has granted me as I slam the log against his head. When he collapses to the ground next to me, I don't hesitate as I leap to my feet to hit him again. But I don't stop with one hit; I continue until I am confident he will not get up. Standing over him, panting wildly, I am startled by a voice behind me.

"A?" Spinning, I discover the one person I wasn't sure I would ever find again.

"Suki?"

"Is that really you, Avalon?" Her voice is thick from the emotions building within her.

"Where the hell have you been, Suk? I've looked everywhere for you."

"Well, I can sure as shit tell you I haven't been hanging out in bandit camps." We look at each other for several seconds before she rushes over to where I stand to pull me into her embrace.

"What happened to you, A?" Thoughts of the last several months flood me, but it's not until I see his face that my breath catches. "A?"

"Learning how to live again," I whisper.

"Where's the horseman?" clenching her tighter against me, the hurt of losing him fills me up and threatens to overflow.

"Gone."

"You beat him? You sent him back to wherever the hell he came from?" Her excitement that I may have hurt my horseman has me choking back a sob. I know Suki doesn't understand. How could she? The last time we spoke was when I told her I was leaving. She doesn't know how close we became or that he somehow made me fall in love with him, and as much as he changed me, I changed him too. I want to tell her how wrong we were about him, but after the events of the day, I don't think I have it in me to convince anyone of anything. Still, I will not allow her to think I killed him.

"No, he left to save us." Suki pulls back to look into my eyes, glistening with all the emotions I have been burying for months. I know she has questions, but she must sense how much I do not want to talk about this since she does not press me for those answers right now.

"Did you do this?" she asks as she kicks the dead guy lying at our feet. When I nod, she grins before declaring, "So badass."

We both stand in the middle of the destroyed bandit camp, laughing like we've lost our damn minds.

Which, by the way, is still up for debate.

Chapter Four: Perfect

~ Greer Late Winter 2025~

RUNNING TO KEEP UP WITH THE little ball of energy scampering away from me, I laugh as I tell him, "I'm going to catch you, Renny."

His sweet giggles are like music to my ears. This is the first time since the thunderstorm he hasn't been clinging to my legs.

Since the world took a hard right turn, he has had to learn how to cope with the way things are now. It took centuries to advance our technologies to where we were two years ago, and only a few brief minutes for a being people keep claiming is one of the fabled horsemen to show us how insignificant we really are. Or should I say claimed, since everything I keep hearing is that someone finally defeated the rider and sent him back to wherever he came from.

"Gotcha," I laugh as I scoop Renny up to pepper his face with kisses. He responds by forming flattened O's with his hands and repeatedly tapping his fingers together.

"You want more, huh?" he squirms to break my hold on him so we can continue our game. The instant his feet touch the ground, his little legs work overtime as he tries to put as much distance between us as possible. Watching him run away from me, I can't help but think how far he's come over the last two years. As the world regressed, Renny bloomed.

~ *Flashback Spring 2022~*

March

Dealing with this particular mom is nothing short of a lesson in patience. Trying to hold my temper in check has quickly become an exercise in futility. She insists on meeting every Friday afternoon so she can yell at me about her perceived lack of progress Wren has made. Her words, not mine. I think his improvements are leaps and bounds over where he was six months ago; sadly, she doesn't see it. What's most frustrating about this entire situation is I would love to be Renny's mom. He's the sweetest little boy I have ever had the pleasure of having in my class.

"Lynn, you have to understand Wren is trying his best."

"I know my son is. My question is whether or not you are doing your job."

"There's no magic answer here."

"He's been coming to this place for six months, and he's no different today than the first day he walked through that damn door."

"That's not true, Lynn; he's learned to do many things independently."

"I have a maid to clean. I don't need him to learn how to pick up a few toys.

"He's learning how to interact with other children—"

"Wren doesn't need to learn how to play with other kids. He needs to know how to fucking talk. That's what I'm paying you to do. Teach him how to talk, eat by himself, dress himself, not how to play with other fucking kids."

"He has to learn how to do all of these things."

"Are you calling my kid stupid?" She screams as she leaps from the chair.

Lifting my hands, I know I need to get control of this situation before she does what she normally does, including acting like a petulant child and throwing the classroom supplies all over the place. Last week I was here an hour after she stormed out just to put everything away.

"I never said that. The truth of the matter is Wren is a very smart little boy, but Lynn, he's autistic."

"You don't think I know what my son is?"

"Of course you do, but you have to understand he doesn't process things the same way a child without autism does. He has to learn how to do many of the things other neurotypical children know how to do."

"I want to hear my son call me mother," her confession shocks me, but not how you would think. Most parents tell me their only wish is to hear their child say, daddy or mommy. Never in all my years as a teacher have I heard a parent say mother or father. "and I want it to happen by next week, or I'll pull him out of this joke of a program."

"First off, this is a preschool, not a program, and second I can't make promises when Renny will—"

"My. Son's. Name. Is. Wren. Not Renny."

"My apologies. Wren will talk when he's ready," I retort, allowing my frustration to seep out with my response.

"Just do your damn job," she gripes as she storms out of the classroom, pulling Wren behind her. Taking a deep breath, I need to learn how to handle her better. One good bit of news is I won't have to deal with her again until next week.

April

"Go on now, Wren. Go sit at the table like a big boy," Lynn says while she pushes him into the class. The preschool also functions as a daycare for some children. The director did this to cater to some clientele, like Wren's mom. We open at seven in the morning, and when Lynn drops him off, she normally meets us at the door, practically dumping him on our doorstep before scurrying away to do whatever she deems more important. If you haven't figured this out, I won't be putting this vile woman up for a mother-of-the-year award for the foreseeable future.

I don't know what happened, but I have noticed Wren has regressed in the last several weeks. Lynn is noticeably cold when she drops him off or picks him up. I think this woman could benefit from some counseling. She has to learn how to cope with having an autistic child; the sooner she does, the better off he will be.

"Ms. McNealy."

"Ms. Harvey."

Our interaction has diminished to little more than minimal conversation and simple platitudes. Had I known what was about to happen, I would have pushed her ass out the door faster.

The first thing that occurred was the lights flickered before going out altogether. And not just lights; all electronics mysteriously stopped. Cars, trucks, heck, even the battery-operated clock hanging above the welcome sign has ceased to function.

"What the hell?" Lynn says as she pulls her coat around her to block out the wind that has oddly whipped up.

"Has to be some kind of electromagnetic pulse," one dad named Mac announces as he repeatedly tries to turn on his phone.

"A what?"

"A burst of energy that can affect anything from computers to cars," he says, pointing at the cars holding their confused-faced drivers and passengers. "To electronics like smartwatches and cell phones." This time, he shows us both devices are dead.

"So, how long does this last?" Lynn asks as she pulls her phone out of her pocket, confirming what Mac already told her.

"I have no damn idea. Hell, until thirty seconds ago, I would have said there was no way something like this was possible, at least not to this magnitude."

"Give me a timeframe, not what you think." I can't believe she's treating someone she doesn't know like this.

"Lady, your guess is as good as mine. As I told you before, I thought it was all bullshit."

"So you're just talking to talk," Lynn huffs as she storms over towards her ninety-thousand-dollar paperweight, mumbling her car is not like the pieces of junk on the road. When she arrives, she repeatedly presses the button to unlock the door; when this doesn't work, she scowls before returning to where Mac and I are standing.

"May I use the school's phone?"

"I don't care, but if I had to venture a guess, I would have to say it probably isn't going to work—"

"Let's not speculate, shall we?" she snaps as she storms back into the school. I watch her until she disappears around the corner.

"How long before she figures out everything stopped working?" I ask Mac sarcastically.

"In three, two—"

"Damn it." She yells from the office.

"One," he says with a laugh.

Turning, I watch as people mill about, inspecting the objects that have been rendered useless. It seems they are just as perplexed by the turn this day has taken as we are. "Any idea what could cause this?"

"No." An explosion occurs somewhere in the distance, shattering the illusion that this is an isolated incident. Instinctually, I reach out to grab Mac's arm. I needed to reassure myself I wasn't alone as much as to confirm it was actually happening.

"Is that normal when one of those pulse things happen?"

"No damn idea, but we should head back inside until we know what the hell is going on. Surely the police or fire department will figure out a way to get directives out to the masses."

After four hours, most parents have had enough of Lynn's constant bitching about missing lunch with her holier-than-thou, hoity-toity Country Club friends. While most people are worried about their loved ones, this chick is concerned about her sixty-dollar-a-plate lobster and pear arugula salad. Yep, you heard me right, sixty damn dollars for a freaking salad.

By four o'clock, Mac announced he wanted to get home to see if his wife was waiting there. By six o'clock, Lynn looks much different from her normal, perfectly put-together self. Large chunks of her hair have fallen out of her tight bun, her clothes are a disheveled mess, and she has makeup running down her face. The only thing that could make her appear any worse would be lipstick on her teeth and one broken high heel. Although I admit, picturing her like this makes me chuckle, something I haven't done all day.

"Lynn, I think I'm going to lock up and—"

"I am not leaving my car here unattended, and I am certainly not walking home, so if you are about to suggest you want to lock up and go home, you can rethink that thought. We'll be on our way as soon as they figure out this mess and fix whatever caused all this foolishness."

Knowing we couldn't leave her and Wren in the school, I volunteered to stay, telling the administrator to go home to her family. Lord knows no one is waiting for me to come home.

That school became our safe haven over the next four days, with Wren's mom being a constant thorn in my side the entire time. The last night we were all together, Lynn stopped talking to me entirely when I yelled at her for taking the food I had scraped together for Wren. Pouting, she stretched out across the couch, leaving Wren and me to sleep on the floor again, and the next morning she was gone. She left only a half-hearted note reading; she couldn't deal with it or him if this was what our life had become.

I waited for Lynn to return for two days, but when people began looting the surrounding businesses, I decided we weren't safe there any longer. Having no other option nor idea what else to do, I scribbled a quick note in case she came back to tell her where she would find her son before I took him to my house.

The whole thing was extremely hard on Wren. I don't think he understood what happened to his mom and would start crying randomly. He had no more than settled into a routine when a gang moved into the neighborhood and began terrorizing the residents. My neighbors convinced me to leave with them, and everything was fine until we were separated from each other during a freak snowstorm.

This is how we ended up on our own, but more importantly, it's how Renny became my son.

*****

~ Greer Present Day ~

Renny ducks around an outcrop of trees, making me pick up my pace to catch up. The way the world is today, it's not safe for me, let alone my six-year-old autistic son.

"Wren, stop," I yell, sprinting round the corner, and my heart falls to my feet when I find someone looming over him.

Chapter Five: Push

~ Pestilence Late Winter 2025~

HOW MY BROTHER LIVED AMONG these humans without killing them is a testament to his patience. I long believed I was the calmer one out of the four of us, but having dealt with them over the last several weeks proves how wrong I am.

Starting with the cretins who demanded my meager possessions. I killed several of them with my bow but left the leader. This individual does not deserve a quick death. For him, I released my tendrils of plague. They leach out of me and slither along the ground before twisting their way up his body. He fought against them frantically. My brother War would declare almost valiantly, but in the end, he lost. The simple truth is you cannot fight against something so small you cannot see it. While the tendrils that reach out to my intended target are visible with each slash from their blade, they merely split, divide, and surge toward their waiting victim.

Watching my disease weaving around the leader's legs, I know it will only be a matter of hours before the first symptoms begin. And as he returns to the rest of his gang, the black death will have him firmly held within its grip. Unfortunately, those unlucky enough to come across him will fall to the same fate he does. They will also be infected by the time they realize anything is amiss. This only makes my job easier since everyone who chooses to run from my disease will only spread it to every soul they come across.

"What the fuck are you?" his yells make it easier for my rot to slip into his gaped mouth.

"I am Pestilence."

"It can't be." His response does not merit a reply. Tilting my head, I assess how much more I should give him before I recall the tendrils of death back. As the disease plunges down his throat, spreading to his vital organs, he crumples to the ground, racked by wave after wave of choking spasms followed by uncontrolled coughing spells. His face turns red, and tears stream from his eyes as he struggles to take his next breath. When I know he has taken enough to spell not only his demise but anyone who ventures near him, I retract my weapon before mounting my horse.

As I prepare to continue my trek, he pushes up to his hands and knees, coughing and gasping for the oxygen my disease deprived him of. This is the beginning of his end. He will be nothing more than a bloated, rotting corpse in a few short days. My judgment has been delivered, and until he speaks again, I thought I was done with this human.

"She said you'd come." He states each word between a sucked breath.

"She?"

"Some bitch rambling about how another horseman was coming."

"A mortal woman told you I would come?"

"Bitch called you by name."

"I have no name, human."

"You just said you're Pestilence."

Dismounting my horse, I stalk closer to him, curious if the one he speaks of could be the lamb my brother asked me to seek. "What the fuck did you do to me?"

"Nothing less than what you deserved. Now tell me about the woman."

"Fucking bitch killed my brother."

"Why?"

"Who the hell knows? One minute she's moaning, and the next, she split his fucking head open."

"Moaning?"

"Yeah, when my brother.... You know."

"I don't. Enlighten me."

"When he was getting ready to fuck her."

"An act she consented to?"

"She wanted it; we all heard her."

"Doubtful."

"I'm telling you, the whore was into it."

I am not sure who the lamb is exactly, nor do I fully understand what happened between her and my brother, but the expression he wore as we discussed finding her leads me to believe he would not approve of any who would disparage her the way this mortal has. With his throat firmly encased in my grip, I bring his face in line with mine.

"You will not speak of the lamb like this again."

"Lamb?"

"The human female."

Another round of coughing cripples him. "What did you do to me?"

Ignoring his question, I continue with one of my own, "You advised this woman said I was coming."

"Said she called you." His strangled response confirms the plague has taken hold.

"Where is she?"

"I don't fucking know where she is." His eyes grow wide when he swipes his hand under his nose and finds it covered in blood. "What the hell. Did you do this to me?"

"What am I?"

"One of the bloody fuckin horsemen of the apocalypse."

"Precisely. So what did you believe I would do to you? Is this all you know of the girl?"

"I'm going to die?" I think he finally understands what is happening here. As he paws at the blood oozing from his nose, I can hear the rhythm of his heart speed up.

"Yes, you will die. The girl?"

"Take it back, and I'll tell you everything I know."

"Tell me what I seek."

"Will you take it back?" When I do not offer a response, he must think I have agreed with his terms as he rushes to tell me what he believes will save his life. "It pissed me off when my brother claimed the bit—" the look I give him silences him as he corrects, "the chick. It was my turn to take one of them, but my brother decided he wanted her. When I heard her moaning, I was livid that he had taken someone so.... Willing. Listening to her made me.... You know."

While I understand the proclivities of most men's desires, I do not know why it holds so much appeal that one would force themself upon another. I do not hide my disdain for what he has confessed.

"What am I saying? You're a guy, so of course you understand how hearing a woman moaning can affect you." I make no attempt to correct him regarding me not being a man or understanding their baser needs. "...so I went into my tent to take care of it. I remember thinking I should be the one fucking her until I heard him yell. By the time I got my pants up, she was standing over him with a bat or something, and several others had invaded our camp. Since I didn't have a weapon, I bolted into the woods and hid until they left."

"She left with the others?"

"I think she knew them."

"This is everything you know?"

"Yeah. So will you take whatever the hell you did to me back now?"

"I am the spreader of disease. I do not recall what I have freely given," I say, shoving him away before I remount my horse. The lamb is close; I must be on my way if I wish to find her. Whistling, my horse continues down the path I traveled prior to the fool's interference. The only sounds remaining are from the man whose screams fill the air around me and the joyful song of the birds perched in the trees.

~ *Death* ~

I felt powerless as I observed the mortal descend upon Avalon, still lying unconscious from the one who struck her. I attempted to intercede when their debate began regarding which of them would claim her, but unfortunately, I am nothing more than an observer in their world at the moment. They are no more aware of my presence than the water droplets in the air surrounding them.

As he began removing her clothes, I reached out for my brother. If I cannot protect her, I need him to do it, and as much as it hurts me to think of her sharing herself with my brother, I cannot allow my feelings to interfere if it is the only way he will understand how special she is.

Even though he is not mortal, I can no more speak to him than I can with Apple when he is within their realm until he fully acclimates to his new form. But I can push, which is what I do. I force my will upon him, shoving until he mounts his horse and heads in her direction. I realize he will not arrive in time to save her from the man who intends to claim her now, but I cannot allow Avalon to suffer as she did when her parents gave her to Calvin.

With Pestilence en route, I return my attention to the man who will suffer for what he plans to do to her. I admit hearing the gentle moans I once elicited from her slipping from those soft lips causes my chest to ache, much in the same way it did when I denied how she affected me.

Does she wish this man to touch her as I did? No, I will not believe this. She is still not awake. She is unaware of what is happening to her, yet those sounds.... Those beautiful moans would suggest otherwise. Closing my eyes, I realize I have no claims to her. I left her. So, she owes me nothing, but this does not stop the pain from building within me.

When I open my eyes, I do not find any signs she is enjoying this. I witness pain and confusion, not desire etched within her features. Rushing towards her, I attempt to yank him off her, but my hands pass through him. For all my power, I cannot stop this man from hurting her, and this thought alone sends me into a frenzy as I hurl myself at him. To my amazement, I realize I have somehow slipped into her dream and am not alone. I brought the soul of the man attacking her with me. Clenching it within my grip, I finally understand why she is moaning and what is causing her distress. Apple believes my hands are the ones roaming over her body, but she senses something is wrong. When her eyes land on mine, I think it is only then she realizes none of this is as it seems.

"Avalon, you are lost in a dream. It is not me doing this; please wake up."

I watch as she blinks several times, looking back down at the man she still sees as me. Moving closer, I drag the soul of the fucker who is hurting her with me. She needs to know it is him, not me touching her.

Even though I hold his essence, I cannot halt his behavior. If I could reap his soul, he would die, but because I exist only in her dream, I am incapable of doing this, yet I am no longer helpless. I can....

"Stop, please," hearing her beg gives me the strength to fully slip into her dream, and when she looks down this time, it is my eyes looking back.

"Avalon, wake up."

"What?"

"You need to open your eyes." It pains me to see her helpless. I would give anything, including my immortality, to protect her. A wisp of hair has fallen across her face during her struggles, concealing a slice of the eyes I long to see. Reaching up, I swipe it away, knowing our time is ending. If Avalon has any chance of coming out of this unscathed, she needs to... "Open your eyes and see the truth, Apple."

The words no sooner leave my lips than I am forced to merely watch as understanding fills her eyes. This is when her struggle begins as she fights to break free from the one who will regret his actions. My rage has reached a boiling point. My roar shakes the ground of her realm, resulting in a log tumbling off the pile and landing within her grasp.

Pushing with all my might, I growl, "Above you, Apple, your salvation lies within your reach. Take it, and I will do the rest."

Forcing my will upon Pestilence, I spur his horse until he is galloping toward the camp my brother will locate Avalon.

Avalon's first swing stuns the man, but her second brings him to me. Snatching him by his throat, he mutters, "What the hell is happening?"

"Your death," I snarl before shredding his soul, ending his fleeting existence. There will be repercussions for what I just did, but I will gladly face them all as long as she is safe. I suppose they can add this to my growing list of transgressions, starting with when I interceded two days ago and went against every order my father decreed. Our creator does not permit us to interfere with their lives. Yet she now finds herself in danger because of us, so I forgo his rules to guide Avalon toward Xander, and tonight my efforts have paid off.

Chapter Six: Protecting the Innocent

~ Avalon Late Winter 2025~

LUCK. THIS IS THE ONLY WORD I can use to describe it, a stroke of long-overdue fortune. Of all the places I thought I would find Suki, a bandit camp was not one of them. It's crazy; after searching for her for weeks, I ran into her in the one place I never thought I would find her. Although I admit she has this innate ability to locate me during the lowest points in my life. After all, it was how I first met her.

Suki moved across the hall from me when I hit one of those low points. I was alone and broke; my unwillingness to compromise had cost me yet another job, and the landlord threatened to lock me out of my apartment. After living on the streets for more years than I care to admit, I had no desire to return there. In truth, I questioned if I would survive it. Back then, I was very much the glass-is-half-empty kind of gal. I was ill-prepared for the ball of fire, who would become the only family I have.

I remember the first time I met her. To prevent the padlock from keeping me out of my tiny studio apartment, I had given my landlord the last of the money I possessed. Broke, hungry, and at a loss for what I should do next, I stood at the same window looking down at the same street I would one day watch the soul I love being stabbed. The darkness surrounding me pulled me into its embrace, and I let the tranquility of night replace the turmoil of the day.

With the last job interview bombed and having handed over the last dime in my bank account to my landlord to buy me a few more weeks for the first time since I fled Calvin's house, I did not know what I was going to do. That is until a five-foot-four-inch fiery redhead refused to stop knocking on my door.

No matter how many times or how many ways I told her to get lost, she refused to take no for an answer. I'd be lying if I didn't admit the bottle of bourbon helped her cross that threshold. Halfway through the bottle, she was on the phone with her cousin. Before I could cough my protest, I had a job, a two-hundred-dollar advance, and a lifelong friend I would one-day call sister.

This is why it should have come as no surprise when I looked up and found her standing there, dagger in hand, a messy mop of red hair dancing in the wind around her.

Our time apart has changed her. Given her a strength she previously did not possess. Seeing her standing here clad in leather, prepared for battle, is a far cry from the girl I pulled from a falling city all those years ago. But it isn't just Suki who appeared out of nowhere; Xander is here too, along with several of the men from the group they have been staying with.

"Avalon, we've been looking everywhere for you. Suk was going crazy with worry, wondering what had happened to you," Xander declares as he pulls me in for a hug.

"Doesn't surprise me," I say with a grin.

"We might have found you sooner if my sexy as sin and loving boyfriend...." Hearing her call Xander her boyfriend makes me happy, and I can't help the smile creeping across my face. "...would have listened to me."

I know she is trying to feign anger, but she's doing a shitty job. Especially since she can't stop giving him those big doe-eyed, I love you to the moon and stars side glances.

"Baby, I told you Thanatos—"

"Thanatos, Smanatos. That asshole not only all but chased away my best friend and sister but raced after her to haul her ass back to the horde when she tried to start over. I don't think I need to remind you how much she didn't want to be a part of his legion any longer. Isn't that right, A? You didn't want to be there?"

"I—" This is all I get out before she starts her tirade again.

"Only to turn around and leave her to fend for herself shortly after he found her."

"Babe—"

"Don't you babe me, and don't you dare defend him after he left Avalon defenseless. Left her, Xander. As in alone... to travel these roads by herself. Defenseless!"

"Suk, I'm not exactly some frail helpless—"

Suki slaps her hand over my mouth to silence me so she can continue yelling at Xander, who looks like a little kid being chastised by their parents. I hope to help him and shield Thanatos from her wrath, but with her hand firmly clamped in place, the best I can manage is a muffled defense.

I know she is doing this because she was worried about me, but she shouldn't be taking it out on Xander and, most definitely, not Thanatos. Shaking her hand off, I growl, "Suki."

"A, you have to—"

"No, Suk, you need to stop. Thanatos didn't want to leave me. They forced him to return to his realm, and Xander's only crime was overseeing the people in the horde as Thanatos asked." She drops her head, and the defeated look on her face instantly makes me regret yelling at her.

Taking her arm, I softly say, "I love that you love me this much, but there are some things you don't understand." She opens her mouth to ask what it is that she doesn't understand, but I continue cutting off her inquiry. "And before you ask, I'm not ready to talk about any of it yet. Someday, yes. Just not right now."

Thankfully, she accepted my response and hugged me again in true Suki style, murmuring how much she missed me. Xander proves he is the perfect man for her when he walks over to wrap his arm around her shoulder.

"So, Avalon, I have to ask, what the hell are you doing here in this shithole?" Xander is a good man. I'm almost ashamed of myself for ever thinking otherwise.

"I could ask you two the same thing."

"We heard about the camp and what currency they dealt in." His eyes refuse to meet mine. Yeah, he didn't have to say it. I know what he meant. "Even if I didn't already want to end it the second we found out about these vile pieces of shit, Suki wouldn't have stood for it. She rallied the troops, and we left less than twelve hours after the first woman reached our camp."

"Let me guess, the currency was women?" Xander gives me a sympathetic smile recognizing what my presence here must mean, but he doesn't ask me to elaborate because he is such a good guy.

"Sadly, it seems to be the case, yes."

"How did they get you, A?" Seeing Suki standing here with her arms wrapped around Xander's waist, I know I made the right decision to leave her behind. If I had told her goodbye the morning I decided it was time to go, she would have insisted on coming with me, ruining this great thing she has going with him.

Without thinking about what I was saying, I rattle off something stupid. "I got caught with my pants down."

Now you all know I didn't really have my pants down. This was more of a figurative statement than a literal one, but Suk doesn't get this if her slack-jaw wide-eye expression is anything to go by.

"What I mean is I fell asleep on the side of the road, and one of these assholes found me."

"Oh my god, I was worried for a second there," she declares with a whoosh of air.

"I know you said you didn't want to talk about it, but based on what you said, can I assume the rumors are true? Thanatos really is gone?" I know Xander deserves to know the truth, but even after all these months, my emotions are still too raw. The best I can give him is a nod.

After scavenging what we could from the camp, we bid farewell to the other men who traveled here with my friends. Xander, Suki, and I are making a side trip to where one of the women we liberated from this shithole said she left a stash of supplies. The guys offered to come along with us, but Xander thought it would be better for them to take the other women back to their stronghold. He figured the three of us could handle collecting whatever we found there before returning.

*****

We traveled last night until we found a place to rest. It would have been nice to sleep in this morning, but we need to get on the road if we want to make it to the location where Nehra indicated we would find her supplies. Everything was going fine until something I never thought would happen happened. As shocking as it was to discover Suki at the camp, seeing the little blonde-haired boy running towards us alone is significantly more startling.

He skids to a halt directly in front of us. Looking from him to my travel companions, I can't stop the laugh when he snorts before swiping his entire arm under his nose, making Suki retreat several steps. Suki has often told me she can handle anything except feet and phlegm, and apparently, her newfound ass-kicking mentality still doesn't include the gruesome twosome.

"Shoo," Suki says with a wave of her hands.

"Shoe," the little guy mimics as he lifts his foot up to show us his shoe.

"Shoo-shoo," she tries again, only to have him stomp one foot after the other as he continues repeating her.

"Wren, stop," someone shouts from around the bend. On instinct, I reach down and move the child behind me as we pull our blades and prepare for whatever we must face.

The woman who rounds the corner is not what I expected. The terror that springs to life when she finds us standing between her and the boy is apparent.

"Please. Please don't take my son," she begs as she lifts a hand and takes one tentative step after another in our direction.

When we make no effort to move or give her the boy she calls son, desperation seeps into her request, "Renny, come to momma. Come on now, son, we should let these nice people be on their way."

I look over my shoulder at the still-smiling little boy. One thought keeps plaguing me: if the little guy really is her son, then why hasn't this woman taught him how dangerous it is in the world today? I can't in good conscience hand this boy over to her without knowing for certain. "Do you know her?"

"Know her," he repeats with the same beaming smile he has worn the entire time.

"That's what I asked. Is she your mother?"

"Mudder." Like a parrot, his words mirror my own.

"He can't give you the answer you seek."

"And why not?" I snap as I turn my attention back to her.

"He doesn't understand what you want from him."

"Bullshit, he can hear me just fine."

"I didn't say he couldn't hear you; I said he couldn't understand you."

"And why not?" I ask, moving with her steps to keep myself between her and him.

"Wren, come to mommy," she says. Her gaze drops from mine before she beckons the little boy to return to her.

Dropping my free arm behind me, I take his little hand in mine to ensure he doesn't slip away.

"Let him go," she yells, pulling the dagger she had concealed behind her back before leveling it at me. I'm not sure what she thought she could do against three armed individuals. She has guts; I'll give her that. I think she realizes the recklessness of her actions since her eyes glisten from unshed tears. "Renny, baby, come to momma."

"If you think I'm going to turn this child over to you when he refuses to acknowledge you are his mother, you're fucking crazy." I suppose having a mother who turned me over for something else she wanted more makes me a bit skeptical about what people will or will not do where children are concerned.

"I said he can't." Her desperation seems to increase with every passing second I keep him from her.

"And I asked you, why not?"

Her eyes shift from one face to the next before she exhales loudly; her shoulders slump as she says, "He's autistic."

Dropping my gaze back to his little face, I reassess him. Something in this woman's admission rings true. This little guy is entirely too trusting, even for someone of his young age. Releasing his hand, she calls him once more, and there is no delay as he scampers past my legs and into the waiting arms of the woman who hugs him tight. She kisses his head before smoothing the hair away from his face as she inspects every inch of her son.

Trying not to scare her off, I return my blade to my belt and softly say, "Sorry, you just can't be too careful nowadays."

Her focus meets mine, and as much as I sense she wants to tell me to fuck off, she responds with a nod, but when she circles us to proceed in the direction we just came from, I know I can't let her do this.

"You don't want to go that way."

"Why not?"

"Let's just say there are some people who are not as friendly as we are that way," Xander calmly says.

"Well, there's nothing for us the other way either," she cautiously advises us as her eyes flick from the direction she wants to travel to where she just came from.

"Why don't you come with us?" I know Xander is only trying to protect them. He's a good man. Unfortunately, we all know traveling with me can be dangerous, and the last thing I want to do is put this kid and his mom in harm's way.

"No." "Not happening." the mom and I say simultaneously.

Her eyes shoot to mine before she elaborates, "That's really very kind of you, but I think it's better if we—"

"A." Suki's harsh use of my nickname informs me she is as opposed to letting this woman wander these roads by herself as Xander is.

"Suk, you know what we face."

"And you know what they face being out here alone. I like their odds with us a hell of a lot better than them being alone on these roads without any help," she snaps, slamming her hands to her hips as her foot taps angrily against the ground. A clear sign she has no intention of budging on this subject.

"Avalon, we can't just leave them here. You know better than any of us what kind of people are out here. What do you think they will do to him when they decide to take her?" Xander implores as he places his hand on my arm.

"Really, it's okay. We'll be fine. We've been on our own for a while now."

I know with the arrival of another horseman, letting this woman leave would be nothing short of signing her death warrant. Taking a tentative step towards her, she instinctually wraps her arms around the little boy, hugging him tighter against her.

"My name is Avalon, and my friends are right. It's no longer safe to roam these roads alone, and things are bound to get a shit load worse in the coming weeks." Suki hits me for my use of profanity in front of the little boy, even though she had no problem using the word *'hell'* when she was yelling at me.

"Why?" The woman cautiously asks, turning slightly to move the boy further out of my reach. I have to respect her protectiveness. Her unwillingness to listen, not so much.

"Because another horseman is coming," Suki says as she steps up next to Xander, taking his hand in hers.

"And you know this how?"

Sighing, I confess, "Because I called him here."

~ Greer~

At first, I didn't know what to think of the people who held my son from me. They refused to return him even when I told them who I was, yet I would be remiss if I did not acknowledge that this woman appeared to be protecting him. I have to respect them for doing this even if I don't appreciate it or trust them yet. Still, I am all too aware what they said is true; remaining out here alone with my son is dangerous.

So, for Wren's sake, I must do what I believe is best, which includes traveling with these people for now. These people have been nothing but kind to Wren and me, but kindness only goes so far in today's world and can quickly morph into dangerous in a matter of seconds.

"Bye-bye," Wren laughs as he waves at the woman beside us.

"Nope, little dude, we're going the same way." I know this one's name; it's easy to remember since it happens to be the same as a character from a vampire series I watched. Here's hoping she's as trustworthy as the girl from the show.

"What do you want?" This is a new phrase Renny started using anytime he wanted something. The problem is that he no longer tells me what he needs, so it becomes a guessing game. "Peas."

"I'm all good, little dude. What about you?"

"What do you want?" He repeats.

"Renny, use your words and tell mommy do you want a drink or a snack? Are you hungry?"

He clicks his tongue, a new tick he has picked up in the last couple of months, before repeating, "Hun-gee."

"Do you think we could stop so I could feed Wren?"

"If I remember correctly, there's a farmhouse not much farther up the road. It should offer us protection to rest and grab something to eat. Do you think he'll be alright for a little while longer?" Avalon asks.

Nodding my head, we continue walking until the house comes into view. It's not the worst place we have had to stay since leaving my house. It even has intact beds we can sleep in tonight. My back should be thankful for that at the very least, and I admit having three other sets of eyes to help watch over Renny is a welcome relief. I love my son, but he can be a handful, especially since I have yet to make Wren understand that not everyone is as nice as the ones we ran into today.

"So, how long have you been out here?"

"We stayed in my house for a couple months after everything fell, and when we left, we went with a couple of my neighbors."

"So what happened to them?"

"Don't know. We got separated from them during a storm."

"You never found them after?" Suki asks as she sits down with us.

"No."

"Well, then it's settled. You'll stay with us. We only have one rule."

"We do?" Avalon asks as she tilts her head to one side, pulling her eyebrows together.

"As a matter of fact, we do," Suki declares as she reclines back against the couch.

"Since when?"

"Since now, A," Suki grumbles through her gritted teeth.

"This I have to hear," Avalon declares.

"Okay, what's the rule?" I ask because, let's face it, curiosity has gotten the better of me now too.

"No touching Xander. He's spoken for."

"Really, Suk?" Avalon mutters as she rolls her eyes. Hey, I respect a woman who isn't afraid to stake her claim.

"Yep, it's easier to establish boundaries from the jump than to deal with hurt feelings or busted asses," she mumbles the 'busted asses' part under her breath before returning to her normal volume for the rest. "...later on."

"I can live with that." My confirmation has her bouncing as she claps her hands.

"Then welcome to team A."

"Team A?"

"It's what she calls me," Avalon confesses as she shoves Suki over. We spend the rest of the night chatting and getting to know one another. I answer as many questions as I can. The only one I'm not ready to talk about is Lynn Harvey, Wren's biological mom. It's not that I'm worried they will judge me. If I had to venture a guess, I would say Suki would congratulate me, and Avalon might want to show her the error of abandoning her son. Painfully. It's more because I don't feel like she deserves the acknowledgment. Lynn may have given birth to Wren, but she abandoned him when he needed her the most. Something I could never do.

After the day slipped away and night took over, Renny and I went to bed. For the first time since we got separated from the others, I could sleep without the fear of someone or something hurting us.

It feels like I have no more than closed my eyes when they snap open. Awakened in the wee hours of dawn by shouts from Xander followed by the screams of Suki.

Chapter Seven: Stand

~ Pestilence Late Winter 2025~

AS HARD AS THANATOS PUSHED, WE did not arrive in time to find her. The lamb left the camp in shambles, but the ones who survived and were complicit in harming her do not escape my judgment. They will all linger only long enough to realize the foolishness of their actions. As I walk among the stench of decay and rot, I know their suffering will not end even with their passing because any who harmed the lamb will not find my brother waiting to lead them out of purgatory. Thanatos will never ferry their souls to the afterlife, leaving them to wander lost and alone for all eternity. This again makes me wonder what happened between Thanatos and the lamb.

He may not have told me who this person is to him, but he cannot hide his desire to protect her. Regardless of why he still watches over her, I have a task to fulfill, and the more she moves, the easier it is for me to complete my assignment. City after city, soul after soul, they all fall when they find themselves unlucky enough to cross paths with me.

As much as I would prefer to be on my way, I know if I do not scour this camp and search for any clues to where I might locate the lamb, Thanatos will hound my horse and me until I do. After wandering around for several minutes, I come across the body of a man most mortals would believe died from a massive head injury caused by the log lying next to his body, but I can sense his death came at my brother's hands. It doesn't take long to figure out what fate befell this man.

The ground shows signs of a struggle. Based on what the first victim of my plague advised, I believe I have found the spot where his brother tried to force himself on the lamb who woke me. Since our creator has refused to allow Thanatos to return, he would have been forced to stand by and watch helplessly. Unless the mortal he protects could somehow render the man incapacitated, lingering amidst life and death, between my judgment and that of my brother's. I fear the brother he found was not in a forgiving mood. The instant he teetered on the edge of existence, he was well within my brother's grasp, and Thanatos wasted no time snatching him away from this realm so he could rip his soul apart.

Crouching next to the spot she occupied, I sweep my hand across the ground, gathering the loose dirt in my fist. As I allow it to shift through my fingers, I sense him nearby. And I realize I am no longer on their plane.

"Hello, brother."

"Pestilence."

"It will not please our creator when he discovers you interceded on her behalf."

"And when he does, I will accept his punishment." Glancing up, I find Thanatos looking every bit as deadly as he ever has, yet there is something one could easily miss if not looking; a sadness has settled deep within his eyes.

"Who is she to you, brother?"

"She is the one who showed me their worth. It is by her grace I found my way home."

Brushing away the only remnants of their plane to have traveled with me from my hands, I stand to properly greet my brother. Grasping his shoulders to ensure I have his full attention, I exclaim, "I know she is more than what you claim. Do you believe I do not know one of my brothers well enough to sense you are conflicted, and if you could return to her world, you would? So I ask you, who is this woman to you?"

Thanatos meets my gaze, and I watch the turmoil brewing within him. He struggles with doing as our father wants and what his heart desires. Which I imagine is exceedingly difficult since this is a foreign emotion for us both.

"She is the lamb—"

"You may tell the others this nonsense, but you cannot lie to me. Who. Is. She?"

"Someone I respect."

"Thanatos."

"Someone I grew close to during my time in their realm," he confesses, dropping his eyes from mine. An action he does to hide the half-truth he just spoke, but as I previously stated, he is my brother. His pain is my pain; his joy is mine. Thanatos's feelings for her break through the walls he has carefully constructed and floods through me, filling my heart with a sense I can only equate to how I feel about our father until I am certain Avalon is so much more than someone he merely cares for.

"You don't just care for the lamb. You love her, don't you?"

"I am Death, brother. What do I know of love?"

"And yet you do."

"Pestilence, if anyone were to find out how I feel about her, Avalon's life—"

"Would be in danger."

"Yes. Besides, the next time I see her will be to ferry her soul to the afterlife. Therefore, I must ask you again to please find her. Xander is a good man but can only protect her so much, and if they made him choose between the woman he loves and the one I... Avalon, his choice will not be in her favor. No matter what consequence she may face, Avalon would not permit him to choose her over her friend, the little one named Suki."

Before I can respond, pain slices through my arm, and my horse grunts angrily. When my eyes snap open again, Thanatos is gone, and I am back in their realm.

"I said drop it, fucker."

Unlike when our father recalls us, my physical body remained on this plane while my essence walked within purgatory with Thanatos. After bearing witness to his pain, I know I need to find the lamb before returning to my task. I will do as my brother has asked because requesting anything is something he has never done before, while I have made many of him. So concerning his request, I will not let him down. Shaking off the lingering confusion caused by Thanatos pulling me from this realm to our own, I try to refocus from my brother to the one who addressed me.

"It would seem our creator has smiled upon you today."

"What the fuck are you talking about?"

"I have an urgent issue I must see to. A matter that requires my immediate attention, so I do not have the time or patience for your judgment this day. You should be thankful since it is the only thing sparing your life."

"There are six of us and only one of you. What the fuck do you think you can do?"

"I seek the lamb. Her name is Avalon; if you know where she is, it will behoove you to tell me now."

"Who the hell do you think you're talking to?"

"A son of Adam."

"You got the wrong man because my dad's name sure as shit wasn't Adam."

"You misconstrue my meaning. You are one of Adam's offspring. One my father and the lamb have sent me to judge."

"Ever since that asshole came here claiming to be one of those fucking horsemen sent from the creator...." The disrespect he displays with his mocking tone when referring to our father is something that will not go unanswered. "to judge us, every asshole thinks they can claim this shit. Listen up, dipshit, I didn't buy what the last fucker was selling, and I don't buy it from you either."

Standing to full height, I turn to face the mortal so I can better explain the error he just made. "The fucking horseman, as you called him, is my brother Thanatos, but you may know him better as Death. I am Pestilence, the bringer of scourge and disease, and today you will receive your judgment."

Yanking my bow from where it rests across my back, I nock an arrow and fire before he reaches for his weapon. The projectile flies true and strikes the man between his eyes. I would have rather released my plague, but if I hope to catch up with the lamb, I do not have enough time to sentence him as he deserved. If I had sent my tendrils of plague to claim him, he would continue fighting, so it is best to take the ones who will oppose me out of the battle straight away. As suspected, the one who did not know his place was not the only mortal to challenge me. One of the men who traveled with him returned fire. Dropping to one knee, I twist, and the next second he stares up at the blue skies with vacant, dead eyes. The others show more wisdom when they turn and flee before they share the same fate as their fallen companions.

Releasing my tendrils, they slither along the ground, catching the ones who retreat. I will use them as another vessel to deliver a slow death to all they come across. Mounting my horse, I begin my search for Avalon.

~ *Avalon* ~

Xander's shouts and Suki's screams shatter the tranquility of the night. Leaping to my feet, I sprint through the house to find him standing over some unknown invader, a random ass guy currently on his knees with his hands behind his head.

"I'm sorry, man. I didn't know anyone was in here. You got to believe me," the newcomer begs.

"I asked you what the hell you're doing here."

"I was just looking for a place to stay for the night." After this, everything happens in a flurry of activity. Xander and the other man continued yelling, each trying to be heard over the other. Xander is demanding one way or another; he will tell us why he's there while the guy on the ground is screaming he found the place by accident. Neither man is listening to the other. Both men are giving me a headache, so for the sake of my pounding head, I take matters into my own hands when I walked up behind the newcomer and slammed the butt of the gun we found here against the back of his skull. The impact results in him crumpling to the ground and the sweet return of silence. At least I found a use for this thing since using it for its intended purpose seems to be out of the question. Who the hell has a gun but no bullets? Even if we found them, the pistol still wouldn't work. The reason is that whatever Thanatos did to the rest of our technology seems to afflict any weapon we could use against them that our hand does not power... like, for instance, arrows. This doesn't mean we don't keep checking them every chance we get.

"Do we have anything to tie him up with?" I ask Suki, who stands next to Xander as she frantically pulls on his arm. When she doesn't reply, I ask again with more force, "Suk! Do we have anything to restrain him?"

"I think I saw some rope in one of the kitchen drawers," Greer tells me as she scampers past.

"Xander, are you okay?" Suki has moved from pawing at his arm to inspecting a wound on his face. Until now, I had not realized he was injured. I understand why she needs to make sure he's okay. I can't fault her for this because had it been Thanatos, I would have reacted the same way.

"Sweetheart, I'm fine."

"You're bleeding."

"He caught me off guard when I rounded the corner. He got in one good hit before I regained the upper hand, but I'm fine."

"No, we need to clean that up and—"

"Suk, baby, I'm fine," Xander says, taking her face in his hands before kissing her.

"Here," Greer yells as she runs back into the room, holding the rope out in front of her. We tie his arms and legs before securing him to the only furniture in the room. After Xander checks the perimeter, and we are sure the dumbass will not be waking up in the foreseeable future, I offer to take the first watch so the others can sleep.

Leaning against the window frame with my arms resting against my chest, I watch the sun crest the tree line, coloring the sky in amazing reds, oranges, and yellows. Everything is so peaceful. I almost lose myself in the tranquility I always find in the dark. On any other evening, this would have been fine. The issue is, tonight I'm on guard duty, and I almost forgot about the asshole tied up behind me. Almost. Until his groans remind me why I'm standing here watching the sunrise in the eastern sky.

"What the hell. Did you hit me?"

"Call it repayment." He doesn't have to ask me what I'm talking about. He knows it was repayment for hitting Xander.

"How long have I been out?"

"A couple hours."

"We really need to get out of here." I can just make out his reflection in the glass as he whips his head toward the door when the house creaks from the wind.

"Like any of us care what you have to say," Suki says as she strolls into the room, stopping next to me.

"The guy is probably still searching."

"Searching.... What the fuck does searching mean, asshole?" Suk yells.

"Searching as in looking for, seeking, stalking. Take your damn pick."

"Hey, mind your manners, prick," I interject without turning my attention from the splendor of this beautiful sunrise.

"He has to be getting close. We should have left last night. You never should have knocked me out," he yells the last part, but something in his tone tells me this is more from fear than bravado. I turn to face him for the first time since he woke up as he mumbles several obscenities and struggles to break free of the ropes restraining him.

"What was he looking for?" Xander asks, stepping in front of Suki, protectively putting himself between the man who may have merely stumbled across the woman he loves and us. The asshole's eyes flick to mine; however, he doesn't say anything.

"For. What?" I think I have a good idea. Even so, I need to hear him say it.

"You. At least, I think the woman he wants is you."

"What the fuck did he say?" I snarl. I know I shouldn't show any reaction, but after everything that has happened since Thanatos first arrived in my life, I think I have earned the right to react.

"He said he needed to find the lamb." Goosebumps form over my entire body. This is the first time I have heard this name since the raven previously known as Jared called me this shit the day I broke the first seal.

"And what the hell makes you think I'm this lamb?" Yeah, I know technically I am one and the same, but I'm sure as hell not going to share this information with him.

"He called you by name, and I don't imagine there are many Avalons around these parts."

"What did he look like?" When the guy glares in my direction, I take a menacing step closer before saying through clenched teeth. "I'll give you to the count of three, and then I promise you're going to wish you never walked through that door."

"Big guy. Massive horse. Bow strapped to his back. Said he was one of those riders."

"Which rider?!"

"Does it matter?" He snaps his response, confirming he is as tired of answering my questions as I am asking them.

"Yeah, it kinda fucking matters."

"Pestilence. He said his name was fucking Pestilence."

Well, fuck.

Chapter Eight: Force Meets Foe

~ *Death Late Winter 2025* ~

SENSING MY BROTHER WAS IN DANGER, I fought to return to their world. I know I am being irrational. Pestilence does not require my assistance. Regardless, it was because of me they could take him by surprise. He would have sensed their approach if I had not pulled him to me. They would have never got a shot off, let alone the one that struck him.

I decide to appeal to our father again. Perhaps if I can speak to him alone, he will hear me out and permit my return. If I return, freeing my brother from his duty will be a priority, but assuring Avalon's safety will be my number one mission. Do I plan on disclosing this in my plea to our creator? No. Will I lie if he asks me directly? I will not. Realistically, I physically cannot outright lie to him. I may have omitted some details as I discussed their world. Although I would be a fool if I did not admit he already knew the answers I would give and the truth even with my obvious omissions.

I need only figure out when his guard Michael has vacated his post; only then will this allow me an opportunity to make my plea without his interference. Before this thought has fully materialized, I sense his approach. But not just Michael; he has brought one of his brethren.

Without turning to acknowledge him, I state, "For all your bluster and bravado, I see you are too afraid to face me alone."

"His was a soul you had no right to take."

"I don't know why it matters to you, Michael. Isn't this precisely what you want? All of humanity exterminated."

"While I do not have the same affinity you seem to have for these mortals, I only wish to carry out our father's plan."

"Bullshit, you want them gone, although I'm unsure why. Let's call that one soul a prepayment on the ones I will reap when she calls me there."

"You did not take his soul as part of your calling. You did this to save the life of another."

"You should be happy since she is the mortal task with calling us to her world. If she dies, how—"

"You don't believe we have measures in place for this precise reason?"

Hearing him confirm this makes me realize how precarious her position truly is. If the mortals in her world find out she is responsible for releasing us, I don't think I need to tell you what her life would be worth. And as much as Xander would try to protect her, he would have to choose.

"You will answer for your misconduct."

"Is that how you see it as well, Gabriel?" I ask the angel who accompanied Michael to dole out my punishment, which is the first time I have acknowledged his presence since they entered my space. If he wishes to follow Michael's lead, I have no more use for him than I do the warrior angel, who will soon realize his mistake.

"We all have our assigned missions. Even you, Death."

"Yes, I suppose we do." My wings flare behind me just as Michael's sword slashes through the space I previously occupied. Twisting away from Gabriel's whip, I lash out, landing a blow on Michael. Seeing they do not stand a chance against me on their own, they regroup to attack as one. The fight continues until the only thing filling the room is the flashing glints of steel, the crack with each snap of the whip, and the sounds of flesh hitting flesh every time I land a strike between blocking theirs.

Michael makes a mistake when he lunges in my direction, allowing me to move behind him. Before he can react, I have his throat locked in the crook of my arm. Ending any further fight from the two who thought they were strong enough to face me and win.

"You have been weighed and found wanting." I am preparing to prove to them each action and every decision they made since I was called home will be met with an equal reaction when I am pulled away by a soul slipping from the realm of man. I will not leave this innocent soul to toil or become lost in limbo to deliver my retribution.

Michael and Gabriel will have to wait, but their time will come. For none can escape my final decree.

~ *Pestilence* ~

My brother has gone quiet; his push is no longer here. I can't say if this is because he knows I will look for her or if his true calling keeps him busy. My plague has been within this realm for long enough that the ones who crossed paths with my carriers should be faltering. As each one dies, my brother will be there waiting to help them cross over to the next stage of their existence.

I have a purpose, a task, and even though I have given my word to Thanatos, it does not release me from our father's decree. Yet I do not feel rushed to find her because I sense I am on the right path. She is not too far ahead of me, so as I travel, I release my disease in waves of darkness. The tendrils seep out of me and twist their way through the trees surrounding me. You may wonder why I have done this. The answer is simple: the plague is not deadly to the animals it will cling to; they will carry it with them, infecting any soul unlucky enough to cross their path. And for those who feast upon their flesh will fall as if they stood before me themselves.

The time of man is slated to end, and I don't see how one human will persuade me any differently. I know Thanatos argued Raum tricked the lamb into releasing me. I am simply having difficulty reconciling how anyone would make such a mistake. Unless everyone's perception of this lamb is incorrect. I need to approach this situation with that in mind.

Rounding the corner, I come face to face with a being I know is anything but mortal. He is standing in the middle of the path I am traveling, where he is confident I could not miss him. His hands are behind his back, looking down as he works to loosen a rock stuck in the ground with the toe of his boots.

Pulling on the reins, my horse stops short of the being who still has not lifted his head. I would release the tendrils of my slow death, but I know as well as he does it will have no effect on him.

"Pestilence."

"You seem to have me at a disadvantage." Lifting his head, I instantly know who has stopped my progress. I am unsure how I want to proceed with this vile creature. He is, without a doubt, wicked. You can feel the evil emanating from him, much the same as the mortals feel my rot wrapping around them.

"Raum."

"It is good to see you here among the mortals. I have also felt your gift clinging to the ones who have had the misfortune of meeting you."

"If I am to believe my brother, it is a gift you alone are responsible for releasing."

"And do you? Believe your brother?" The glare I give him is the only answer he will receive regarding this question.

"I merely led the little lamb to her destiny; she is the one who chased it."

"Led by deceit."

"I prefer to call it a necessity," He says, reaching out to stroke my horse's nose. An act that almost has his head removed from his shoulders when my horse rears up before lunging at the demon who should have known better.

"Why interfere?" His answer will not change the circumstances I find myself in. I want to know why a demon, a high-ranking one at that, would interfere with our creator's divine plan.

"Let's just say I'm tired of bowing to these mortals, of living in darkness while they bask in the light. It is our turn to rule this realm. They have had their time; it is our time now. Would you not agree?"

"I do not." The smirk he has been wearing falls away, and the wickedness of the being before me creeps out. I know many beings would slink away from the demon. I am not most beings, and he does not frighten me. He is irritating me because he stands between me and my side mission. I think he finally understands that I will do as Thanatos has asked; because of this, I believe he sees his plan slipping away.

"There must be something you want." I lift my brow, knowing there is nothing this being can offer I want. "A home? Power? Prestige? Women? Men? Name it, and I will see it done."

"Nothing."

"I'll make you a deal, rider."

"I do not make bargains with anyone, least of all a being of your low moral compass."

"Regardless, you only need to turn back. If you do, I promise you will never have to return to your long rest again."

"Why?" His refusal to answer me confirms what I already know. "Because you want to get to the Lamb first."

"Just... Turn back. Give me two days which will allow—"

"Let me make this simple for you. If I catch you anywhere around Avalon, you will answer directly to me."

Raum's roars shatter the quiet surrounding us. His fist clenches around the spear strapped on his back. He whips it around, trying to slash my traveling companion. My horse takes offense to this act, and this time when he slams his hooves on the ground, Raum barely escapes his retribution. Yanking my bow from its position on my back, I level it on him. He rolls at the last second, narrowly avoiding the arrow I released.

"You better hope your horse can run faster than I can fly," he snarls before transforming into his raven form to fly in the direction I know we will find her.

He may be a demon, but he meant what he said; Raum will not rest until he finds Avalon. If he gets to her before me, I will have to choose which path I take. Carry out my father's decree or rescue the lamb who can wake my brothers. Which makes my decision easy. I need to find her before he does; when I do, I will protect her whether she likes it or not.

Chapter Nine: Hunted

~ Avalon Late Winter 2025~

"GREER, GET RENNY; WE NEED TO go. Right now," I instruct as I pack any supplies we can use while Suki and Xander scour the house to ensure we haven't overlooked anything.

"Untie me," the asshole whose only redeeming quality is giving me this information begs. Well, he can plead until the world ends... Okay, I admit it was a terrible analogy since this is precisely what the man I am preparing to run from is here to do. Regardless, let's get back to the dumbass; if he thinks I'm going to release him, he is woefully mistaken. If the damn raven has taught me anything, it's this... don't trust assholes, and this guy is the epitome of an asshole.

"Shut up before I gag you."

"You can't just leave me here. Tied up. Defenseless. I don't deserve to die like this."

Grabbing the gag, I prepare to do exactly what I threaten until Renny's smiling face appears around the corner. I don't want to tarnish this sweet boy. If anything, I want to protect him from the evils of this world.

"Please. At least promise you'll untie me before you leave. Give me a chance to outrun death."

Watching Renny standing there with his thumb in his mouth, taking in everything around him, I absentmindedly say, "Pestilence."

"What?"

"Pestilence is the horsemen you want to outrun, not Death."

"Does it really matter which horseman is coming to kill us?" He yells.

"It does to me." It matters to me which horseman is coming our way because if it were Thanatos, I would already be out the door running in the direction I suspect he is traveling from. Pestilence is a different story.

"Avalon, we're not really going to leave him like this, are we?" Greer asks, looking past me at the man lying on the floor.

"It's better than this a-hole deserves," Suki snaps as she dashes into the room, her arms overflowing with the last supplies they found in the house.

"Why? Tell me what I did that is so horrendous I deserve death."

"You hit Xander for one."

"Because I was afraid. I wasn't expecting to find anyone in the house. I panicked when he came around the corner and ran into me."

"Avalon?" Greer's tone is close to pleading.

For the next fifteen minutes, I tried to convince her of all the reasons letting this guy go was a bad idea, but she gave me as many examples to prove otherwise. The last one is the most compelling.

"You trusted Renny and me enough to take us in."

"It's your call, Avalon," Xander says as he covers Suki's mouth to stifle her objections.

"Greer, can you honestly tell me you would trust this guy around Wren?" This is my last-ditch effort to make her understand why I prefer leaving him to meet Pestilence. Greer's eyes shift from me to the man looking at her like she is his only hope in the world of walking away from this. Which, if I'm being honest, she is. If this was where her focus remained, I would have said I lost the battle, but she falters when her gaze lands on Wren's big blue innocent eyes. Greer knows she would trust no one around her son. Not me... not Suk... not Xander... and certainly not some guy who attacked the people who helped shelter her and Wren for the last twenty-four hours. I know I've won the war when she closes her eyes.

"Come on, Renny. Let's get your blanket." Wren's response is to stick his thumb in his mouth as he pulls on his ear opposite his free hand.

"You can't leave me. Please, I'm a good man." Hearing him say this takes me back to a time when men declared how good and honorable they were while delivering me as a sacrifice to Thanatos. In the end, it worked out in my favor. The problem is, I didn't see it that way while we were traveling to his camp.

Leaning over so he is the only one who will hear me. I whisper, "In my experience, the ones who have to declare themself good or honorable are the ones responsible for the most reprehensible acts."

As Greer and I turn to exit the house, he says the one thing that halts us in our tracks, "Then kill me. If you're so hell-bent on giving me a death sentence for defending myself, then I prefer you do it now. Quick and easy rather than slow and painful."

Greer glances over at me, and I realize I have allowed the damn raven to turn me into an uncaring asshole who would do something like this. Damn it!

"A, don't," Suki mumbles.

"Suk, would you feel the same if he hadn't hit Xander?"

"Doesn't matter because he did."

"Do you think Xander would have done anything less if we stumbled across someone when we took over this place? This has to be a group decision. It's all or nothing."

"But—"

Xander intercedes on the guy's behalf when he turns Suk to face him. "Babe, Avalon is right. We're not the kind of people who do things like this. I vote we release him."

He looks over at Greer. "Oh, I don't think Avalon was referring to me."

"Yes, I was. Greer, it's all or nothing; you get a vote too."

"If it makes any difference, I vote you release me," the guy whose fate hangs in the balance of this decision imparts.

"I didn't ask you, and you don't get a vote. Now shut up before I gag your dumb ass," I deliver my huffed response without turning to acknowledge him.

"I vote we release him," Greer confirms as she shifts a squirming Wren from one hip to the other.

"Suk?"

"Well, if I say no now, I just look like the a-hole in the group." The smile I give her is all the confirmation she needs. "I swear to God if you fuc—" she quickly corrects from saying fuck to a more Wren-friendly word which is a good thing since he immediately repeats her. "Fudge us; I will slice and dice your man bits."

"Udge us."

"That's right, little man, fudge is delicious. Especially peanut butter, it's my favorite. Maybe if we're lucky, we'll find it somewhere along the way," I tell him as I ruffle his hair. My nod to Greer causes her to understand it's time to move Wren out of the room.

Pulling the knife from my waistband, I look at each of them to give them a second to reconsider. Greer kisses Wren's head while he plays with her necklace. Suki refuses to look at me, finding the ceiling significantly more interesting even though her crossed-arm, tapping foot stance confirms she is not happy about any of this. It's Xander who finally gets me moving when he nods his agreement.

Squatting in front of the guy, I warn him in a hushed hiss, "Don't fucking make me regret this."

I admit I was ready for him to lash out, scramble away from me or try to grab my knife; his response is something I was unprepared for.

"Thank you. All of you." This last part was meant for Suki since his eyes are focused on her as he rubs his wrist. "My name's Jay."

"Don't care!" Suki snaps before asking, "Can we go now?"

"Babe."

"I wanted to tell you again how sorry I am for hitting you." Xander dips his chin. I guess he's ready to move past the events that ended with this guy Jay tied up and a nasty bump on his head.

"All is forgiven. Right?" I ask, even though it's more a demand than a question. At least he's smart enough to agree, even if it's nothing more than a simple bob of his head.

"Don't follow us." My tone may come across as friendly, done purposefully for the benefit of the little guy intently watching me; I can assure you it is anything but.

"Alright, it's past time we got our as-behinds," this whole not cussing thing is going to be difficult, "on the road."

Jay doesn't stand until I'm across the room. His cautious approach better imply he agrees with my last command; otherwise, our deal is off. My eyes remain on him until I twist the door handle and come face to face with....

"Hello, little lamb."

Chapter Ten: Meet and Greet

Therefore, I have come out to meet you, to seek your presence earnestly, and I have found you. Proverbs 7:15.

~ *Pestilence Late Winter 2025*~

IT SEEMS I ARRIVED JUST IN time to halt the lamb from fleeing. An act that would have led to her death because just as I can sense the woman standing before me is the lamb, I can also feel Raum lingering inside the tree line. The instant she walked out of the safety of this dwelling, he would have snatched her away. All with only one hope in mind, keeping her away from me. Yet it seems our little lamb is not alone. I suspect the man who is pulling her away from me is none other than the one my brother called Xander.

"You have been most elusive in tracking down, little lamb."

"It's Avalon, actually."

"So it is."

"And I'm going to take a stab in the dark here and say you must be Pestilence."

Adjusting the quiver slung over my shoulder, I tilt my head, wondering if she has seen any mortals who could be mistaken for a rider. Each of their faces displays discomfort at having me standing so close. The only one among them still smiling is the youngest of this group, who giggles before declaring in song what would be obvious if my horse was born of this realm.

"Orse, say nay-nay-nay." Looking over my shoulder, my horse huffs while twitching his ears.

The child has no more than sung this when the lamb asks a one-word question. One I am uncertain how I should respond. "Ghost?"

"Since there are no spirits around us, I must ask who or what is a Ghost?"

Without answering my question, she pushes past me, which is an act I am surprised by since most mortals would do anything to avoid me. Yet this daughter of Eve had no issues putting her hands on my chest to move me out of her path. One which leads her in the direction of my horse.

I cannot say what she hoped to find; whatever it is must not be what she discovered since she halts her progress as her shoulders slump.

"A," the little woman mumbles as she slinks around me. To say the least, this is an odd group of mortals. The only one among them who seems to understand what my arrival here could represent is the one sneaking around the corner.

"You will stop, or I will send my tendrils to retrieve you." His head whips in my direction, leading me to believe he is aware of what this will mean for him. Until I know who these people are, none will leave, and only one is safe. With the lamb removed from the others, it would be prudent to extricate her from this place so I can return to my rightful task.

"Come, lamb, it is past time for us to be on our way."

"I'm not going anywhere with you."

"This was not a request."

"I don't give a rat's ass."

"I am unsure how the lesser end of a rodent would have any bearing. Regardless, trying to find you has delayed me from my task long enough."

"If you mean killing off humanity, then I'm doing the world a favor."

"Yeah, Avalon's not going anywhere with you," the tiny woman held back by a son of Adam yells from the porch. Yet when I turn my gaze to assess her, she loses much of her false bravado and cowers from my wrath.

"Suk, I got this," the little lamb says in a rush. I believe she understands I am losing my patience and will not hesitate to eliminate the ones blocking me from my goal.

Her refusal to leave may be misguided. I sense she feels responsible for saving the ones who travel with her. She does not know their lives are in greater danger by being with her. Raum will not be as forgiving or patient. He will kill them if only to get her moving. Perhaps if I tell her this, she will relent, allowing me to return to my father's task.

"The instant you leave this dwelling," her eyes snapping to me is perplexing since I have not yet told her about Raum. Nonetheless, I inform her of the fate she is choosing for the rest of her party if she refuses my demand. "Raum awaits you and your companions. If you do not come with me, their lives will end at his hand."

"Raum?"

"You may know him better as the raven."

"That fucker is around here?" She yells as she shifts her focus from me to the trees. "Come out, you asshole. Come out and face me."

My hand flies out to grab her arm as she storms in the direction I sense Raum waiting. Her actions remove any doubts. She will not leave the others or back down when faced with a high earl from hell. I cannot leave her here if I wish to honor my brother's request.

"Either you proceed away from here with me, or I follow you and your party. The choice is yours, but you will make it quick, or I shall make it for you."

"I can't just leave them here."

"Then I can assume I will be coming with you."

"And if I refuse—"

"How do you propose to stop me?"

"I can't take you back to their camp. You'll kill them."

"You have my word; no harm shall come to the ones you protect. Once they are safe, you must give me your word that you will come with me without further delay."

"I'm supposed to believe you'll forgo every instinct and let the ones they have sent you to kill go free?"

"Were my words confusing to you, mortal?"

"We make sure my friends get back to their base, and you will leave the entire camp alive and well?"

Huffing my frustration that she is making me repeat myself, I give her a one-word response I hope will end any further argument. "Yes."

"Fine, I'll go with you."

The rest of her party slowly exits the dwelling they have remained in during our argument, all but one. The man who tried to slip away once already.

"You too," I demand.

"No!" Avalon is quick to respond.

"He is with your group."

"Not by choice."

"He comes. This is not open for debate." I do not want to tell her Raum will capture this man the second we are out of view and force him to reveal where we travel. If she wishes to keep her companions safe, this is the only way to do it.

*****

We have been traveling for several hours. Except for the one our little lamb did not want to bring, each adult takes a turn watching the child. In my short time here, I have witnessed what the mortals of this world have to offer. Because of this, I am astonished the child yet lives. I have also noticed the child is not the only one whose eyes float toward my horse. I cannot say if they hoped he would permit them to ride him; they are mistaken. Our horses will let none but their chosen rider on unless we grant permission first. Something we would not do.

"How's Ghost doing?" the lamb asks as her eyes stay on my horse.

"Ghost? I am unsure who you are referring to."

"Death's horse."

"Why do you keep referring to my brother's companion as Ghost?"

"Because it's the name I gave him while he was here."

"My brother permitted you to name his horse?" I admit this shocks me. None of us have ever named any of the creatures who aid us.

"Yeah. Why?"

"Our horse is an extension of us. They do not exist without us, and we cannot function without them. To name our horse is akin to separating it from its rider."

"Well, he did, but if it's any consolation, Ghost helped me pick his name."

"My brother's horse helped you pick his name?" Without looking at me, she nods. "And he did this how?"

"With a lot of snorts and several hoof stomps."

"And Death did not advise this was in reaction to you speaking to him?"

"Since it was only Ghost and I out there, Thanatos—" Hearing her call my brother this name causes me to raise an eyebrow in question. None have ever been so informal when talking about my brother. "–didn't have a say."

"My brother permitted you to travel with his horse without his presence?"

"Seeing as he told his horse to follow me, there was no permission needed."

"Thanatos did what?"

"He told Ghost to watch over me. When I slipped away, Ghost followed. It was during this trip we picked his name."

"Where was my brother?"

"I don't have any idea. We weren't on the best terms, so he didn't feel an overwhelming desire to share his comings and goings with me."

"To answer your question, my brother's *horse* is fine. He awaits the time you call him here, as do the rest of them."

"Who the hell said I would be calling any more of you here? It was a one-time error in judgment because I had no idea what the hell I was doing. Which, by the way, your father really should put a warning on those things."

"Things?"

"The seals. I mean, do you know how easy the damn seal is to break? Even if the one unlucky enough to find the damn thing didn't want to break it. The act of picking it up alone could do it."

"You are mistaken."

"No, I'm not. It was as simple as snapping some damn wax. I'm still amazed the wax held on as long as it did without pulling away from the parchment."

"The seal remains intact until the day the lamb breaks it, thereby releasing the riders to perform their task."

"What? You're trying to tell me a human has to be the one to open it?"

"Not just any mortal. Only the chosen lamb can break it." Our conversation is interrupted when the child falls, and the wailing cries begin. The one most protective of him rushes over to comfort him, as does the one named Suki. It only takes a couple minutes to quiet him, but it is long enough the lamb does not return to our previous conversation. This is for the best because I fear what she may do if she knew everything.

"How did the other mortals come to be in your comradeship?"

"You know, if you plan on staying in this world, you might want to drop the highfalutin way you talk. It's off-putting."

"It's... off-putting?"

"Yeah, the way you talk doesn't scream, '*Hey, come get to know me.*'"

"You believe I wish for mortals to acquaint themself with me?"

"See, you could have just said, 'You think I care if people talk to me?' Doesn't this sound better?"

"It sounds like something a mortal would say."

"Precisely."

"I hold no desire to be mortal."

She rolls her eyes before exhaling forcefully. "Suki, I've known since before Thanatos came. Xander was one of his advisors. Greer, we met shortly after...." She hesitates before changing whatever she was prepared to say. "She's been with us for a few days. Wren or Renny is her son, and the guy you made us bring along is some asshole who broke into the house you found us in."

"The child is a liability. Why keep it?"

"First, his name is Renny, not child, and certainly not it. Second, he is not a liability. He's everything right in this shithole world. Third, don't ever say something like that again."

"Or what?"

"Ask your brother," she snaps before storming off to see how the child... Renny is doing. *Perhaps I shall do just that.*

Chapter Eleven: Raid

He trains my hands for battle, so that my arms can bend a bow of bronze. Psalm 18:34.

~ *Avalon Spring 2026*~

WHEN WE ARRIVED AT THE CAMP that had sheltered Xander and Suki for several months, it wasn't the warm welcome they believed we would receive. It didn't take them long to figure out who the mammoth man on the horse was. I can tell you the instant they put it all together, had it not been for Xander rushing in front of Pestilence's horse, the men and women who live here would have started an all-out war with one of the riders sent to judge us. The problem is that the deaths we would have been grieving are theirs, not his.

The inhabitants were none too happy I willingly brought Pestilence to their doorstep. I have little doubt if they did not fear what he would do to them, they would have killed me for it. They refused to talk to me for the first week we were here. It wasn't until the horseman did something I never thought he would that they finally stopped looking at me like I was a traitor. He told them they had nothing to fear from him. He confessed they would not fall from his disease because of a bargain I struck for their safety. I notice how often the rider uses the word he, him, or his when assuring their safety which means this community may yet fall if another horseman is inadvertently released. He will be the only rider to uphold the promise.

Suki and Xander are both trusted members of this group of survivors. I said it before, and I'll say it again, there is something about Xander you can't help but feel at ease around. Like the men and women of Death's horde, these people look to him for guidance, and Xander seems only too happy to help. Even with all the other beautiful women in this group Xander still only has eyes for the spitfire I call sister. Which is a good thing because I would hate to have to stab him.

The asshole isn't quite as big an ass as I originally thought. Jay helps the community by doing whatever they ask, no matter how menial the task is, and he does it even if he thinks no one is watching. He's attentive to Wren, who requires the entire community to help keep him safe. It's a testament to Greer's fortitude that she did it alone for so long. Then there's the way Jay fusses over Greer. I'm not sure what is going on there, but if I had to guess, I would say Jay wants to explore things further. This doesn't mean I fully trust him, but I'm willing to give him a chance.

Marcelle Valentine

Renny has settled in nicely. Like the rest of the people who meet him, he completely enthralls the members of this community. For all the horrible things this world has left to offer, it did get one thing right. A blonde-haired, blue-eyed angel named Wren. To look at him, other than his small stature, you would not realize anything was different. But for this sweet little boy, this is where the similarities to other children end. Wren cannot communicate with us; his vocabulary is limited to a few words, phrases, or songs. He clicks his tongue between most of the things he can say. He requires a routine to help him from becoming overwhelmed. When this happens, he can only express himself by crying. The biggest obstacle is he has no fear, not of other people, not of hurting himself, not of a certain rider who scares the shit out of the biggest of men. And the one thing little Renny loves above anything other than Greer is the horse I have yet to name. Give me some more time, and I'll also figure out this horse's name.

It took Greer slightly longer to find her stride here. She had a hard time processing all the help she now has with Wren. Including several of the children who recognize Renny is not like them but work with him every day so he can learn how to interact with kids. I have found Greer on more than one occasion with tears filling her eyes as she watches her son playing with the other children. As for Jay, she seems to enjoy spending time with him, though I'm unsure if she feels the same about him as he does about her. I can tell you one thing I have noticed: she watches Pestilence... a lot. More than any of the others living here. It reminds me of a time when I would gaze at another rider.

I want to encourage it since we all know how it turned out for me and my rider. Well, apart from the whole 'him being called home' shit. The problem is twofold. First, Greer seems too shy to act on it, even if she is attracted to him. Second, I can't get a read on this new horseman to know if he has any interest in mortals, let alone the timid woman who barely talks to him and spends most of the time sneaking glances from the corner of her eye.

After I told Pestilence off for calling Renny a liability, I refused to speak to him for days. I realize he could give a shit less if we lowly mortals talked to him or not, but I did. I wanted him to know his observation was wrong and unwanted. If it hadn't been for him agreeing to stay here until we could fortify the camp, thus ensuring Suki, Xander, Greer, and Wren's safety, I still would not be talking to him. Thankfully, he agreed to do this because a band of thirty men raided the camp four nights after we were due to depart.

They had been planning it for weeks, learning how the patrols worked, when they switched out, where every man resided, and if they had wives or children.

~

Avalon the night of the raid~

I walk over to help Greer pick up the rest of the dishes from tonight's dinner. "It looks like Renny is having a blast."

"He loves it when the kids let him play hide-n-seek. He doesn't understand what he's supposed to do, so they don't expect him to be the seeker even when they catch him. They also don't get mad when he runs out to tag them when he gets tired of hiding."

"They're a wonderful group of kids."

"More than good. They're the best," she says with a smile as she watches Wren running away as he giggles loud enough for them to find him no matter where he hides. Regardless of whether he laughed or not, the kids could walk straight to where he hid since it was the same place every time. He hides next to Pestilence's horse. Which I admit is amazing in its own right since if it were anyone else, the horse would have no issues warning you away, but Renny gets a pass. I guess even the horse isn't immune to this sweet little boy.

I laugh whenever I hear the adults saying, "If I didn't know any better, I would swear that horse is hiding him." If only they knew what one of the rider's horses is capable of.

"Are you going to the bonfire tonight?"

"If Renny doesn't wear himself out before they light it."

"You know, I'm sure if you bribed one of the kids with chocolate, they will keep an eye on him if he falls asleep."

"I don't know, maybe."

"I heard Jay's hoping you'll be there," Suki announces as she comes over and plops her ass on the table we just cleaned.

"What's the deal with you two?" I ask, wiping the last of the crumbs away.

"Yeah, give us all the dirty details," Suki purrs as she wiggles her eyebrows, making me snap her with the towel I'm holding. "Ow, damn it, A, that hurt."

"I meant it too," I reply with a laugh.

"He's nice, but I don't know."

"What's not to know, girl? You need some adult time, and he wants to be the one to bring the hammer home."

"Seriously, Suki, where the hell do you come up with this shit?"

"Playboy."

"You mean, Playgirl?"

"Nope, I mean Playboy. The best way to learn how to please your man is to read what turns them on." Her response leaves Greer and me standing here with our mouths hanging open. "What? Don't tell me you never read one."

"I didn't even know Playboy has words," I confess.

"Yeah, I'm with Avalon on this one. I thought it was nothing but pictures."

"I have a couple if you want to learn a thing or two."

"I'm good," I confess. It's not like I'll be having sex anytime soon since the only man I want no longer exists in this world.

"Greer?"

"I'll keep it in mind." Suki lifts her hand before pretending it's a gun and fires it in her direction.

"So you're not into Jay?" Suk pushes.

"I don't know. It's just...." I don't miss her eyes flicking toward a certain muscled rider tending to his horse. Thankfully, Suki does, or Greer would regret letting her eyes wander. "I think he wants more than I'm ready to give."

"I get it. Keep things simple until you're sure." Or you figure out how you feel about the man you can't keep your eyes off. I don't lend a voice to these thoughts, opting to keep them to myself. "This way, there are no messy breakups to deal with, especially since the camp isn't all that big."

"I mean, I do like talking with him, and when it comes to Wren, he is sweet."

"Say no more; it's a maybe but not a today. Besides, I want to hear all about A's time with a certain someone."

"Not going to happen, Suk."

"Oh — come on, it's been months. It's time to dish out all the dirty deets."

"You assume there are dirty details to reveal."

"See, I don't even know that, and I'm your best friend. This is something I should know. Isn't that right, Greer?"

"Don't bring me in on this. If Avalon doesn't want—"

"You can take her answer as political. She wants to know, but she's too polite to ask."

"No, Suki," I say, tossing the towel on the table as I make my way over to the closest soul to Thanatos I can get, Pestilence.

"Just tell me if it was big or not. I imagine it was huge." Several other residents stop to glare at Suk, who, in true Suki form, comes up with something fast. "What? I'm talking about a rabbit she saw out in the woods today. I wanted to know if it was big enough to satisfy or not." She yells the last part to ensure I know her reference has nothing to do with some fictitious rabbit. Looking at the group of women staring at me, I shake my head before continuing toward the other rider in my life.

"What was the little one yelling about?" Pestilence asks as he continues to brush his horse.

"You don't want to know." When he looks at me, I swear I glimpse the hint of a smile. There is no way he knows what happened. Sweet Jesus, please tell me this rider doesn't know all the dirty details Suki is dying to learn.

For thirty minutes, we stand there. Neither of us talks, but somehow it's comforting to be this close to one of Death's brothers. Especially since I no longer have to worry about him killing off the men and women of this camp or the rest of the world. Because if he's here with me, he's not out there spreading his disease.

"I think I'm going to go to bed."

"Sleep well, little lamb."

"Okay, what's the deal with the nicknames you and your brother call me?"

"Lamb is what you are. Apple is fitting."

"This is the same damn thing Thanatos said. Care to elaborate?"

"He did not tell you why he calls you this?"

Seeing an opportunity, I reply, "Of course he did. I just wanted to get your perspective."

"You do understand I can sense when a mortal is lying.

"Well, shit. I do now," I mumble, realizing any hope of discovering the deal with the nickname just evaporated.

"If Thanatos did not elaborate on why he calls you this, neither shall I."

"You're all a bunch of assholes. You know that... right?"

"As you say, little lamb. See you in the morning."

I have only moved a few feet when I hear a scream which results in Pestilence pulling me protectively against his chest.

"What the hell—" Pestilence's hand comes across my mouth, silencing any further questions. Loosening his grip, he turns me to face him before bringing his finger to his mouth. I know he's not mortal, so I'm sure most of the residents would not understand why he is using caution, but they don't know what I do; the horsemen are not invincible.

Another scream has me jerking to see what the hell is happening. This is when I see the waves of men storming into camp, attacking the men and immobilizing the women.

"You do not know who I am, but you will soon enough. For now, you should know we are the ones who run this camp from here on out. Everything you have belongs to us. Your supplies, your homes, your... women," he declares as he steps up to Greer to run his finger over her face. I swear Pestilence's grip tightens painfully on my arms. I don't know if he meant this as a warning to me to keep my mouth shut or something else, but if the glare he is giving the man touching Greer is anything to go by, I would have to say it was the latter.

"Tie the men up. I'll deal with them later," Suki screams as she charges toward an unconscious Xander. They must have caught him out on patrol and beat him because his face is covered in blood, and his eyes are so swollen he couldn't open them even if he were awake. I jerk, wanting to help my friend, but the rider holding me whips me back before I can expose where we are standing.

"No." This is the only response I get.

"Fuck you," I hiss as I try again to shake off his grip.

"You will remain quiet," his hushed warning is every bit the demand he meant it to be.

"If you think I'm going to stand by and watch my friends—" I'm cut off when I hear Greer shriek. We yank our heads in the direction of where she is standing. This is when I see what has her screaming and the catalyst that brought a horseman into the fray.

Wren, who does not understand what's going on, has wandered up to the man running this show. His smiling face beams up at the newcomer as he slaps his hands together as if in prayer before clicking, "Dink, peas."

"Get the fuck away from me," the soon-to-be-dead man snarls.

"Fuck, fuck, fuck, fuck," Wren mimics as he marches in a little circle.

This is when the asshole makes the biggest mistake of his life. He lifts his foot and knocks Wren to the ground. Greer's screams, and Renny's sobs are only outdone by Pestilence's roar as he comes to full height. Before I can follow, he plucks me up, tosses me on his horse, and delivers his instructions. "If I fall, take her to safety."

If I try to climb down from the horse to follow, I know he will bolt and carry me away before I can confirm they are all safe. So instead, I am left feeling helpless as Pestilence makes his presence known. He marches across the area with only one intention. Several men who accompanied the one whose life is not worth spit charge Pestilence only to be sent sailing back to where they started in a heap.

The leader is wise enough to back away, giving him a clear path to his goal; a crying Wren. Who is currently trying to stand up while wiping the dirt from his hands and face. I didn't think Pestilence possessed the ability to be gentle, but the way he is with Wren proves he can. With Renny held safely in his arms, the rider whispers something to Wren before yanking his bow from his shoulder. I'm amazed at what I see. Wren's arms and legs are locked around the horseman, eyes closed tight, his face buried in his neck, hands covering his ears, and he's singing.

Before any invader can react, Pestilence whips around, drops to one knee, and begins firing one arrow after another. What is more shocking than the rate at which he can release them; is the black smoke oozing out of him and tracking only the ones who shouldn't be here.

One fool gets a shot off before the horseman can stop him, and seeing it flying at them, I am terrified Wren is the one who will take the hit. At the last second, Pestilence wraps him protectively in his arms and twists to take the shot meant for Wren. Payback for our resistance. The arrow drives deep into his side, and his pained expression is only rivaled by his horse's urgent huffs.

"Come on, boy, we can't let them fight this alone," I quietly tell him as I stroke his neck. Thank goodness the horse is more aware of his surroundings than I am because I feel his shift before his back legs kick out. I feel a thud vibrate through the air, and I realize he has just fought off the man who was trying to sneak up on us. Knocking him several feet away from where we stand.

I right myself in time to discover Jay holding Greer from rushing out to her son's side, Pestilence is back up firing a volley of arrows, and Wren is singing what I can only guess is Baa-baa Black Sheep as loudly as he can. With Pestilence's horse momentarily distracted, I flip my leg over him and slide off the horse faster than he can react. I grab the blade left behind by the asshole who wanted to stab me and race out to the clearing.

With his objective no longer a deterrent, Pestilence's horse joins the fight. Leaving me to dole out a little of my own brand of justice. I dodge the fist of the first man while dropping low enough to drag the blade across his shins as I slide by.

My next obstacle doesn't come from the invaders; it's a courtesy from the rider. A death I have no desire to experience, forcing me to dive over one of the black tendrils; I slam my head into the groin of the next man. Before he can react, an arrow buries deep between his eyes. I nod my thanks to the rider while rushing toward my next target.

The next man in the line focuses solely on the rider as Pestilence tries to protect me while I make my way through the line of men opposing him. I watch as my next target levels a nocked arrow at the only one who stands between us and the asshole who invaded. I fear the worst when he releases it before I can stop him. The shot finds its mark in Pestilence's chest. This time he doesn't merely wince; he howls from the pain. Another arrow nocked, and another projectile pierces Pestilence's calf. As I reach the one doing all the damage, I slash my blade out, cutting through muscles and tendons, forcing him to drop the damn weapon. The problem is the one I took out is not the only one focusing their attack on Pestilence now. The rest of the cowards who attacked us are firing at him in rapid succession.

Fury fills Pestilence's eyes as he throws his bow aside to cocoon Wren in his embrace before the shouts in his native tongue release more tendrils. They do not simply slither toward their target this time; they streak. How they manage to avoid the residents in this community is a miracle in itself, but realistically it proves he is the master of the plague he commands. Seeing the men responsible for attacking us writhing on the ground as the smoke forces its way down their throats is nothing short of terrifying.

The attack lasted for several minutes. By the time the smoke clears, I find most of the invaders dead, Pestilence lying on the ground and Wren standing next to him with his eyes closed and hands still covering his ears.

Chapter Twelve: Naïve

~ Greer the night of the raid~

SEEING MY SON SHUFFLING TOWARDS THE one who invaded our home made my heart leap into my throat. Watching as the asshole kicked him shattered it. Wren has made so many strides since we arrived here, and in less than two seconds, one careless act reversed all his progress. I rush the asshole responsible for my son's tears, but someone yanks me back before I get anywhere near him.

"Let me go," I yell as I flail wildly against the one holding me.

"Greer, don't." Jay stopped me. Who the hell does he think he is?

"Damn it, Jay, let me go. My son is out there."

"I know." If he knows this, then why in the hell is he pulling me further away from Wren? Slamming my head back, hoping to shatter his nose, he dodges my incoming attack.

"I'm not letting you go out...." His words trail off while his grip on me loosens, giving me more space to maneuver. "What the hell?"

Twisting to see what has him so rattled, I don't know if what I discover is a good thing or not. Pestilence is stalking from the area he keeps his horse. One thing seems to have garnered his unwavering focus, Wren. Terrified he'll hurt Renny more than he can help, I struggle to break free from Jay's hold. Unfortunately, I wasted my opportunity because Jay's determination to keep me safely away from the invaders, and the horsemen are back in full force.

"Let me fucking go."

"No."

The rider sent to kill us does something I never expected. He picks my son up, whispering something that only Renny can hear before he begins his assault against the raiders. Realizing my son is in the middle of this fight, I scream, begging them to stop. If one of those arrows hits Wren, there is no way he will survive. The last couple of years flash before my eyes. All the times I have kept him safe, all the advances and regressions. The fears, the dreams, the hopes for a better life all come down to one rider of the apocalypse protecting my son from the arrows flying towards them.

A rider of the damn apocalypse.

A being sent to destroy us.

A bringer of plague is the sole being standing between the assholes who came to enslave us and my life. If Wren dies, I'll have no reason to live.

Marcelle Valentine

I realize my biggest fear has come to pass when I see the arrow flying, not at the horseman but at my son. My strangled sob produces no sound as I try to warn the horseman, but it makes no difference because the rider twists at the last second, taking the shot meant for my Renny. A newfound respect for this man surges to life. The relief is short-lived as another thought occurs to me: if he can feel pain, can he also succumb to it? And if he falls, no one other than me will be left to protect my son.

Avalon streaks out from wherever she is hiding. When she slices her blade across one man's legs, I realize her intention is to join the fight rather than run; I know my time of standing by has also ended. Another arrow impales the horseman, and this time he doesn't grimace; he groans. Wrestling away from Jay, any thought of helping them ends abruptly when I see what is rolling off Pestilence in waves.

"NO!" I scream, knowing Renny will never survive his plague, and I have no doubt what I'm looking at is precisely that.

Jay dives on top of me. I don't know if he thought he could save me from whatever the horsemen released. I can assure him nothing could be further from the truth, and what the hell gives him the right to decide this for me? But there's no point in fighting him; he outweighs me by more than a few pounds, making any attempt to push him off me feeble and ridiculous.

After more minutes than what is comfortable, I feel Jay shift on top of me as several people begin coughing. Oh god, has it started already? My only thought is getting to Wren. Thankfully, Jay slides off me, allowing me to survey my surroundings for the first time since he threw himself over me.

What I find is the men and women of this community are alive, well, and seemingly unaffected by his plague; as is....

"Renny," I scream as I run towards him while Avalon sprints towards the horsemen, who did not fare as well as the rest of us. Oh my god, they riddled him with arrows; however, Wren doesn't have so much as a scratch anywhere on him. This rider, the one who is supposed to be our end, protected my son when no one else could.

"Pestilence, get up," Avalon pleads. If not for the fact he saved my son, I would question her sanity. But after everything this man did for me, I know I need to help him. Doing one more thorough check to ensure Wren has no injuries I missed the first time I inspected him, I turn my attention to the being I know needs my help.

"Nehra, take Renny back to my place. I'll be there soon." Nehra is a young woman they saved from the camp where Xander and Suki discovered Avalon. The place they kept me from wandering into a few days later. She's a sweet woman who Renny took to immediately.

Lord only knows if the rest of the community helped Avalon and I carry the horseman into one of the unclaimed structures because they realized the sacrifice he made for them. They could be afraid of what will happen when he wakes up. Or it's possible what drives the people here is the fear of what the other riders will do if they arrive. Especially if they were to discover the survivors did nothing to help their brother. Whether it be kindness, concern, or self-preservation, their help was necessary because I'm not sure Avalon and I alone could have moved him.

After we have him settled, Avalon removes one arrow after another. The pained expression on her face leads me to believe this is not the first time she has done this. If I didn't know any better, I would swear Avalon counts each arrow as she pulls it out. The precision of how she treats each wound lends credence to her having medical experience.

"Maybe we should let him die." I hate being this person, but if letting the unconscious being lying before me die saves my son, I have to do whatever I can to protect him.

"Never going to happen."

"He's here to kill us, Avalon. How can you defend him?"

"Because."

"That's not an answer."

"I defend him because I find him worth my loyalty," I begin to interject, but Avalon raises her hand to silence my objection. "I know what he's here to do. Have you or any of these other people stopped to think about why he's doing it?"

"You think there is any reason that justifies our extermination?"

"We've been doing it to each other since the beginning of time. Humanity does it for a piece of land, jealousy, desire, and a whole host of other bullshit reasons, but for him, it's what his father created him for. To deliver his father's divine justice."

"So you're fine with him killing us? You don't even believe in God or like him, for that matter."

"There are worse things than death. And the believing part, well, it's pretty damn impossible to not believe with one of his horsemen lying there. As for the liking part, we haven't always seen eye to eye about things, but that doesn't mean I will take out my frustration on another of his creations."

"Worse things than death? Avalon, death is final."

"But is it really? None of us know what happens after we die."

"You can't be serious. Do you think Renny deserves this? Does he deserve to die?"

"No, but I can tell you his chances of survival are a hell of a lot better with the being sent here to judge us than the good and honorable men of this world."

"Avalon."

"Do I have to remind you it was a man who cared so little for Wren he kicked him because he asked a fucking question? And it was the man lying over there who saved him at the risk of his own survival."

"He's not a man."

"He's as real as any of us. Besides, I'm betting that we may still come out of this alive if we can show him our worth. Especially since it is my fault he's here."

"You may have to elaborate on that 'your fault he's here' part." The problem is she has no intention of disclosing any further details regarding this issue, and after she pointed out it was Pestilence who saved my son from a mortal man, I felt like a massive piece of work.

Twenty minutes later, Suki shuffles into the room where we are nursing the horseman back to health, confirming Xander will survive. She delivers the sad news one community member fell during the attack, a man they caught out on patrol. Thankfully, she also checked on Wren, who doesn't seem as affected by all this as I feared he would be since she confirmed he was sound asleep. After all the craziness from the night, the most insane part is I think Pestilence's horse is eager to know his outcome. He hasn't left the front of the shelter since we brought the rider in here.

"I'm going to get his horse settled. Will you be okay until I get back?" Avalon asks as she takes one last look at his wounds.

"Yes."

"Are you sure you're okay with watching over him?"

"I should never have suggested we let him die. He doesn't deserve it. So yes, I'm sure we'll be fine. Do whatever you need to do. I promise I'll look after him."

"If you need me, just yell."

"I can do that," I say with a smile. Avalon fusses over Pestilence for another second before she goes to the door.

Avalon's tender voice as she tries to reassure the horse his rider will be fine is confusing. Then again, what isn't baffling when it comes to the man lying in this bed, the horse forever at his side, or the woman who seems to know more about these horsemen than anyone else? I listen to Avalon's comforting words until her voice fades to little more than murmurs in the distance. She must have persuaded the horse to return to the area Pestilence had established for him.

After I'm confident we are alone, I say the things I would never have the guts to say if he were awake, "Thank you. Thank you for saving my son. You will never understand how much this means to me."

His soft groan leads me to take his hand in mine. I did it on instinct, wanting to comfort another soul who was suffering. The fact he's a horseman sent to kill us never enters my mind.

*****

"You are drooling on me," the deep rumble of his words cause my eyes to snap open. What the hell? Without moving my head, I scan the room, trying to figure out what happened when it all comes back to me in a rush. The fight, the injured horsemen, helping Avalon, talking to an unconscious rider, and... Oh. My. God. Falling asleep on his chest with his hand still clasped in mine.

"Sorry!" I reply as I jerk away from him, wiping my mouth, still damp from sweat and, god forgive me, slobber. He reaches for one of the bloody rags we used to clean his wounds to sop up the puddle I left behind. I don't think I have ever been this mortified before.

"Is there a reason you are here? Sleeping on my chest? Showering me with your saliv—"

"Please don't finish your sentence," I plead, jumping up from the chair I had pulled up next to his bed. "They injured you during the fight last night. I wanted to watch over you."

"And you are able to do this with your eyes closed?"

"Oh, god, grant me strength." My plea is a feeble attempt to give me a second to think of any probable response to explain why he found me the way he did.

"My father would also be interested in knowing how you are so adept you can watch without using your eyes."

"I fell asleep. Which never would have happened if Avalon would have come back."

"The lamb did not return because she knew I would survive."

"Who?"

"The one you call Avalon."

"She knew you didn't need our help?" Why the hell didn't she tell me this? I see a long conversation in our future. A discussion about her withholding information. Or could he be mistaken about what she knew? "Are you sure? Because she seemed pretty distraught last night. Especially when she was removing the arrows from you."

"I believe this has more to do with Thanatos than me."

"Thanatos? I don't know who or what a Thanatos is."

"Who he is would be my brother. What he is is the final rider. He is Death."

"Wait, I thought Death was the first horseman? He already came and lost."

My question causes him to laugh, although I'm not sure what I said that he could find amusing. Since I've already drooled all over his large, firm chest, I figure I can't do anything else to embarrass myself, so I push forward, "I don't know what you're laughing at."

"You are very naïve."

"I'll thank you not to insult me. Especially after I spent the entire night looking after you." Before I can move, he sits up, planting one enormous leg on either side of the chair I flopped back down on. When he leans closer, I withdraw, attempting to put some space between him and me. But apparently, he has other ideas since he pulls the chair closer.

"You are right. I owe you a debt of gratitude. I should have chosen my words more carefully."

"Or, at the very least, thank me," I mumble, which causes a small smile to appear. This, in itself, is a phenomenon. I think I've only seen it happen a handful of times, mostly when he and Avalon are off by themselves, murmuring about only God knows what. It's a pleasant smile; he should do it more often.

"Thank you, Greer." Shit, he knows my name. I'm not so sure having a rider of the apocalypse knowing your name is a good thing. When he moves to put his shirt on, I scramble off the chair, careful not to let my legs touch his. I don't wait around to find out if he has anything else to say as I hurry out of the quarters we slept in. Okay, let me rephrase what I said. I didn't sleep with him; I fell asleep watching over him. Big difference. The first person I see also happens to be the one person I want to talk to.

"What happened to you last night, Avalon?" I ask, trying not to let too much attitude slip into my question.

"It took me a while to get Pestilence's horse calmed down—Hey, I think I came up with a name for him; want to hear it?"

"No, I do not want to hear the horse's name. What I want to know is what took you so long?"

"Are you pissed at me?"

"Well, you're not high on my list of favorite people right now."

"I'm sorry, Greer. Truly." She says when she realizes her first attempt didn't have the desired effect. "It took longer to calm his horse than I thought, then I checked on Xander and Suki. Afterward, I popped in to see how Wren and Nehra were doing. I helped move some of the... people—" Thankfully, she used this word rather than bodies, which I know is what she means. "out of camp, and by the time I got back, you were already asleep. Pestilence seemed much better, so I left you both alone so you could get some needed rest."

"Well, you shouldn't have."

"Did he say something to upset you? If he did, then he'll answer to me."

"For one, he told me he didn't need our help."

Avalon tilts her head, giving me a sympathetic smile. "Do you really think one of the fabled horsemen wants to admit he needed one of us lowly mortal's help?" I give her an incredulous sigh, followed by an eye roll to drive home how irritating this entire situation is. "Alright, so would he have died? Probably not. Was he suffering? Absolutely. Would I do it again if the situation arose? Without a doubt."

"Why?"

"I don't know... I guess it's because he reminds me of someone. Besides, I don't know why you're so upset. So you fell asleep in the same space as Pestilence. It's no big deal."

"No big deal? Avalon, I drooled on him. Big. Wet. Slobbery. Drool puddle right in the middle of his chest."

She pulls her lips into her mouth, biting down on them, in what I can only imagine is her trying not to laugh at me. She only manages it for a few seconds before laughing hysterically at my misfortune.

"Go ahead, laugh it up."

"What did Pestilence say?"

"He woke me up because he had spit on his chest. What the hell do you think he said?"

"I don't imagine the word thanks was part of it."

"The word thanks," I grumble in my best, *you're an idiot tone*. "Was definitely not part of the conversation."

"Hey, you were upright in the chair when I came in. The head on his chest thing was all you." The sound of the door slamming behind me has me whipping my head around, only to find the object of my humiliation standing there, adjusting the armor covering his arms. "I wonder if I should show him to the shower, or do you think he is satisfied with the bath you gave him?"

Smacking her arm, I snap, "Not funny. I blame you for this."

"I'm not the one who slept with a rider last night," she says as she backs away, with an annoying grin spreading over her face. The most irritating part is she isn't wrong.

I glanced in the direction where he was standing a second ago, only to discover him moving to his horse. I watch as he strides through the camp, and with each person he passes, he gets the same damn thing. A stupid half-hearted thanks from the people who owe him so much more than a meaningless word mumbled as he passed them by. I'm so wrapped up in his movements that I am unaware someone else is standing next to me. And honestly, I wish it had been anyone other than the person I discovered.

"Who slept with a rider?" Suki. It had to be Suki.

Chapter Thirteen: Storm

~*Pestilence The day after the raid*~

I ADMIT TO BEING CONFUSED AS to why the one named Greer stayed with me last night. Especially since I believe she would have rather been with the tiny child she cares for. Waking to her head on my chest and my hand held in hers was an odd sensation. Most mortals will not enter the city I am invading, let alone the same space. She looked so peaceful I contemplated allowing her to remain until I felt the warm liquid trickling from her mouth onto me. I can tolerate many things; evidently, this is not one of them.

She must know I would have recovered. Or does she? Had it not been for the arrow piercing my heart, I would never have faltered enough for the other projectiles to take me out.

Not to mention I expelled a significant amount of energy, focusing my plague to only affect the invaders. I swore an oath to Avalon and the other mortals at this camp that they would not fall by my hand. A promise I do not take lightly.

I cannot say why I felt inclined to intercede when I did other than to say the small human has never hurt another soul. He is also incapable of protecting himself. The men who attacked this camp did so with one thought in mind; to take what did not belong to them and dispose of the ones they did not want. The child fell into the latter category.

After Greer rushed from the dwelling they placed me in to recover, I felt it prudent to check on my horse and the little lamb I swore to protect.

"Nice to see you up and about."

"I am told you removed the arrows they attempted to end me with. Is this true, lamb?"

"Do you think we could do away with the lamb nickname, and I don't know, maybe call me Avalon? Hell, even A is better than lamb."

"You would prefer to forgo the honor of being the lamb and have me reference you as nothing more than a letter?"

"Ah, yeah. Listen, I understand that you all think the one who breaks the seals is all special and shit, but I can assure you humanity would not. The truth is, they would be only too happy to string my ass up and leave me for dead."

"No one would harm the lamb—"

"What world are you living in? We're talking about the same assholes whose action resulted in your father questioning our worth. The same assholes who tried to kill Thanatos several times and you at least once now."

"This is simply self-preservation."

"The same assholes who would hurt someone like Wren," she interjects while cocking her head to the side, and as much as I would like to, I cannot argue with her statement. The cowards who stormed this small community didn't think twice about him. She apparently realizes her point has been made since her eyebrows are raised to her hairline, and she sports a crooked smile while rocking back on her heels.

"I concede." Her crooked smile morphs into the beaming grin one can only experience when one believes they are triumphant. Well, this will not do. "On this one thing only. I will not refer to you as the lamb when we are with others."

"I guess I'll take it."

"Orsey," the child I saved yells as he runs over to where Avalon and I are standing. When he pulls on my shirt, I look at the lamb to explain why he continues to do this.

"He wants you to pick him up."

"Why?"

"I guess he likes you."

"Why?"

"Hell if I know. I'm still trying to figure out why I like you," the lamb replies, but she corrects her comment when my gaze moves over to where she is standing. "If you have to know, I guess it's probably because you did something decent for him. He must feel safe around you."

"And you? Why do you like me, little lamb?"

"The jury is still out on that one, and I would like to point out we are not alone."

I attempt to ignore him until he progresses from pulling to yanking. Huffing, I lean over to pick him up. He immediately begins singing a song.

"Orse, say nay-nay-nay. Cow, says moo-moo-moo."

Looking over at Avalon, I ask, "He realizes there are no cows around us?"

"It's a song Greer sings to him all the time. He's singing it because of your horse, just as he would if he saw a pig or a dog."

"A pig?"

"Yes, Pestilence, a pig. As in the pig, says oink, oink, oink." I cannot help the sigh I give her, but she must find it entertaining since she is now laughing at me, and based on the grin from the little one I'm holding, so did he.

"Oggy, says woof-woof-woof."

"How long will he persist with this, lamb?"

"Lamb says bah-bah-bah," the little one sings as he looks at me.

"Until he gets tired of singing it."

"Which takes how long?"

"Better settle in for the long version," she says over her shoulder, waving as she walks away. Why she would leave me to tend to the child is something I cannot comprehend. Perhaps she merely forgot.

"Wait, you should take the child with you."

"Nope, I think he's perfectly happy right where he is." Avalon and I will need to discuss this when we talk next. Looking back down at the child, he smiles briefly.

"What do you want?" The child's question baffles me. I am unsure why he would ask me this since I did not indicate I needed anything. "Peas."

"No, Renny, you have to tell him what you want. Do you want something to eat?" When the child does not respond, Greer proceeds to her next question.

"Do you want something to drink?"

"He is not responding."

"He will. When we say the thing he wants, you'll know." She redirects her attention to the little boy, who refuses to let me put him down. "Do you want to pet Pestilence's horse?"

"Peas... Tank you." He says, bringing his hand to his chin and pulling it away.

"There you go. Wren wants to pet your horse."

"Pet my horse? No mortal has ever wished to do this before."

"Well, I guess Renny will be the first." The young child wiggles in my arms, attempting to move closer to my companion. Without further thought, Greer places a hand on my back, bringing her close enough to take the little one's hand in hers so she can guide him on how she believes is the proper way to pat my horse's snout. I admit I am somewhat amazed he does not shy away; quite the contrary, if I did not know any better, I would say my horse is enjoying this attention. I am also keenly aware of her hand still resting on my back. To have a mortal seemingly unafraid to touch me is surprising since most of them give me a wide berth.

When the child finally tires of stroking my horse, I place him down. He immediately runs to play by himself. I often witness him alone. The other children ask him to play, but he seems content to play on his own today.

"Can I ask you something?"

"Of course," I reply, moving over to begin my daily ritual of tending to my horse.

"What did you say to Wren?"

I know she is referring to my action from last night when I silenced him with a few words. I can tell her what she wants to know; however, she will not understand the effect of these words relates directly to how I spoke them to him. This, beyond anything else, is what calmed him. I am not magical.

My creator made me for only one thing, spreading disease, but my father also understood some of the beings who would fall from my plague would not necessarily deserve it. In those times, he granted me the ability to calm. And while I'm certain my father never intended me to use it while sparing a soul, he did not stipulate how I should use it. I could think of nothing more worthy of this gift than the little one who shines so brightly.

"Will you please tell me?"

"I told him to close his eyes and cover his ears. I told him no matter what, he was to remain like this until you told him otherwise."

"That's all?"

"I also asked him to sing me a song."

~ Avalon four weeks after the raid~

I get a distinct feeling whatever he is about to say will only piss me off since his stance is rigid, his expression is stone, and the rate he stalks toward me tells me he is not in the mood for any argument from me. Too bad for him because I'm not the compliant little lamb he hoped for.

"We need to leave." Pestilence demands.

"Why? And to where?"

"The why is because I told you we are leaving. The where does not matter."

"If you think I'm leaving without a damn good reason, especially since the community is still trying to rebuild after the raid, then you're going to be pissed because I am not going anywhere."

"It is time, little lamb. I have delayed my mission far longer than I should have."

"So you're planning on killing people."

"I was sent here for a reason. Guarding this community and the ones who live here was not it," his eyes drift briefly towards Greer, who is laughing at something Jay said. He continues to watch their interaction before his body goes rigid. "We leave today."

"I don't want to go."

"This is not the deal we made. I have upheld my end; it is time for you to do the same. Unless you wish for me to retract my promise."

He's not joking. If I want to keep these people safe, I must leave with him. I had hoped his growing affection for Wren and Greer would change his mind and heart concerning his task, but I guess not. His eyes flick over to where she is standing again. His gaze seems to trace the lines of her frame until he realizes he is not the only one watching another. He drops his eyes when he becomes aware I am looking at him and where his focus is fixed. He cares for Greer, or at least he seems intrigued, and if he is fascinated with her, there is still a chance I can change his mind. I can work with this.

"Will we ever return?"

"I suppose anything is possible," his stoic response as he abruptly turns away confirms it's more than possible. It's highly likely, especially if Greer is still here.

*****

Pestilence wasted no time gathering our stuff before he practically tossed my ass on his horse to head out of town. I thought Suki was going to attack him. Hell, if Xander hadn't been there to stop her, she may have done just that. I admit watching Xander holding her back almost made me laugh. It wasn't because he was restraining her; it was how he did it I found most amusing. He had her back held against his chest as her legs dangled a good foot off the ground. She looked like a baby strapped to her parent's chest in one of those stupid ass baby carriers. Only this baby wasn't smiling or cooing; she was cussing and screaming.

I should be upset he is forcing me to leave her behind, especially when I tried so damn hard to find her. Not to mention Thanatos told me to return to Xander because he would keep me safe. But I'm not worried about it. For one, something tells me Pestilence, not Xander, is better suited for the 'keeping my ass out of trouble' job, and two, I have little doubt I will see her again soon.

We ride for an hour without seeing a single soul. Something that makes me infinitely happy.

"You seem uncharacteristically cheerful, a rather abrupt emotion, I might add. So tell me, little lamb, what has you grinning like this?"

"No people."

"The lack of mortals causes you joy?"

"Well, let's face it, Pestilence, no people means no one for you to kill. So yes, the entire you not decimating humanity part makes me extremely happy."

"You believe I can only deliver my plague if I see them?"

"Well... yes?" He turns without answering my obvious question, which informs me how wrong my assumption was, making me mumble from the distress I am currently feeling. "Shit."

"I assume you realize the folly of your belief?"

"Does this mean the entire time we were back at camp—"

"I was releasing my plague to the surrounding territories?" He turns, his brown eyes assessing me as he searches my face for the answer. I have to force myself to swallow. The fear mounting inside me sits like a lump in my throat. A massive choke me to death, you didn't do shit to help anyone, blob stuck right in the middle of my damn windpipe. The sense of pending death hangs heavy in the air as I realize the lack of people is because of the man I travel with, not because they are smart enough to stay away.

"Can you stop Storm? I need... I need... Shit, I don't know what I need.... Down. I want down."

"I sense no incoming inclement weather."

"What?"

"You asked me to stop the storm, but no foul weather approaches us."

"No, not weather. Storm." He looks at me like the only thing I did was repeat what he already said, just in a different manner. Or maybe he thinks I'm an idiot. When I take a second to look at him, I would have to say he thinks I'm dumb, but right now, I don't care about what he believes because I'm working hard to not lose the breakfast we ate a few hours ago. As a result, I mumble, "Your horse."

"Storm?"

"His name."

"My horse has no name, little lamb."

"He does now."

"Ah, yes, I recall you like to name our horses. Why do you do this?" Pestilence asks as I throw my leg over the side of

Storm to slide off him. The second my feet hit the ground, I know all the swallowing in the world won't halt the inevitable. Leaving me little options other than to scramble off the road into the thick overgrowth so Pestilence doesn't have to witness what is erupting out of me.

"Are you feeling better, little lamb?" he asks five minutes later when I rejoin him on the road.

"I don't know what happened," I lie, hoping he can't sense the untruth I spoke like Death always could.

"You have a caring heart. One that does not like to see others suffer. I should not have revealed the truth in the manner I did. For this, I apologize."

"Only for how you told me, not for what you're doing?"

"Avalon, you know my purpose. This has never changed," he tells me as he rests a hand on my shoulder.

I know I should hate this being. Should despise him with every breath I take, but I can't. I can't because I don't see an evil monster when I look at him. I see someone who is following what they were created for, and that's not his fault. It's his father's. Besides, I don't think he enjoys killing us off any more than I like knowing he's doing it.

Surprisingly, instead of climbing back on Storm, he opts to walk next to me as we continue toward wherever he plans to take us.

As different as he is from Death, I also find similarities; they both battle with what they were tasked with versus what I think they want to do. What their heart tells them is right. I know this because they wouldn't feel drawn to any of us if they didn't have doubts. Death would never have cared for me, at least I hope he cared for me, and Pestilence wouldn't look at Greer like she holds all the secrets this world has to offer.

"You never answered my question, little lamb." His words pull me out of my private thoughts.

"What question did you ask?"

"Why do you feel a need to name our horses?"

"Because everything and everyone should have its own identity, even a horse for one of the notorious riders of the apocalypse."

"Notorious?" I shrug my shoulders because, honestly, I figure that for most of the people in this world, it's probably the best word to describe them or what they represent. "Okay, I accept your sentiment, but tell me why you selected Storm as his name?"

"He will only heed the call of his true owner. He's deadly and unpredictable, yet at the same time, he's beautiful. Watching him is like observing a storm roll in. You know it's coming, but you can't tear your eyes off it, nor do you want to."

"Do you agree, horse? Is your name Storm?" And like Ghost before him, Storm nods his approval, confirming he does.

Chapter Fourteen: Return to Normal

~ Greer Early Summer 2025 ~

IT'S BEEN A MONTH SINCE AVALON and Pestilence left camp, and I still don't know how I feel about it. Even though Pestilence's sole reason for being here was to bring about our end, I only truly felt safe when he was with us. After the brazen attack on our community, the truth of how precarious our situation was became abundantly obvious to me and several others.

Wren misses them too. I discovered him countless times standing where Pestilence used to keep his horse when they were here. I know he's looking for them, and the saddest part is no matter how much I try to explain they're gone, he doesn't understand. I think this is why I miss him too, because as terrible as his task might be when it came to Renny, he was patient and gentle. He did so much for my son that I will never forget. It is only because of his actions that my son is still alive.

As intriguing as we found Pestilence, I believe he found Wren just as fascinating. I can't say I blame him. I know the second Wren came into my life, he captured a piece of my heart. The best word I can use to describe my feelings is smitten. I was utterly smitten by the wonderful little boy who would someday become my beautiful son.

"Are we still on for tonight, Greer?" Jay's sudden appearance startles me. Jay must realize he scared me when he saw me jump because he immediately grasped my arms in his hands.

"I'm sorry. I didn't mean to frighten you."

"No, it's alright. I just didn't hear you coming up behind me." He rubs his hand down my arms, trying to comfort me.

"So, about tonight?" Jay has been asking me to go out with him for weeks now. I've used every reason I could come up with as to why I couldn't go until yesterday when I ran out of excuses. It's not that I think Jay is a bad guy, and he is handsome. Before the first rider showed up, I would have happily accepted his invitation, but now it's no longer only me. I need to think about Renny. While Jay is good to Wren, I don't know if he's ready for everything it entails to care for him. I finally agreed when Suki and Nehra reminded me it was only dinner, not a marriage proposal.

"Looking forward to it."

"Great, I'll see you around six?"

"Nehra said she be at my place by six, so that time works for me," I tell him, which leads him to do something I never expected. He lifts my hand to his mouth and kisses it. Gosh, I hope this isn't a glimpse of what's coming tonight because if it is, this may be a long evening.

*****

Looking in the small mirror in my cottage, I briefly contemplate calling the whole thing off. The place I now call home was once a camp for rich kids. The biggest difference between this place and every other camp I've seen before is instead of the kids staying in barrack-style bunkhouses, they received a small cottage with its own bathroom. A room that would be useless if not for the engineers living here who restored some functionality to them. While the showers are not hot, the water goes through a warmer, so it's no longer frigid. It works as long as no one spends twenty minutes in their shower with the water running.

"Is that what you're wearing?"

"It was, but based on your reaction, maybe not. What's wrong with it?"

"It's a damn good thing I came over here because that outfit is great if you want him to think you're a fifties housewife on the verge of joining a convent," Suki says with a laugh while she tosses a couple of outfits on the bed. "And that we're the same size."

Picking up the outfit on top, I am momentarily left speechless. It's covered in lace and sequins. It would be great if it was 1970, and we were going to a disco, but it's 2025, in a post-Death current Pestilence world where discos, bars, restaurants, and damn near everything else is gone, "I don't think so, Suki."

"I'm going to tell you the same thing I told A. I have game, Greer. Not to mention skills in the art of—"

"Seduction?" I finish for her because I remember Avalon teasing her about this on more than one occasion.

"Don't mock. It's annoying when Avalon does it, and it pisses me off when anyone else does."

When she holds up the next dress, it's not awful, and somehow I end up in it with my hair pulled up and knotted on top of my head because Suk told me men love seeing women's necks. Here I always thought it was another part of a woman's anatomy a little further south.

Suki turns me, allowing me to see her handy work. "Perfect. Now go forth and procreate."

I almost choke on the glass of homemade wine Mitch makes for the entire camp. Thankfully, a quick swipe of my chin saves the yellow dress I'm wearing as I sputter, "What?"

"Do the deed, get busy, screw like bunnies, ride his coc—"

Slamming my hand over her mouth before she could finish her thought. My eyes grow wide as I glance at Wren, who is playing in the corner but tends to repeat Suki like she's his own foul-mouth tutor. I can feel her growing smile against the palm of my hand.

Her thoughts about what this evening will entail tell me what I fear Jay may also expect. If so, I need to reconsider this entire night. I've never had sex on a first date. If I'm being honest, I've never had sex on a second date either. I've always been a three-date or more kind of girl.

I have almost convinced myself to scrap the whole thing when a knock on the door halts any further thoughts of blowing him off. Especially since Suki is already opening the door for him.

"Greer, you look... beautiful." He says, stepping into the room with a bouquet of wildflowers.

I timidly tuck a loose strand of hair behind my ear, relishing the cold air on my neck as I lower my gaze to my dress instead of meeting his eyes. Say something, Greer. You can't just stand here like some ungrateful buffoon.

"You... umm... thanks."

"Are you ready?"

"Yes." I want to say no, but if this is where our world has landed, I need to start living life again, not just survive it.

Jay leads me out of camp down to the stream, where a picnic is waiting for us. There is food, wine, and a blanket spread out. He thought of everything right down to the candles flickering in the gentle breeze, but when he takes my hand to escort me the rest of the way, I can't help the sense of dread pooling in my belly.

Over the next hour, we chat about nothing in particular. Our conversation is light... easy. Exactly what I've needed, and the tension I've had across my shoulders all day slowly slips away.

"So, what are your plans? Do you want to stay in the camp, or do you plan to move on someday?"

"For now, I enjoy being at camp. I love the people who live here, and it's nice having the extra help with Wren. It's hard on him being on the road."

"But don't you want a place of your own?"

"We have a place—" I start to tell him, but he doesn't wait for me to finish.

"No, I'm not talking about a summer camp cottage repurposed into a survival camp. I'm talking about a proper home. One where Wren could have a yard to play in, a place just for you, Greer. Away from the demands that come with living in a survival camp." Why in the world does this matter to him, and why would I ever want to move Wren out of the only place we have both felt safe in? I could tell him these things, but what would be the point? If he doesn't recognize the security we feel in this place, he will never understand why I don't want to leave.

Thankfully, he must sense the shift in my demeanor. One that is now screaming this subject is off limits.

"Sorry, I never should have pushed you for answers or suggested you leave this place." After his apology, I think it was safe to say the evening was done. Fortunately, he realized it at the same time I did since he immediately began packing everything before we made our way back to my place.

I wonder what the protocol is for dating in this post-Death world. Do you shake hands, thank each other... kiss. Definitely not kissing. Gosh, I hope he doesn't want to kiss me because I'm not sure I feel the same way about Jay as he does about me. I am not left wondering for long.

"I had a pleasant time with you until I opened my mouth and inserted my foot." The fact he is acknowledging his mistake goes a long way with me, and I can't help the little chuckle I give him.

"You really look beautiful." With his confession made, he brings his hand up to cup my neck as his thumb slides over my cheek. When he drops his gaze to my lips, I know he is debating if he should kiss me. I am not opposed to kissing. The longer I stand here with him, the more obvious it becomes that it means something different to him than it does to me. If I'm being truthful, it simply isn't something I thought about.

His tongue darting out to moisten his lips confirms his intention. His thumb under my chin prevents me from dropping my head as he moves to kiss me goodnight. The problem is the second his lips touch mine, it is not his face I see flash through my mind. What the heck is that about? Did I really imagine the lips against mine belong to Pestilence? At least Jay won't be able to press for another since Nehra saves the day when she opens the door to go home.

Pulling away from Jay, I thank him for a lovely evening before I slip through the door. What the hell was that all about? Why would I imagine it was Pestilence, not Jay kissing me? I'm not attracted to a rider sent to destroy us. I can't be.... It's not possible. Is it?

Panic swells inside me as I repeatedly tell myself I am not attracted to him. That the entire reason I imagined his face instead of Jay's is because I had been thinking of Avalon earlier today and, by extension, the horseman she is traveling with. The truth is A, and the riders go hand in hand. It has nothing to do with attraction.

Besides, he's long gone. I'll probably never see him again. It was a fluke event. A one-time phenomenon. One I'm sure will never happen again. So why is it that the only time I felt anything close to attraction was not when I imagined Jay's face... It is when I picture his.

Chapter Fifteen: Answer for an Answer

~ Pestilence Summer 2025 ~

AVALON'S BEAMING GRIN IS MADDENING AS she enthusiastically declares, "Bullshit. You can't lie to me."

Has she never heard the term numerous mortals have used in this situation?

"It was nothing more than an inadvertent mistake. Or, as you mortals like to say, a Freudian slip."

"Do you even know what a Freudian slip implies, Rider?"

"I do not lack intellect, nor am I missing the portion of my brain necessary to ascertain the meaning of something so trivial." What has the lamb so riled with the certainty I wish to return to the camp we left nearly two months prior? A foregone conclusion she was willing to bet her life on, which is something she should know better than doing. My grievous mistake was in calling her Greer. A clear sign in Avalon's mind I wish to return to them.

What I find most frustrating about the entire conversation is my thoughts should no longer linger on the woman or the child we left back there. The instant I left them behind, I should have forgotten them... as I'm confident they have surely forgotten me.

"Nope. I still say you're full of—"

"Shit. Yes, I am aware since you have repeated it ad nauseam."

"Hey, I simply call it as I see it."

"Surely."

"Don't be salty."

"I do not understand you at times, lamb. This would be an example of one of those times." I sigh my frustration. Exasperated, we are still discussing the subject I felt we closed long ago.

"Salty, as in mad. As in angry for no damn reason. Especially since it was you, not me thinking about Greer."

Again, I cannot control the sigh escaping me, "And as I have repeatedly informed you, I was not thinking of the mortal woman."

"Uh-huh," she declares as she returns to reading the book she always has close at hand.

"How did my brother tolerate such insolence?"

"Much the same as you do. With a shit ton of frustration."

"A shit ton?" I repeat questioningly.

"It's an expression," she says in a sing-song response without lifting her eyes.

"It's ridiculous."

"I like to express myself."

"A trait nearly as infuriating as you are."

"You're just pissed that I figured out you like Wren's mommy more than you care to admit." I can no more control the growl she elicits than the woman who provokes it. Apparently, if I want to end this inane conversation, I will have to extricate myself from our camp, and since it seems my horse would prefer the company of the lamb over mine, I am left to trudge through the brush around us without his aid.

Ten minutes after leaving camp, I discovered a small pond filled with aquatic life. I am fascinated watching them living so utterly unaffected by the state we have reduced this world to and so blissfully unaware the mortals of this realm are facing annihilation.

It is the most peace I have had since waking up. I do not hate having the lamb traveling with me, but she can sometimes be difficult. She has placed herself between my intended target and me more than once. I know she believes this will save them, and truthfully a few times it has, but it mostly only delays what I have already decided.

I remain next to the pond until the moon rises high in the night sky. The peaceful tranquility of this place is the calm I need to refocus myself and concentrate on the task at hand. It should not surprise me when I return to camp only to find Avalon curled up next to the fire book in hand.

"What are you reading?"

"A book."

"I am aware it is a book; what I meant is, what is it about?" Her eyes lift to meet mine, but she does not respond. "Okay, if you do not wish to answer my previous inquiry, tell me why you read it so often?"

"Because."

"This is not an answer, Avalon."

"It is today."

"What could you possibly find within the pages that could retain your attention this long?" She attempts to restrain the smirk playing at the corners of her lips but fails miserably.

"Well?"

"Maybe ask your brother," she says before returning her attention to the object we are discussing.

"Thanatos?"

"I haven't met any of your other brothers yet, so he would be a good guess."

"Why do you believe he would have the answer to my question?"

"Because he read it."

"My brother... Thanatos... Read your book?"

"Trust me, I was almost as surprised as you are." Hmm, perhaps I shall query him when we next speak. If I understand what she finds so appealing on the pages of her story, I might figure out how to get her to better listen when I speak.

"I think Storm is hungry."

"First, he does not get hungry, lamb. Second, can we not return to calling him horse?"

"Sure, as soon as you refrain from calling me lamb. Besides, he likes his new name."

"How do you know this?"

"Storm, come here, boy," she says before clicking her tongue, much the same as Thanatos does when directing his horse. And, of course, my traitorous horse responds to her call, moving from where he was waiting directly next to the reclining lamb, who absentmindedly reaches up to rub his side.

"Anything else, Pestilence?" She asks while turning the page of her book. Taking a seat next to the fire, my horse wanders over to me to nudge my arm so I will pat him. When did my warrior horse become an obedient pet? There is no point in pushing this topic any further. Avalon has given him a name he approves of, and since I have no intention of refraining from calling her what she is, I find it prudent to shift subjects.

"Tell me of my brother's time here."

She clears her throat. For a brief moment, I believe the lamb will refuse to answer this inquiry, as she has done with several other questions I have asked, until she closes the book, straightens, and looks directly at me.

"What do you want to know?"

"How did he come across you?"

"The first, second, or third time. Which one do you want to know about?"

"How many times did you two cross paths before he allowed you to travel with him?"

"He didn't let me do shit; he demanded I go with him."

"It was my brother who wanted this?"

"It was."

"And he pursued you three times."

"No, he let me go once. I was given to him the second time we met, and his pursuit of me resulted in our third and final meeting."

"Proceed."

"Yeah, now I understand the whole brother thing."

"Explain." The over-exuberant exhale I receive from the little lamb informs me I have angered her. I shall have to retain this knowledge for further use. Perhaps I can use this when she pesters me nonstop on things like returning to a camp we already stayed in.

"You sound like him. He likes to give one-word commands too. Something that annoyed the shit out of me when he did it and apparently still does when it comes from you."

"At last, I have found something to exasperate you. My father only knows how often you have done this to me."

"Really?"

"I believe I should not have disclosed this to you."

"Probably not. Listen, I'll make you a deal. In fact, it's the same offer I made him once. An answer for an answer."

"You will have to explain this."

"For every answer I give, you have to give one as well."

"I am not permitted to reveal—"

"Let me make this clear. I could care less about the inner workings of your world. I promise I won't ask you about the creator or where you come from. Deal?"

"Okay, I agree with your terms. An answer for an answer. Why did Death let you go?"

"I saved him."

"How?"

"That's two questions. Is the reason you called me Greer because you think about her?"

"There are times I wonder how she and the child are faring. How did you save him?"

"An asshole from my neighborhood somehow got the upper hand against him and stabbed Thanatos several times, after which they left him to die in the building across the street from me. When I discovered he had survived the attack, I took him to my place, where he remained until his body was healed. To show his appreciation, he let me live and gave me a chance to escape the city before he destroyed it."

"You realize he would not have died at their hands." The raised eyebrow she gives me infers I have yet again asked a second question.

"Do you think we might return to their camp someday?"

"I don't know what you believe our returning would accomplish."

"It would give you a chance to tell her you are attracted to her."

"I am not attracted to her," I rebuff, but her laugh implies she does not believe me. "You are not following your own rules since this is more than one question."

"The last one was a statement, and you never actually answered my question."

"My brothers and I do not covet the mortals of this realm. Tell me about your second meeting."

"I was captured and presented to him as an offering so he would not destroy their city. Are you sure about that?"

"Sure about what?"

"That the horsemen do not covet the mortals of this realm." I cannot tell if the look she gives me is more knowing or questioning. Is it possible her statement was made hoping it would satiate her own curiosity?

"Is there something you wish to disclose to me, lamb?"

"Only if you knock that lamb shit off." I will come back to this question; there are others I am more interested in knowing.

"My brother accepted humans as an offering?"

"Ah-ah, you still haven't answered my question. Will we ever return?"

"I imagine one day we will. If only to halt your constant nagging."

"He didn't accept or want humans offered to him, but it didn't stop people from doing it. Do you have wings too?"

"No, only Thanatos is capable of flying. Why did he pursue you?"

"I imagine because he hated losing members of his horde." Something in her response is off. She is not telling me the entire truth, yet she is not outright lying to me. Both cannot be true unless she is unsure which is the truth. "Since you can't fly, do you have any other supernatural abilities?"

"You have witnessed my ability. I hold within me a plague that kills all others. How long did you travel with my brother?"

"Months. What is the thing I see you holding sometimes?"

"A reminder. Is Thanatos the reason you left his group?"

"His horde."

"His horde?" The look crossing her face must indicate my confusion and her willingness to answer what could be considered a second question.

"I'll give you this one for free, big guy, but no more. It's what the mortal's called it, and to answer your questions, at times yes and other times no. What do you mean by a reminder?"

"Of what my being here means. Beyond this, I do not care to discuss it. At least not now. Did you wish to travel in Thanatos's horde?"

"Absolutely not. Do you agree we should be erased from existence?"

"No, but my opinion matters little. What did you hope to accomplish by traveling with him?"

"To show him humanity deserves another chance. If you could stop this, would you?"

"Yes. Did you accomplish your goal?"

"Not really. Do you think Thanatos told your father we should not face judgment?"

"Not only do I think he did this, but I also know he did. If you failed, why did my brother speak against waking us?"

"At some point during our travels, he came to his own conclusion. Why are you here if he told your father not to wake you?" She requires no response to this question. Avalon knows the reason I was awakened. "Oh, right. Dumb question. Sorry."

"You may ask me another if you like, little lamb."

"Do you think a horseman could ever love a mortal?"

"I don't know. Do you miss him?"

"Very much so," she whispers. "Do you think he would come back if he could?"

"If permitted, I believe he never would have left. Do you think a horseman is capable of love?"

"I hope so." I know this is against the rules, but I ask her one last question. One I have wondered about myself.

"Do you believe a mortal could ever love one of the riders sent to remove you?"

"I know they can." She quietly confirms before turning over, thus ending our question-and-answer session.

Once I am certain she is asleep and the fire I built will not burn out while I am gone, I direct my horse to watch over her. I plan on traveling to the one being who has the answers both Avalon and I seek... I travel to purgatory, hoping to find my brother Thanatos waiting.

Chapter Sixteen: Purpose

~ Death Summer 2025 ~

I ADMIT HAVING MY BROTHER SUDDENLY arrive in Purgatory does not surprise me. Although it's possible if our father is aware of his return, his warrior will not be far behind. I realize I pulled him here once already, but he needed to understand what I was asking of him. The importance of protecting Apple. He has his assignment, and we do not typically return to our realm until we have completed the task. Yet, the level of the immorality most of these mortals... mortals my brother has always had a soft spot for, a kindness many of them are not worthy of... possess has to be troubling for him. Not to mention traveling with my Apple must lend itself to questions. Questions only I may hold the answers to.

"The little lamb is an interesting human."

"I assume you have seen her stubborn side."

"I will admit she can be difficult, but her capacity to protect the ones she deems worthwhile is admirable." I laugh, hearing him explaining what I am all too aware of.

"Has she attempted to flee from you yet?"

"I believe she would have left long ago if not for the oath she swore to me."

"What oath?" I ask, feeling the slightest hint of jealousy rising within me. I acknowledge it was me who asked him to seek her out, but now I wish it were me she was with. And what of this oath she swore. What could she possibly need to pledge to?

"She swore to come with me once we assured her friend's safety."

"If?" I know my Avalon. With her, there will always be a give and take. She would not be willing to give unless Pestilence gave something in return.

"I promised to spare the ones she cares for." Yes, her negotiations are always to benefit someone other than herself. If you wish for something from Avalon, you must give something in return, but it is not one-sided. She also offers a compromise when asking for something.

"And she has honored her deal?" The emotion I felt before I knew what their deal was, loosens its grip around my heart, allowing me to laugh as I ask this question.

"She has." The grin he gives me confirms she may be doing it, but not without her typical obstinate temperament.

"Does she know this oath will only be upheld by you? That when our other brothers wake, the lives of the souls she bargained for will be taken then?"

"She is not unwise, Thanatos. While she has never outright asked this question, I believe she understands the promise made was mine alone."

"Thank you for watching after her, brother. How is she doing?"

"Well. The lamb is well. She reads a lot; one series, in particular, seems to hold much of her attention." Her books. The ones I read and felt jealous of. Jealous that a fictional character was able to do what I could not.

"Truly?" I asked, trying to hold at bay the longing to watch her with her legs crossed and flung over the arm of a chair as she twirled her hair around her finger while reading a book. The mere image in my mind pains me. I remember watching her so intently. From the smile that played at the sides of her lips when she read something she liked or the crease in her brow when my Apple read about the one she disliked the most, a character named Tap. I instinctively knew what section she was reading by watching her face. If she ever realized I was doing it, she never implied as much.

"I asked her what the appeal of the story was."

"What did she say?"

"She said to ask you. She confessed you would know because you read them as well." How do I tell my brother I read the books first to understand her and then learn what a mortal woman might want? The answer is I cannot. I cannot tell my brother how desperate I was to connect with her. So, for this reason, I remain silent. Thankfully, he must understand my silence means I do not intend to reveal this any more than Avalon did, but with his next confession, I wished we were still discussing the books.

"She asked if a rider could ever love a human." Why did it have to be Pestilence she posed this question to? If it had been

War or Famine, they would have done as I asked, forsaking any hope she holds for the answers she seeks. But Pestilence... he has always held an affinity for mortals. Of the four of us, he is the one who would speak in favor of absolution. Where Famine would preach retribution and War indifference. In fact, my militant brother would most likely shrug his shoulders before recommending we flip a coin. Heads they live, tails we bring destruction to their world. I suppose this is why my father appointed me to judge them. I neither love nor hate them but would give them a chance rather than allow fate to decide their existence.

"What did you tell her?"

"The truth. I told her I did not know. But I believe you hold the answer she seeks." I want to answer every question she has; however, if I wish for her to live, and I mean truly live... I cannot. Because it is my affection for her, I will sacrifice every desire I have buried deep within my heart. For it is in my yearning for her that I must not waiver. I want Avalon to have a long, happy mortal life filled with friends, laughter, children, marriage... love. If I wish these things for her as I do... she needs to let go of any hope she holds for me. If I answer Pestilence's questions, he will feel honor-bound to reveal every detail, which will hurt her more than it will help.

"You should advise her we are incapable of such an emotion," I tell him as I return my focus back to the soul I await to ferry to their next life.

"I-I had believed you would answer this differently. Are you certain?"

"Are you asking for her or for yourself?

"The lamb."

"Are you sure? Because, like you, I can sense when one of my brothers is conflicted."

It seems my brother has secrets he prefers to keep to himself. And since I have not been honest with him, I cannot expect him to give me what I refuse to give him. He will have to come to his own conclusion regarding this. And if our Father's grace is objective, I believe he will.

Mercifully, he does not push the issue further, allowing us to speak of other things. Unimportant nonmortal things. Which mostly is what he likes about their world. We talk for a while until I feel the life of the one I watch fading fast. I know they will soon pass, and I plan to be there to greet them when they slip from Avalon's realm, a task my brother will not delay me from.

~ *Avalon* ~

I wake up shivering. The moon is high in the sky, and a thin layer of frost coats the grass beyond where the fire would have reached. If this is a precursor for the day to come, I would have to say it's not starting out so great.

"Pestilence, the fire went out." I was expecting some surly comment along the lines of '*Well, light it*,' but a response never comes. I scan the area where we set up camp, and it takes me much longer than it should have to realize I'm alone, compliments of the dim light the moon offers.

"Pestilence?" I say to the empty space around me. Thankfully, when Storm clomps towards me, I realize I am not entirely out here by myself. Since Storm is anything but a normal horse, he has a keen ability to put me at ease.

"Pestilence." This time I yell his name as I push off the blanket he placed across me so I can stand up. The process is slower than I like since my bones ache as I force them to move. This time of year, the ground is still trying to thaw from winter, and lying on it with nothing in between can quickly zap the heat from you. I imagine this is what happened to me and why my body is so unwilling to cooperate. I think the riders forget I'm not like them. I am affected by cold weather, and as much as I'm sure he attempted to ensure my comfort when the fire died out, the area around me changed, shifting drastically as the temperature dropped, and as a result, I woke up with my teeth chattering.

"Well, Storm, it looks like it's just you and me for a little while. Now, if I could only figure out how to restart this damn fire, I might not freeze my ass off before your rider returns." I tell him as I stack the wood on the faintly glowing embers.

I am almost ready to light the fire when I hear something moving somewhere off to my right. Ordinarily, I would have dismissed it as Pestilence, but when Storm snorts as he stomps his hoof on the ground, I instinctually know this is not his rider.

"What is it, boy?" I ask as I move closer to the horse. I do this to calm him as much as compose myself or at least slow down my racing heart. Without thinking, I bury my hand under his mane as I scan the woods around us. For the first time in quite a while, I am afraid. During the day, when I can see what's coming at me, I don't let nerves get the best of me, but in the dark, when I don't know if it's friend or foe, animal or man stalking me, I can't help but feel vulnerable. An emotion I hate almost as much as pity.

Grabbing the only thing I have to help ward off anything that may want to harm us, I pull the dagger I always keep close at hand from my belt. My shaking hand isn't going to do anything to assist me even though I know this is as much from the chilly night air as it is equal part nerves. I know it certainly doesn't convey badass bitch to anyone watching; it's probably closer to a meek little mouse.

I am smart enough to know that holding it out in front of me only invites my enemies to knock it from my hand, so I hold it close rather than waving it around like a loon. I flip the blade opposite my thumb to leverage more force if I need to drive the knife into someone as I place my arm across my chest. Holding it closer to my body makes it more difficult to snatch it away.

"Pestilence?" I recognize this is pointless because I am now absolutely certain who or whatever is moving inside the tree line is not the rider. I know this because Storm's muscles are coiled tight as he prepares to fight or flee. Unfortunately, he is preparing to fight because I know he will not leave me, but if I could climb on him, he would be able to bolt if we cannot fend off whatever is lingering at the edge of the clearing.

Shoving my foot into the saddle's stirrup, I quickly figure out that hoisting myself on this mammoth beast isn't happening anytime soon since my legs are still cramping from the cold, and my arms feel as useful as a wet noodle in a sword fight.

Okay, running is not an option. Riding out of here on Storm doesn't seem viable right now. The horseman is nowhere around here. The topper on this shit cake is the clouds moving across the moon have reduced my visibility to a couple feet in any direction. Which leaves only one option, fight. Lowering my stance, I grip the blade tighter, keeping my head on a swivel as I prepare for whatever is to come. And when the invaders finally reveal themselves, I know this situation has gone from bad to a worst-case scenario.

"My, my, imagine our surprise. Here we thought we were coming to kill the man pretending to be a rider, and what we find is a pretty little thing left to her own devices." Men. Why did it have to be men? I would rather it be any animal this world has to offer, as long as it isn't the kind that walks on two legs.

"Who said I'm alone, asshole?"

"Tsk-tsk-tsk," he responds with a click of his tongue. Backing closer to Storm, he snorts several times as he slams his foot furiously at the ground in front of him. I reach my hand up to loop in his reins. If need be, he can drag my ass along with him. I imagine the damage I will sustain from the horse will be significantly less than whatever they have planned.

"Because we've been watching you," a second voice somewhere to my left says, followed by a twig snapping off to my right. So there are at least three, and they are moving closer but are smart enough to remain just outside my line of sight.

"Then you know I'm not alone." I must admit I impressed myself with this response because I somehow succeeded in keeping the fear building within me from leaching out in it.

"Well, since we've been watching you for nearly two hours, and the beast behind you is the only other living soul we've seen, I will have to politely disagree." Two fucking hours. Pestilence has been gone for goddamn hours. Shit, I know he doesn't have wings, so it means the horseman left on foot, and lord only knows where he went or when he plans on returning.

The breaking of twigs informs me they are moving closer. Okay, think Avalon, think. If I smack Storm's ass, will he do what I want and take off? Fuck! Why the hell did I have to fall asleep? I know better, especially when we light a fire. The orange glow always brings in the biggest and worse predators.

"So tell me, pretty little thing—"

"Don't fucking call me that, asshole."

"A name for a name, then. You stop calling me an asshole, and I'll stop calling you the name you seem to dislike." The one talking is attempting to hide how close they have moved. He keeps lowering his voice as they move closer to where I stand. The problem is I saw the glint coming from what I imagine is a blade of some kind not fifty feet in front of me. I don't want him to know he has given away his location, not yet. I need them to think they still have the upper hand.

"Nah, I think asshole fits you best."

"So be it. Now, why don't you tell me, pretty little thing, where is the man you were traveling with?"

"Who said I was traveling with anyone?"

"Careful, or else I might think you're trying to protect him. Can you imagine what my men would do to you if they thought you were protecting some asshole pretending—"

"You don't know shit."

"Well, if he is an actual horseman sent to kill us, I gotta say," he clicks his tongue and releases a loud sigh before finishing. "This is about to get so much fucking worse for you. I don't think I need to explain to you how screwed you would be."

"I bet that's what she's doing," the one to my left snarls.

"What's that?" the seeming leader of this group asks.

"Screwing him." This time his response is closer to a growl.

"Oh, tell me it isn't true, pretty little thing. You're not screwing one of them, are you?"

I know the prudent thing to do here is to keep my mouth shut. These assholes came looking for trouble, and it appears it doesn't matter who suffers their wrath... but like I have said before, when dealing with an asshole it is best to let them know from the start they are, in fact, an asshole.

"If the choice is between assholes like you or the horseman, I'll take the horseman."

"Good to know." his calm demeanor never slipped during our entire interaction, and when it remained intact after my last declaration, I knew I was in trouble.

The first sign things have taken a drastic turn is when Storm kicks out his back legs. The thud followed by a howl of pain reveals they were within striking distance. I spin to where the man is lying on the ground groaning and can barely make out the silhouette of the man writhing in the mud. Again Storm rears up, but this time it's to slam his front legs down on whoever was trying to sneak in from the front.

"Fuck," I mutter, realizing I should have figured out how to get my ass on his back when I had the opportunity to because the second he reared up, he yanked his reins out of my hand and threw me off balance.

And then my day went from bad to completely screwed.

Chapter Seventeen: Paltry

Blessed are those who act justly, who always do what is right. Psalms 106:3.

~ Pestilence Summer 2025 ~

NOT WANTING TO SCARE AVALON WHEN I returned, I opted to materialize away from camp and then trek back to where I left her resting on foot. The closer I get to where I left her, the more I realize something is amiss. The telltale glow of the campfire is missing. The sounds I have grown accustomed to hearing when she is asleep are absent, yet it is the knowledge that I cannot feel the presence of my horse I am most disturbed by. But when my brother reaches out to me urging me to hurry, I pick up my pace until I am streaking through the night.

The instant I enter the camp, all my fears are realized. My horse is missing, the fire is out, and the blanket I used to cover her is tossed aside. However, it is in observing the obvious struggle that occurred here I am left with little doubt that Avalon is gone, and she did not leave of her own volition.

"Avalon." The only sound to answer me is the rustle of the wind through the barely budding branches.

"Horse."

Pestilence, she is in trouble. You need to find her. Now! My brother presses his will upon mine, forcing me forward before I have the opportunity to examine the camp.

Death, return my free will to me. The words escape me in a growl because I know his actions will not help her. But when I feel him battering against the walls holding him from this realm, I know he is on the verge of losing control.

Hurry! His plea is filled with pain, concern, and love. For the first time in my existence, I can feel it. He loves the lamb even if he refuses to admit it. He loves her, and the thought of her in danger drives him to do what nothing else ever could. Defy our father. His intention is to bring the veil down. In doing so, allow him access to this world.

Not willing to waste any further time, I race through the woods around us, tracking the faint trace the mortals left behind. What I do not understand is my horse. Everything points to the fact he is not with the ones who took Avalon, yet he did not await my return where I left them.

His hoof prints in the soft ground confirm he traveled this way. The way the earth is kicked up, it appears he is moving rapidly in the direction I travel. Much faster than the ones who have Avalon. Thinking back to the state of the camp, I now register something I missed upon my arrival. My horse was bound or incapacitated for a time because there was a perfect imprint of my companion compressing the dry brush. Does this mean he is attempting to save the lamb? This is unheard of. Our horses never stray far from their rider, yet he has moved miles away.

I feel my brother's anxiety ramp up as he screams, *Release me!*

I know the command he issues is meant for our father, for it is his will alone holding Thanatos in our realm.

The closer I get to the ones who invaded our camp, it is no longer Thanatos alone who feels her. I can as well, and the terror filling her invades every atom in my vessel. Until this second, I would have said the fear filling her and me was the worst thing I have ever experienced, but now I know how wrong I was as pain replaces the terror she felt. Red hot unbearable pain fills every muscle. It is so intense it drops me to my knees.

Pestilence! my brother screams, and as this one word echoes around me, I can feel the first fracture between our world and this one occur before he slams against the barrier again. If I don't get to her soon, Thanatos will bring down the veil and rip this world apart to save her.

Pushing through the pain, I stumble as I take one shaky step after another toward where I know I will find her. Thankfully, I can also feel my horse, who has sensed my arrival and is currently galloping back to me. When he arrived at my side, I managed to block out her emotions. If I wish to save Avalon, I must be at full strength. Swinging my leg over my horse, he wastes no time turning to charge in the direction I sense she is being held. But Thanatos forces his will upon my horse, and before long, we are racing headlong into what will most likely be a trap.

"*Brother*, you need to trust me. I will not let them harm the lamb, but they may kill her if I race in there unprepared." This alone is the sole reason he releases my horse. Slowing him down, I prepare to enter the camp but with a plan in place.

~ Avalon ~

The instant Storm's attack resulted in me on my ass; they didn't waste any time. Several men charged me while others occupied the horse who was still trying to save me. Three large men pinned me down, gagged me, and tied my hands behind my back before the biggest one tossed me over his shoulder.

I can hear Storm struggling, and if I had to guess, one of the pricks who invaded our camp must have roped him before securing him to something. His grunts and whinnies are all the proof I need to know he is aware he is failing the job I imagine Pestilence tasked him with. This being to watch over me. The problem is, I'm willing to bet an absent horseman never thought anyone would be daring enough to take on one of the riders. Especially since he has told me that most mortals run the instant they know he is coming. Yet more proof of how far humanity has fallen. We don't even listen to the little voice inside us anymore.... You know, the one that warns us of pending danger.

I tried unsuccessfully to free myself, only to be dropped on the ground when the one carrying me got tired of my bucking. After that, they drag me behind them. With my hands still bound, I had no means by which to avoid or protect my head from the debris along the path they were traveling.

What I don't understand is why they are taking me. Do they think Pestilence will ride in to save the day? Man, are they going to be pissed when they realize they are banking on him wanting to rescue me more than fulfill his purpose. Idiots.

Even if he plans to rescue me, I know something they don't, something very few people in this world know about Pestilence. He can direct his disease to whomever he wants to give it to while spearing others. Which means he can perch well outside their camp's borders and send his plague to eliminate them without losing one arrow. After the last one has fallen, I imagine if he isn't sick of dealing with the pain in the ass mortal he got stuck with, he will simply stroll into their camp and release me as the last one is gasping for their final breath.

I've witnessed what dying by Pestilence's plague looks like. It's not pretty. I would prefer never to watch it again, but I'm also somewhat partial to living now. So if this is the only way to save my sorry behind without innocent people getting hurt, I have one thing to say to him... release away, but hurry. Because the last branch I hit punctured my upper chest. Unfortunately, I'm bleeding faster than most of his victims die.

~ Pestilence ~

My calm approach allows me to hear the shouts up ahead. They know I am the one approaching their settlement. I have no fear of facing these mortals. What has me on edge is I can no longer sense the lamb. And possibly more disturbing, my brother's attempt to enter this realm stopped, and he went silent several minutes ago. I realize our father may have reached him, but it could also be Michael's interference.

As much as I want to assist Thanatos, I fear Avalon may need me more. Hence I continue to the place where I hope to find her.

It is no surprise the instant I enter the camp, these sons of Adam have no intention of talking when they release the first of several arrows in my direction. Yanking the bow from my back, I swiftly begin returning fire. I can only hope she does not get caught in the crossfire.

These foolish mortals believed they could defeat me with the paltry numbers in attendance. They will soon understand their misstep. I do not want this fight to linger; more pressing issues require my attention. For this reason, my arrows, accompanied by the deadly plague, deliver my justice swiftly.

When the last man has fallen, I climb off my horse. Avalon is close, but she is not well. Her heartbeat is slow, and her breathing is ragged.

I rip the tent flap open, knowing I will find her in here, only to discover her unresponsive on the ground. A large chunk from a tree branch has impaled her chest, and she has lost a significant amount of blood. The wound I can care for. The infection it will cause, I cannot. I give disease, not take it. This means my only option is to return to the one place I know holds the medication she will need if I wish to keep her alive.

I only hope I can make it there in time.

Chapter Eighteen: Fight

~ Greer Summer 2025 ~

AFTER OUR FAILED FIRST DATE, JAY made every attempt to rectify it. He became more attentive to Wren, and it's nice to have someone around to help teach him the things I do not know, but when there is an option, I also take him to Xander instead because I have no expectations of what he should do.

Shortly after our date, Jay overheard Suki teasing me about finding a daddy for Renny, which only resulted in him increasing his efforts for us to begin a relationship. He no longer alludes to being ready to settle down and start a family; he says it repeatedly. My biggest hesitation is there have been times when Jay talks about a future for us where Wren wasn't included in his plan. When I questioned him about it, he claimed, 'Of course, he meant Renny too,' but I don't know; it felt like Jay added my son as an afterthought. Let me clarify: my son is not now, nor will he ever be... an afterthought.

"Hey, Suk, is Wren still with Xander?"

"Nope."

"Are you sure?"

"Well, since I just finished ravaging my sexy boyfriend in an hour-long sexathon, yeah, I'm pretty sure." And, of course, poor Xander had to walk up to us right as she was saying this. His face shifts to a rosy color as he rubs the back of his neck. I think it's endearing how embarrassed he gets by Suki's vivid, sometimes hold nothing back details about their sex life. He is definitely the yin to her yang.

"Sorry, Greer, when Suki required my assistance—"

"Dick," she mouths while pointing at her vagina. Thank goodness the kids aren't around here to witness this. You know who does though, Xander. And the rosy color amps up to scarlet pretty darn quick.

The color of his face isn't the only thing Sukie affects since he has to clear his throat several times before he can finish. "Jay offered to take him fishing."

Leaving Xander to kiss his girl, I go down to the stream, intending to spend some time with my son. When I arrive where I expect to find Wren and Jay, there is a moment of panic when I don't see them.

"Renny."

"Jay," I say as I rush down to the water's edge. My heart feels like it's going to pound out of my chest when I find the fishing poles lying on the bank and Wren's favorite stuffed animal sitting next to them.

"Wren," I yell.

"Hey, momma, over here," Jay calls. I whirl around to find Jay and Wren standing inside the tree line with a butterfly resting on his finger. Wren's unrestrained awe is a sight to behold. One I find utterly amazing. I force myself to calmly walk over to where they are, even though what I want to do is run. Run and scoop my son into my arms and shout at Jay for scaring me.

But I know I'm being ridiculous. Jay didn't do anything wrong other than spend time with my Renny.

"Look, Wren, mommy came to play with us."

"Peas."

"Please, what, Wren?"

"Tank you."

"Do you have a butterfly?"

"Utt-or-fie,"

"Yes, it's a butterfly. It's pretty, huh?"

"Pitty."

"Just like your momma," Jay interjects as he takes my hand. When he leans in to kiss me, I let him because I gave in a week ago. He's a good guy. He cares about Wren and me. But it was him constantly telling me he wanted to take care of Renny and me that finally wore me down. I thought it was time I gave him a chance. A real chance. Not some half-in, half-out bullcrap I'd been giving him prior to this. He deserved better. It was past time for me to get my head out of the clouds. Time to stop living in some fantasy romance novel whirlwind. Time to forget about the man who saved my son. Jay is good to me. Sometimes it's not about what you want; it's about what you need. Jay represents this for me.

So I gave up on the fantasy. Fantasies are meant to remain just that... a fantasy. Not reality. Right? A dream, desire, certainly nothing more. But....

~ Pestilence ~

Since I removed the limb impaled in her chest, Avalon has been dropping in and out of consciousness. That was two days ago. I had hoped we would be back to the camp her friends inhabit. We would have if not for the miscreants who slowed my progress with their feeble attempts to thwart one of the riders.

Over the last couple of hours, the heat from her body has become worrisome. As if this is not enough, she has recently begun talking to my brother as if he was here with us.

"We are almost to your friends, little lamb."

"Thanatos, I'm cold. Tell your dad that's enough with this cold shit."

"Avalon, I am unsure of what you mean."

"You know when you get the wood...."

"Avalon? Avalon!" She has slipped back under. Her frail body, weakened by the rampant infection coursing through her, causes the lamb to slump to the side, and if I hadn't placed her in front of me, she would have fallen off Storm.

This is from a time we traveled together. One night when a storm arose, and I could not shelter her from the cold, she said this to me. Thanatos's words are delivered as a thought. So the lamb is lost in a memory. This cannot be good.

"Run, horse. Run!" my order is both a demand and a plea for him to move faster. She is failing quicker than we are traveling, and if we do not hurry... we will not make it there before the lamb succumbs to her injuries. Her heart rate has slowed, as has her breathing making me realize....

It may already be too late.

~ *Avalon* ~

Shit, I haven't been this cold in a long time. I wonder how long Thanatos will take to return with wood for the fire. Then he can lay back down with me. Wrap his arms around me and keep me warm.

Wait, something is not right. I'm not in bed; I'm moving. There's a sound; I know that sound. Ghost? Yeah, it's the noise Ghost makes when he is galloping. No, not galloping... running. It's the sound he makes when he is running.

When I force my eyes open, the world sways around me. Not Ghost. Another horse. Pestilence. Storm.

Something is very wrong. The world around me is bright, and flowers are blooming. There are leaves on the trees. No snow. Not winter. But then, why am I so cold?

"You are sick, Apple."

"Thanatos?"

"Yes."

"I remember now. You left me."

"Not by choice, Avalon."

"But you left me."

"A decision I now regret."

"How are you here?"

"I didn't come to you, Apple. You came to me."

"But if I'm with you, then that means." As if by magic, his body takes shape and appears before me. There is a pained expression on Thanatos's face when he comes over, running his fingers down my cheek.

"Am I...."

"Not yet, though your body is failing fast. But my brother is taking you to the people who can help you... who will save your life. You only need to hang on for just a little while longer."

"But if I don't, then—"

"No, Apple. I need you to fight. It's not your time." Understanding takes form. Of course, he wants me to fight. I have a task that has not yet been fulfilled. I wonder what the hell these assholes are going to do when I vehemently refuse to break another one of their precious fucking seals.

"I want you to fight."

"I'm sure you do." When he pulls his eyebrows together, I decide to elaborate for him. "You want me to fight because you need me alive to break the damn seals."

"I want you to live, but the seals have no bearing on this. I want you to live because I want you to find happiness. You deserve happiness. I am asking you to fight, not so you are there to break the seals... it is because the thought of you not existing in their world is something I cannot bear," he tells me tenderly before he leans over and brushes his lips softly against mine. When he pulls away, I discover a sea of emotions in his eyes. Every emotion I ever felt for him reflected back to me. I don't know what's worse, believing he didn't care about me or hoping he does.

"I miss you," I tell him, hating how broken I sound when I say it. He takes my face in his hands before gently bringing his mouth to mine. The kiss is everything I have been missing. Every memory of our time together, every promise he made to me and I made to him.

"I need one more thing from you. I want you to promise me you will fight with every ounce of strength you possess. So please, Apple, please wake up."

Something jostles me, causing pain to course through my body. I look up at him again, wanting to argue because I'm tired of fighting. I've been doing it my entire damn life, and the only thing I have to show for it is a few people I love and too many scars to count. It would be so easy to let go. To slip away, to say fuck it.

"Please." But that's not me. I don't give up, so I nod, which causes a slight smile before he kisses my head and whispers, "Time to wake up."

When my eyes snap open, I am held in Pestilence's arms with Suki's worried face peering down at me.

Chapter Nineteen: Nick of Time

~ *Death Summer 2025* ~

THEIR FIRST MISTAKE WAS STORMING INTO my space without my permission.

"Death, I will not say it again. Drop to your knees, place your hands behind your head, and prepare for your sentence." Their second was in making demands I have no intention of abiding by.

"Or—"

"There is no or in this matter. You believe you can get away with nearly bringing down the veil. All so you can save that human." Michael's brows pull together, and his upper lip twists in a snarl.

"You should learn to hold your tongue until one finishes their thoughts. If you had done so, you would have understood I was not questioning if I had another choice. Because I am not. Had you not interrupted, you would have learned I was countering your demand with one of my own."

"You are in no position to make demands." Gabriel's response is as incorrect as it is infuriating, and the growl I reply with tells him as much. He is at least smart enough to step away from me. Michael, not so much.

"You will comply, Death. Retract your wings, drop to your knees, place your hands behind your head, and submit."

"That will not be necessary," Raphael interjects as he strolls into my room.

"Stay out of this, Raphael." Michael does not like anyone overruling him. Even if that someone is his brother. Just as Pestilence, War, and Famine are mine, the archangels are brethren as well. Each with their own responsibility to the mortal realm.

Raphael walks past Michael, ignoring him in favor of addressing me. "Thanatos, if you would please."

"Always the pragmatic one, brother." Michael snaps as his hand moves to the sword strapped to his back.

"Yes, well, I simply see the value of not inciting the ire of the being created for one thing. Ending life. I would suggest you do the same."

There are some souls you respect because they earn it, and then there are souls like Michael who believe you owe it to them simply because they exist. Raphael is the wiser of the two and a being who understands his role within our realm. Overseeing the preservation of humanity. He does his assignment because it is his duty and because he values the lives of the souls he protects. It is a shame he has to safeguard them from the one who should be their guardian, his brother Michael.

I knew my actions would have consequences, but I do not regret anything I did and will do it again if she needs me. If they wish me to stop interfering in their world, perhaps they should allow me to return to her.

I follow him out of the room, leaving Michael and Gabriel seething behind us. When we arrive before our creator, his focus remains on the world beyond. He says nothing. He merely stands there with his hands behind his back, waiting.

Raphael dips his head and leaves me to answer for my misconduct. This conversation is not meant for others. It appears Michael did not receive the same message since he stormed into the room seconds later, sword in hand with his wings extended behind him.

"Death, you went too far this time. You almost shattered the veil put in place to hold the—"

"Michael, I will not require your services. You are free to go."

"But—"

"Thank you." Our father's calm, peaceful demeanor should not be misconstrued as weakness. If pushed, his wrath is infinite. Michael's features twist with rage when he realizes he will not be exacting his punishment. He does not like that I am not at his mercy. Today I face only our father.

Since I have never outright defied him, it is a conversation I am certain he never believed he would need to have with me. Once Michael has left, the silence returns for several minutes. I am left with one thought… this must have been how Avalon felt the day they chained her within my tent while I decided what I wanted to do with her. Just as I watched relief wash over her when I broke the silence, I wonder if my father can see mine now because the silence was oppressive.

"It is a safe assumption to say that you know why the veil is in place?"

"Yes."

"Then it would also be prudent to point out you know your actions almost crumbled it?"

"Yes."

"I can presume this will not happen again?"

I remain silent. This is something I want to give him... the promise he seeks, but I cannot because I know if Avalon needs me, nothing will halt my attempts to return to her.

"You may resume your post." He must realize I will not give him a promise I cannot uphold. As I prepare to leave the room, he quietly informs me, "She will live."

This is the first time I allow the tension to relax from my shoulders. Since I was called home, this is the closest she has come to losing her life. If Pestilence had not gotten to her in time, she would have died, and I would have been tasked with ferrying her soul to her next life. A responsibility I do not wish to fulfill anytime soon.

~ *Greer* ~

Nehra bursts through the tree line and rushes straight to where we still view the butterflies.

"They..." Her heavy pants inform me she ran all the way from camp. When she leans over, trying to catch her breath, the fine hairs on the back of my neck rise as I am overcome with mounting trepidation. I don't know what is happening, but her wide-eyed frazzled state is alarming and makes me worry about her and the rest of the people in our community. If I want to get information from her, I need her to slow her breathing and calm down. To help with this, I place my hand on her back and rub small circles.

"Nehra?"

"Avalon," she puffs.

"What about Avalon?" I ask in a rush as my nerves get the better of me.

"Back... but... she's not... doing good."

"Avalon's here?" Nehra nods as she remains bent with her hands on her knees, sucking in generous gulps of air.

"And... Pestilence."

"He's back?" Jay's rushed response implies he doesn't like having the rider back here, but I couldn't care less what he likes right now. Avalon is hurt, and if we can help her, we must do everything possible to aid her. I mean, it's because of Avalon that Renny and I are here, alive... safe.

"Wren?" I ask as I point to my son.

"Go. I've got him." Nehra thankfully understands how much I owe Avalon. So when I have her confirmation, I turn to run back to camp, but Jay grabs my hand. At first, I believed he was doing it to stop me, but when he started off in the direction of our base, I realized it was more him not wanting me to go alone. It's really very kind of him. Thankfully, he must recognize how much Avalon means to me.

By the time we get back to camp, it's not hard to figure out where I will find Avalon since I can hear Suki yelling.

"What the heck happened?" I ask, busting into the room only to find an extremely pale Avalon incoherent with sweat coating her body. Her hair clings to her face and neck. Black circles surround her eyes, and her cheeks are sunken in. I would swear she was dead if not for the slow rise of her chest.

"Yet again, a rider left her unprotected," Suki yells. "If she dies, it's your damn fault. Death's too. His ass is just as responsible for this shit as you are."

"You are not helping her, little human." My heart slams against my ribs. Of course, I knew he was in the room because I could feel his dominating presence the second I entered, but I dared not look.

It's been months since I've been around him, and even after our time apart, his effect on me has not diminished. The mere sound of his voice sends ripples of longing coursing through me. And now is so not the time for this. Until I slowly swivel my head in his direction, and when I see him standing there, chest bare, arms crossed, pants slung low, basically looking like a Greek god, I have to remind myself to breathe. If I wasn't already out of breath from my sprint to get here, seeing his eyes focused on me would surely have stolen it.

"And you're an asshole, rider!"

"I don't understand... what happened?" I ask as I force my gaze from the man who has captured it to the bed Avalon is lying on.

"Had he left A alone, she never would have been in this situation. But nooo..." Suki theatrically drags out this word as she throws her arms away from her body to point at the rider, "you assholes keep dragging her back into this fucking bullshit."

"She is the lamb—"

"No, she's my family. Not your damn lamb."

"She is our salvation." Pestilence's composure never wavers. I'm not sure how he remains so calm, considering the level of Suki's rage, but he does. He accepts every accusation she hurls at him without reacting, replying, or becoming angry, something many mortals would not have been willing to do, even if she had a point.

"And our damnation," Jay hisses as his icy glare settles on Avalon. Pestilence moves to place himself between an unconscious Avalon and the man whose lips are twisted into a snarl. I suppose this confirms what I already knew... the horseman will protect Avalon no matter what.

"Jay," I snap, shocked he would say something like this. The horsemen coming here have nothing to do with the woman who has placed herself between the riders and humanity more than once and everything to do with our inability to show simple compassion for one another.

"Don't be a dick, dick," Suki's response was not a request. She does not take anyone criticizing her Avalon lightly.

"Oh, come on. You both have to admit—"

"Leave. Now!" Pestilence demands. He must have heard enough since the horseman takes a threatening step closer to Jay when he remains rooted in place.

"Greer?" He can't be serious. Does he really expect me to leave without helping her?

"I shall not repeat myself." This finally gets Jay moving, but I don't miss the exasperated exhale he releases.

"That goes for you too," Suki demands of Pestilence. I am preparing for an all-out war between these two individuals who both want to protect her, but he doesn't fight her. Opting to relent, he follows Jay out the door.

*****

After she received her first round of antibiotics as well as fluids. Suki and I gave her a sponge bath to clean away the blood and sweat from her body. We agreed that one of us should always be with her until she recovers. Suki volunteers to stay so I can go home to give Nehra a break and have dinner with my son before putting him to bed. But as soon as the best babysitter a mom could ask for comes back to stay with Wren, I return to check in on Avalon.

It's only been four hours since they arrived in camp, and while Avalon's fever has dropped from dangerous levels, they linger within the alarming territory. Thankfully, some of the color has returned to her cheeks, but she remains unconscious. I'm no doctor, but I know enough to realize she is still not out of the woods, making the entire situation worrisome.

Suki is curled up, sound asleep on the loveseat she pulled beside the bed. There is no point in both of us staying here, and since it appears that Suki needs the rest, I beckon Xander to come to get her.

"She's going to be pissed I took her out of here," Xander says as he stands over her rubbing his chin. I think he's scared of her. Can't imagine why... couldn't possibly have anything to do with this girl being like a rabid dog with a bone when you piss her off. Which is why I didn't want to wake her.

"Just tell her I thought it would be easier on Wren if I take the night shifts; that way, I can be with him when he's awake. Since we all know Avalon will be incapacitated for a couple of days, I thought it best if she got some rest while I take the first watch."

"I don't think she'll care why I did it."

"She'll understand."

"You do realize this is Suki we're talking about, right? The woman who threatened to remove my..." he clears his throat. "I think you can figure it out. After I left Avalon alone while she was recovering the last time. Suk will want one of us to be here."

"One of us will be here. Me. I promise I won't leave this room until Suk comes back."

It seems fortune is on our side when he lifts her off the loveseat because rather than her bolting upright as he tries desperately not to jostle her awake, she merely curls into him and releases a contented little sigh. Suki is a lucky girl.

I watch Xander from the door as he carries Suki back to their place. It's sweet how much he loves her. This is what every girl wants. A guy who would do anything for you and thinks the sun rises only to shine for you. As much as Jay wants me to believe this is where we are, I don't see it. I guess... maybe someday... way, and I mean way, in the future, anything is possible. I shouldn't complain because Jay is a nice guy.

He's reliable.

Considerate.

Consistent.

Safe. Gosh, why does it sound like I'm buying a sedan when what I want, what I have my heart set on, is a sports car. One of those flashy ones that goes from zero to adrenaline-rushing... throws you back into your seat while your cheeks are flapping in 2.2 seconds, kind of love.

But I'm a mom. I have responsibilities and duties to my son... to this community. I can't zoom around the countryside with my hair flowing in the breeze. Practicality is the way forward.

Who needs an earth-shattering, pulse-pounding, take-your-breath-away kind of guy when logic dictates caution. In today's world, stability is what you need. It's what every person hopes to attain. A worthy goal. Besides, since cars are now long forgotten, my analogy is just as ridiculous as the desire causing it.

I watch them until they disappear into their cottage before returning to Avalon. After taking a few seconds to wipe her face off using the clean water in the basin on the table, I dim the flame on the lantern but leave enough light to read by as I settle in for the first night of watching over my friend. With any luck, she won't discover me sleeping on her with a puddle of drool covering her chest like a certain rider did when I was tasked with watching over him.

"How's she doing?" Jay asks as he quietly slips through the door.

"Better."

"I'm glad to hear it."

"Really?"

"Yeah, why wouldn't I be?"

"I don't know, maybe because you all but blamed her for the end of the damn world."

"I didn't say anything that wasn't true. It is Avalon's fault we are facing another rider. If she hadn't broken the damn seal, Pestilence—"

"May have come anyway. You don't know how any of this would have gone down. None of us do, and for you to blame Avalon when she stuck her neck out to keep you alive is bullshit. Hell, not just you, all of us. Every person who traveled with her and every soul within this camp. We all owe her a debt of gratitude. So why don't you give her a break and stop acting like you are privy to information the rest of us only hope to discover!"

"I know she's your friend, babe. It doesn't change the fact her choices could destroy us. I hate that she has put Renny and you into this position, and I won't apologize for it because you and Wren are the only people that matter to me." I know he thinks I'll be okay with it by confessing he only dislikes her because of Wren and me. I'm not, and I won't pretend I am.

"She needs to rest. Besides, we're trying to limit the number of people around her. She's still not out of the woods yet."

"Why don't we see if one of the other people here will watch over her, and you can come to my place? I thought maybe since Nehra will be with Wren all night—"

"Yeah, so I can stay with Avalon. She's not with my son to let me spend private time in your cabin."

"What? It's not like she'll know."

"I said no, Jay. Now I think it's time for you to go." When someone clears their throat by the door, I look over only to discover Pestilence came in at some point during our argument.

"I came to check on the little lamb."

"Oh, yeah, of course. She seems to be doing much better. I think we got the antibiotics into her just in time. Why don't you come in and see for yourself," I say as I motion for him to enter.

"Wait, I thought you didn't want anyone around her," Jay rebukes.

"Since he's the only reason she made it here in the first place, I think it's fine."

"I thought you were worried about exposing her to illness?" He hisses under his breath as he grabs my arm. I notice Pestilence has moved further into the room, and his gaze is focused on the arm Jay clutches. If you ask me, the contact is a little too tight, and the tick of Pestilence's jaw confirms he agrees with this thought.

"Since she was traveling with the rider, I don't think I have anything to worry about."

"Use your head, woman," Jay snaps. He no longer tries to hide his contempt for a man he should use discretion around as he growls the rest. "This being is the damn definition of illness and disease. It's the entire reason he exists." His grip on my arm tightens, causing me to wince as I yank it away.

"I choose the victims of my plague. I can assure you Avalon has nothing to worry about. However, I cannot say the same for you." Pestilence retorts as he moves directly in front of Jay.

"Thank you for stopping by, but as I said, Avalon needs her rest, so you should go home. Right. Now. Jay." Without giving him another chance to protest, I return my attention to my friend. I don't care if he's mad or not. He's going to have to get over it.

"I'll see you out," Pestilence's tone leaves no room for argument. I'm actually shocked when he doesn't immediately escort Jay out the door since I can assure you his command leaves no room for misinterpretation.

"No, you've got that wrong. I'll see you out where we can have a word about fucking boundaries. Outside, rider," Jay snarls before barging out of the cabin with Pestilence on his heels. I can hear the rider talking, followed by an angry response from Jay, but he falls silent after a few more words from Pestilence. No surprise when the door opens, and the rider, not Jay, comes back inside.

"She looks much better." Okay, so I guess we're not going to discuss what just happened.

"Her fever is coming down, and the makeshift I.V. is helping to replace some fluids she lost."

"Thank you."

"For what?"

"Looking after her."

"You don't have to thank me for doing what she would do for any of us."

"I suppose you have a point."

"Do you mind me asking what happened?" I inquire as I move over to make room for him to sit. It's not surprising when he remains standing. Disappointing but not unexpected.

"A mistake I made. One that put Avalon in danger and nearly ended her life."

"Do you want to elaborate on this further?"

"No."

"You're not very talkative, are you?"

"Avalon would disagree."

"You can sit," I tell him while patting the space on the loveseat next to me.

His eyes drop from my eyes to my mouth before he clears his throat. "Didn't you tell the other mortal she needed her rest?"

"Yeah... well... ah—"

"Greer is trying to ask you to stay without asking you, ya big lunkhead," Avalon mumbles.

"Avalon." "Little lamb." We say together, although mine was spoken with more enthusiasm. The way he rushes to the bed, I would have to say he is just as happy as I am to see her awake and talking.

"Whoa, take it down about ten notches; the ol' noggin is killing me," she mumbles.

"Did you call me a lunkhead?"

"If the big head fits," she says as her lips tilt up in the smallest possible smile. It appears doing this takes effort on her part.

For the next fifteen minutes, I ask questions, to which Avalon gives little nods while Pestilence grunts or groans. It doesn't take long before fatigue overtakes her, and she begins dozing off. After giving her some small sips of water, another round of antibiotics, and some pain medication, she drifts back off to sleep.

It amazes me how attentive Pestilence is as he helps her complete these things. Being a rider of the apocalypse, I didn't expect him to be as gentle as he was when handling her.

Watching how he interacts with her is very sweet. One thing becomes abundantly clear: he cares about her, and I can't say I blame him. There's something about Avalon that draws you in. Makes you trust her. I would never have traveled with Suki, Xander, or her if she didn't have this innate ability. I didn't trust people, especially around my son, but those three managed to convince me to come with them in a matter of minutes.

I figured he would return to his horse after she fell asleep, but when he remained next to her bed, I invited him to sit beside me. To my surprise, he actually joins me this time.

Chapter Twenty: Healing

~ Pestilence Summer 2025 ~

I SHOULD HAVE RETURNED TO MY horse after ensuring Avalon was recovering as much as guaranteeing I had chased away the man I do not trust to be left alone with her, or Greer for that matter. Although from what I have witnessed, I am left with only one conclusion... these two have spent a significant amount of time with one another since our departure. I suppose if this is the mortal Greer has chosen to spend her time with, I should not interfere. Avalon is a different story. One too many times, this son of Adam has made comments I do not appreciate. Disparaging remarks that all focus on the lamb's task.

Rather than following logic or exercising discretion, I chose to stay with Greer. She asked about Avalon and my travels, and I responded with what details I was able to provide her. Thankfully, she did not push the issues further than I could discuss.

I should have left when her eyes grew heavy and her body curled against mine. Perhaps I would have if not for delighting in the feel of her skin or the intoxicating scent surrounding me.

I should have left when her head slid down to lie on my lap; instead, I watched her sleep. Fascinated by the soft sighs and quiet murmurs as she adjusted her head until she was comfortable and content.

I should have done many things, yet I did none.

My mind attempted to rationalize as I told myself it was only done so I could protect Avalon as she fought off the infection trying to overtake her. I deemed it imperative for someone to stand watch, and since Greer had fallen asleep, it left only me.

Yet the truth is, while I wanted to assure the lamb's well-being, the real reason was the woman slumbering against me. It does not matter if my time with her is while she sleeps. Spending time with Greer is the true reason I remain. I despise that Avalon knew my desire long before I did and maintained her stance regarding how I felt about this woman even as I refused to admit it. Of course, I have no intention of telling her any of this. My reason for this is she will never allow me to forget it.

Nor do I intend to admit any of this to Greer.

She has a life, a child... a man. Things I am not capable of providing. What could I ever give her besides rot, disease, and death. Nothing. This is why I will hold my tongue and promise that after tonight I shall return to being nothing more than a rider here for their end as she returns to being nothing more than a wish. But tonight… only for tonight, I will permit myself to enjoy the feel of her against me, the sweet aroma of her surrounding me, and the soft sighs of contentment she offers me while she sleeps comfortably on my lap.

Never in my long existence have I ever wondered what it would be like to be loved by one of the beings my father held in such high esteem until now. Until now. Which is why my fingers trail across her cheek, against her lips, and down the cord of her neck.

"I told you." Avalon's quiet observation is not surprising. I knew I risked her waking only to discover me in my moment of weakness.

"She fell asleep."

"On your lap?"

"Not at first."

"Yet her head has somehow found its way onto your lap."

"Only because she slipped down."

"And the gentle caress… what was that all about?" When I do not immediately answer, offering nothing but a grunt, she continues with an expanding smile. "Let me guess, your fingers just fell against her lips and took on a mind of their own, which caused you to run them down her neck through no fault of yours. Right? Yeah, I can totally see how this could happen. Absolutely believable, Pestilence. Well… of course, only if I am gullible enough to think a leprechaun is about to show up flinging rainbows out his ass while handing over his beloved pot of gold to yours truly."

"Lamb," I growl as I pull my hand away from Greer and rest it along the back of the chair we share.

"Oh shit, hold the phone. Are leprechauns a thing? I mean, until a couple of years ago, I might have said something equally foolish like *'a rider of the apocalypse shows up only to tell us he isn't quite ready to kill us off yet, and we should try snapping his seal again in another millennium,'* you know that kind of stupid shit."

"Avalon! You have demonstrated your point. You may stop at any time."

"I'm glad you finally see reason. You can give me your apology whenever you're ready. I'll wait. Take your time. No need to rush something this big. I'll just stay right over here, you know... resting and waiting. That is unless you want me to leave you two alone."

"Little lamb."

"Yes, P."

"P?"

"Short for Pestilence. We really need to come up with a better damn name for you."

"Pestilence is not a moniker. It is what I am."

"All the more reason. Anyway, you wanted to say something?"

"Yes."

"Well, now's your chance, big guy."

"Go to sleep."

"So you can go back to exploring a sleeping Greer?" The grin she has worn since discovering me in this compromising position doubles in size.

"No, I plan to return to my horse."

"But if you go, who's going to watch over me? I'm still in a precarious way over here."

"Suddenly, you appear fine to me."

"Oh, P, you're breaking my heart. I'm still sick," she says while coughing. Why she would feign illness to the bringer of disease is something I cannot fathom. Yet she continues to cough while her eyes keep shifting over to me. If I am not mistaken, I believe a laugh may be mixed with each of her fake coughs.

"Please stop referring to me as this."

"Nope, I kinda like it. Besides, we're discussing you and Greer."

"No, we're not," I announce, shifting Greer's head so I can stand.

"Are you sure you want to leave, P? Because I'm betting I can make you change your mind."

"And how do you propose to do this, little lamb?"

"Who do you think would take your place as Greer's pillow if you leave now?" The thought of who the lamb is referencing brings a wave of what I can only describe as jealousy. Riders are incapable of such an emotion, but this is what I feel. I am jealous, realizing who the other being is who would happily volunteer to replace me. Avalon winks when a low growl rumbles through me before falling back on her pillow.

"I can't promise anything about the whole nickname thing since you are so hellbent on referring to me as a damn lamb. I can tell you one thing... Storm will be fine until morning," she advises as she rolls over. When I can no longer deny what I long for, my eyes drift back down to Greer's peaceful face, and I cannot help wondering if I will be able to claim the same come morning.

~ Greer ~

I can't believe I fell asleep, especially after I made such a big stink about Xander taking Suki home when she did the same thing. Thankfully, when I bolt upright, I discover Pestilence leaning against the door frame.

The rising sun silhouettes his body in breathtaking colors, and I can't help the sharp inhale it produces because it is the most beautiful thing I have ever witnessed...well, aside from my son.

The oranges and reds from the rays surrounding him blend perfectly with the golden tones of his skin. It perfectly highlighted every muscle and ridge of his upper body, the shadows casting a stunning silhouette. And not for the first time since meeting him, I find my fingers itching to explore them in intimate detail.

I also wonder when he left the loveseat. With any luck, it was before I decided to lie down since the last time I slept on him. I—oh gosh, I don't even want to think about the last time. Even the thought of doing this again makes my heart rate ramp up.

I realize my time admiring him is done when he shifts. Hoping to hide how long I've been awake, I rub my eyes and clear my throat.

"Sorry. I guess I was more tired than I thought."

"No apology needed."

"Thanks for watching over Avalon."

"As with the apology, I require no show of gratitude for this." He speaks the next part more to himself than me. "After all, she would not be in this situation if not for us."

"I'm sure she doesn't see it that way."

"Yes, well, it does not change simple truths."

"Which is?"

"Did you sleep well?" Okay, so evidently, he doesn't plan on telling me his simple truth.

"I guess so," I say as I rub my shoulder. "Did Avalon sleep all night?"

"She woke once."

"Did she say anything?"

He laughs as he pushes off the door frame and looks at me. "Yes, she had much to say."

"Meaning?" Rather than answering my question, he moves closer. The fierceness and intensity of his gaze causes me to squirm uncomfortably. Does he know how much he affects me?

"Hey, how did last—" Jay's sudden arrival in the room ends the rising heat within me. I can assure you this flushed phenomenon has nothing to do with the temperature outside and everything to do with the man who has been in the room with me all night. "I didn't expect to find you here this early."

"Like you, I wanted to check on the lamb's progress."

"Did you just get here?"

"No, Pestilence was kind enough to stay last night when I fell asleep."

"You and he were both here? All night?"

"I felt it prudent, as I suspect some within this camp are displeased with our sudden arrival."

"I'll assume your comment is not directed toward anyone present," Jay snaps as he squares his shoulders while approaching the rider.

"You may assume anything you wish." Pestilence's phlegmatic response should in no way put Jay at ease. If he were smart, he would pay more attention to the man whose posture indicates he is preparing to show Jay the error of speaking to someone like him in this manner. For all his bluster, I don't believe he stands a chance in hell of backing it up if the rider decides he has had enough. Which leaves me to question why the hell Jay is acting like this.

"Jay, what are you doing here?"

"I came to check in on Avalon and you. It seems I arrived just in time."

"In time for what?" I snap, annoyed he would infer Pestilence would actually hurt me.

"Since you are awake, I shall check on my horse."

"You don't have to—" I start to say until Jay interrupts.

"I think that's a great idea," Jay growls as he moves between Pestilence and me. I'm not overly fond of the jealousy thing happening here, specifically since I have never promised him anything. Pestilence looks from Avalon to me. The look on his face says.... Oh hell, I don't have the first damn clue what it means. Is he mad, annoyed, or ready to send out his tendrils? I wish I could read him as easily as Avalon can; however, I haven't spent as much time with him as she has, but if given a few more minutes, I think I could figure it out. I wonder if Jay realizes the same thing since he has moved back to drape his arm around my shoulder.

A new expression surfaces, and this one I have no trouble understanding. Pestilence is pissed. But at who? Me? Jay? Himself? What the hell am I stepping into?

The rider spins and storms out the screen door without saying another word. His sudden departure causes me to jump, but the shock fades almost as quick when Jay slams the door closed before whirling on me.

"What was that all about?" I ask him as I cross my arms over my chest.

"No. You don't get to be the one who's angry right now."

"Hold on a minute—"

"What the hell was he doing here?"

"He told you he was checking on Avalon."

"All goddamn night? I thought you said she needed her rest?"

"She does—"

"So how is that fucking rider helping her accomplish this?"

"He's—"

"Where the hell did you two sleep?"

"What?"

"You heard me, Greer. Where. Did. You. Two. Sleep?"

"First off, I don't think a horseman needs to sleep. Second, I don't owe—"

"Bullshit, Greer, you owe me—"

"She owes you what?" Avalon snaps as she slowly pushes herself upright.

"An answer to start and some damn respect would be nice too!" What in the hell makes him think he has any right to question me? I don't get a chance to ask since someone else does it for me.

"Why? Because you're such a stand-up fucking guy?" This question was posed by Suki since she decided now was the perfect time to show up. Right smack dab in the middle of this shitshow. How did I go from marveling at the glorious body of Pestilence to this? Standing between my two best friends and the man who apparently wants more from me than I do from him. The tension filling this room is escalating quickly, and if I don't do something soon, it will absolutely boil over. And I'm not sure who will be the one it burns.

"Time to fucking go," Suki snarls as she yanks the door open all the way and steps aside for him to leave.

"Come on, Greer," he says as he reaches for my hand. I yank it away before he can grab it.

"Greer stays," Suki demands.

"She's coming with me," he snarls back while stepping closer to Suki.

"She has a mouth and a mind of her own," I yell as I push between them. Now that I have their attention, I proceed. "Jay, I'll talk to you later."

I don't wait for his response as I move next to Avalon's bed.

Chapter Twenty-One: First

~ Avalon Late Summer 2025 ~

IT'S BEEN THREE WEEKS SINCE PESTILENCE rode into camp, begging them to help me. I admit to being more than just slightly shocked when Suki and Xander told me this. I know I'm imperative to their mission, but to beg? Now that's something I never expected.

I realize it has everything to do with me being the lamb, and only the lamb can break the damn seals. But since I have already told him I will not do it again, I can't fathom why he would want to save me or continue looking after me. Yet from what they tell me, he was damn near frantic when he showed up.

While his focus remains on saving me, mine is on Greer and his growing attraction. They can both pretend there is nothing between them all they want because it's all bullshit. There is no denying the way they look at one another, and this is something I can work with. Both in playing matchmaker, remaining with Suki, and, most importantly, saving humanity. Because let's face it, if he's here, he's not out there killing people.

I understand he can send out his tendrils, but how damn far can they reach? Since he already told me he's destroyed all the other communities surrounding this one, I'm hoping he can't extend any further, which means the other people still stand a chance of surviving this rider.

Besides, if Greer and I can't show him humanity is worth saving, I know someone else who can.

"Peas," Wren says as he looks up at Pestilence.

"Please, what?" Since our return to camp, Pestilence no longer needs us to interpret, unlike in the past when Pestilence would look to Greer or me when Renny was talking. It's funny how he so deliberately enunciates the words. It's almost like he's trying to teach Wren.

"What do you want?"

"I desire nothing, little one."

Renny tilts his head before placing his hands together as if praying and continues to express himself the only way he knows how. "Peas. Oh-tay."

"Wren, come here right now." The harshness of Jay's command instantly sets my teeth on edge. After Jay acted like a complete asshole the morning after I arrived here, Greer initially refused to have anything to do with him, but he slowly weaseled his way back in. It's the perfect way to explain it since the term fits more than what he did; it fits the man too. I wish she would have told him to go pound sand, but she believes she owes this jackass something for some unknown damn reason.

When Jay realizes half the camp heard him and is watching this little interaction, he grabs the fishing poles. He must have hoped this little song and dance would cover up the true intention of his command. Yep, this asshole wants us all to believe his tone was all due to excitement as he prepared to extend an invitation, and it had nothing to do with his contempt for a certain rider who has garnered Greer's attention. "Renny, I'm going fishing. You want to come, little buddy?"

"I believe I may know what you desire," Pestilence says, completely ignoring Jay and his stupid fake interest. As does Renny. In fact, this idiot might get more of a response if he was talking to Storm. This thought dissolves almost as quick when I see Storm fiercely stomping the ground. Okay, maybe Storm is a stretch since he gives the impression he despises this man more than his rider.

The rider doesn't leave the little guy waiting long as he pulls something out of his saddlebag and hands it to an impatiently waiting Renny.

"Gummy. Tank you," Wren squeals as he runs over to one of the tables with the gift Pestilence gave him. He carefully lines each fruit snack up, placing every color together before he counts them. Only after he has finished this activity does he eat them.

"Pestilence."

"Yes, little lamb."

"Where did you get fruit snacks from?"

"I may have commandeered them on my last outing."

"Commandeered?"

"Took."

"With the person's permission?"

"By force." When I raise my eyebrows questioningly, he elaborates further. "I took them from a man who did not need them as much as the little one does."

"You didn't...."

"Kill him?"

"Yeah."

"No. The man yet lives only without the sticky sugar blobs the little one seems to enjoy."

"Wren calls them gummies."

"As do you."

" Because it's what they're called."

"That was not the name on the package."

"Trust me on this one, big guy."

"Yes, this is what I should do since it has worked out so well for me thus far." Pestilence's eyes remain fixed on Wren, and I can't help the little chuckle I give when I see a small smile forming.

"I don't know, rider. I think you may be going soft on us."

"Let me assure you nothing could be further from the truth."

"Is that why you get a goofy grin whenever you look at the little guy?"

"Your insolence is not appreciated, nor will I permit it to continue, little lamb."

"And this is supposed to mean...." I drag out the words as I roll my hands. If my question alone wasn't irritating enough, the grin I give him is.

"I shall permit you to ascertain the meaning of my words on your own."

"Oh, are you going to take me out? Put the lamb out to pasture?" The glare he gives me confirms I'm getting under his skin but not enough to make him talk, so onward and upward. "Would your threat possibly bring another of the riders to collect my sassy ass?"

"Something tells me this is something you would enjoy."

Wiggling my eyebrows at him, I confirm his assumption with a smart-ass response. "You are the smart one, aren't you?"

"How you survived Thanatos is a mystery."

"You probably don't want to know." His forced exhale confirms I've pushed him far enough for one day. Slapping his shoulder, I decide to let him off the hook. "Alright, I promise to be a more typical mortal and not talk back. Would that make you happy? Oh, but just so we're clear, I don't cringe."

"Dare I ask?"

"Yeah, as in, Oh God, please save me... a horseman of the Apocalypse has come to ferry my soul away."

"I do not ferry. That is Thanatos's job. Mine is to ensure you cough loud enough that he can find you."

His response causes my mouth to drop open, amazed at what he said. "Pestilence, did you just make a joke?"

I lean around him to confirm my suspicion when his shoulders rise and fall rhythmically. He's laughing. "You did. You just told me a joke. Ah shit, if you keep it up, I might have to call you the fun one."

"War would be devastated. Murderous even."

"And another one. You're on a roll today, big guy." The booming laugh he gives me is a welcome relief. I haven't heard this sound in such a long time, and I'm not ashamed to admit how much I have missed it. I think he still blames himself for what happened to me. But this is ridiculous since it's no more his fault than it is mine, and it's past time he forgives himself for it.

~ *Greer* ~

I don't know what happened today between Jay and my son, but I intend to find out. I learned something was said while I was with a group visiting another community to trade supplies. Nehra didn't like how he spoke to Wren and how Suki told it; he was entirely out of line. Xander admits while Jay's words were initially harsh, he felt it had more to do with Pestilence than Wren. Avalon's only sage advice was to inform me Jay is an ass, and as much as it pained her to give an asshole any amount of leeway, he didn't do anything too egregious *this time*. I wonder if she thought this would help me.

The best way to figure out what is going on is to get to the bottom of it by asking him outright. When I arrive at the stream, Jay is packing up his gear but stops when he hears me approaching.

"Hi babe, I didn't expect you all to be back so soon," he says as he stands and kisses me before I can stop him.

"They didn't have much, so we didn't stay long."

"Great, we can have dinner tonight. Just you and me. What do you say?"

"Um, we ate before we came back. I think my plan for tonight is to make Renny something to eat and then go to bed early. I'm exhausted."

"I suppose another time then," he says as he returns to gathering his fishing supplies.

"Um... can we talk for a minute?"

"Sure," he says, but when he looks up at me, he immediately stands to take my hand. "Is everything alright?"

"Did something happen today with Wren?"

"No, why do you ask?" He may be telling me nothing happened, but his eyes imply another story as they look everywhere except me.

"Are you sure? Someone said you were a bit harsh with him today and for no reason."

"Let me guess, Suki and Avalon. Right?"

"Why do you always have to jump straight to Suki and Avalon? If you need to know, they didn't tell me."

"But when you questioned them, I'm willing to bet they were only too happy to give you their thoughts."

"This is not about Suki or Avalon. I'm talking about whatever you did or said to my son. Not what Suki or Avalon... or anyone else for that matter, said to me about you. It's about your actions, not theirs."

"I don't know what kind of shit they've been feeding you, but it's just that... horseshit. Greer, you have to see they don't want us together. Not to mention Avalon has her own damn agenda."

"What are you talking about?"

"Never mind. Well, let's hear it. What horrific thing did I do to Wren?"

"No one said anything of the such. They just said you were short with him for no reason."

"Of course, you believe them over me."

"Hey, I'm not accusing you of anything. I'm asking. This is what most people refer to as a conversation."

"It seems like these 'conversations' have become a recurring theme over the last couple of weeks."

"I'm not sure where the hostility is coming from—" he smashes his mouth to mine.

"Come to my place," he says when I pull away. His heated tone confirms a trip to his house would include sex. What the hell is this man thinking? He can't actually believe I would be willing to screw him after he mistreated my son. Besides, this is a damn road we haven't traveled yet, and lately, one I'm not so sure I want to continue on.

"I already said I was—"

"Tired, yeah whatever, Greer," he snaps as he snatches his equipment to walk away. Figuring our conversation is finished, I turn to look at the water letting out a frustrated sigh. But my frustration ramps into anger when he continues. "You really should keep your son away from the man who wants to kill him since it seems when I try to do it, everyone gets bent out of fucking shape."

"Pestilence?"

"Yeah, Greer. Pestilence. He's here to end our lives, and you let your kid play with him. Not the smartest fucking thing a mother can do. But then again, you're not really his mother, are you."

"Go to hell, Jay." He stands there for a second, staring at me before he rakes his hand through his hair. He finally takes the hint that I'm done talking to him and spins, leaving me to stand by myself to fume about the entire situation and how he handled it.

After taking several minutes to gain control of my breathing and racing heart, I turn to go home, only to find Pestilence watching me.

"Is everything okay?"

"Yes… actually no. I just talked with Jay, and it didn't go so well." I fully expect Pestilence to inquire about the fight, but he strides over to stand beside me, and rather than asking for details, we watch the fish swimming through the water. He'll probably never understand how much I appreciate this.

It's nice. Being here with him is one of the few times I don't feel I have to pretend. It's my people-pleasing nature to make sure everyone around me is happy. But when I'm with the rider, I can relax. I don't worry about saying the right thing, acting the way people expect, or being the right person. I can be me, and it's better than nice. It's invigorating.

We chat about Wren, his horse, Avalon, and camp life until the sun is replaced by the chirping of crickets, the flickering of lightning bugs, and a sky filled with more stars than I've ever witnessed before. As much as I know I need to return, I am enjoying my time here with him. Probably more than I should.

"Well, I guess I should get back to Wren."

"The little one, Wren, he is very special."

"He is."

"I apologize if the treats I give him make him overly active. Avalon said I must limit how many sugary blobs I give him."

"Sugary blobs? I don't know what that is."

"They are supposed to be fruit, although they contain none of the fruits they proclaim."

"Do you mean gummies? Are you the one who keeps giving him those?"

"I am. Yet, if you prefer, I will stop."

"No, not at all. But I agree with Avalon; you should limit how many you give him."

"I promise no more than one, maybe two packs," this part he mumbles, hoping I wouldn't hear him as he looks toward the sky. "a day."

"I can live with one, maybe two, as long as you can live with me coming to get you to care for him when he's bouncing off the walls."

"He does this?" Pestilence's mouth falls open while his eyes double in size, thinking the gummies can make Wren apparently fly. Initially, I nod, but when he steps away, I can't help laughing as I let him off the hook.

"No, not really. It's a saying a person might use to describe someone who is overstimulated or hyper."

"I was going to say my father needs to be advised of this immediately." The laugh I give him brings out the most breathtaking smile from the rider, who rarely does this.

When Pestilence lifts his hand, suggesting I should proceed him home, I do as he asks since lord only knows if I followed behind, my attention would be focused on his—if I were talking rather than thinking about this next part, it would have been preceded by me clearing my throat first—backside.

Our walk back is significantly more than my trek here since the sun has set and there is very little moonlight. Well, at least for the girl who can stumble over a crack in the sidewalk. And to prove this, I trip over a damn exposed root I didn't see. Thankfully, Pestilence has quick reflexes, and his arms wrap around my waist to halt me from falling face first and embarrassing myself.

"Oh my gosh. Talk about a bumbling idiot."

"Tripping over a root does not make you unintelligent. Clumsy perhaps, but nothing more."

"Well, I guess I've met my daily quota of playing the part of a damsel in distress. Thanks for catching me." I notice his hands are still resting on my hips.

"If you are the damsel, what does this make me?"

"The knight in shining armor."

"I can assure you, Greer, I am anything but." His eyes move over my face until they settle on my lips. The intensity of his gaze sends a shiver coursing across my skin and up my spine before pooling low in my belly. Deciding to bring a fantasy to life, I brush my fingers along his arms, across his chest, and over his jaw. Throwing caution to the wind, I push up on my tiptoes to replace my fingers with something else just before they reach his mouth. When my lips brush over his softly, I admit I half expect him to pull away, but he doesn't. I am jolted by the sensation of being this near to him. I know this is foolish. He's here to end us, not save us, and certainly not to love us. But right here... right now, there is no place else I would rather be.

And the fierceness of his kiss confirms he feels the same.

Chapter Twenty-Two: After Effects

~ *Pestilence Late Summer 2025* ~

I ADMIT I WAS UNPREPARED WHEN Greer kissed me, but the instant I felt her lips against my own, I knew I was incapable of stopping her because the simple truth was the kiss was everything I had wanted since first seeing her.

As much as my hands yearned to explore the curves of her body, I refrained because I also knew this was not my purpose. Our creator, my father, did not send me here to love them. He sent me here to begin their end. Yet how can I continue this path when she and the child have shown me a better way?

A path where growing interest, attraction, dare I say — love takes precedence. As much as I am attracted to Greer, the little guy Wren, I find undeniably fascinating. They both make me wish I could walk away from this task and never look back.

Then there's Jay, who is undoubtedly everything my kind despises about this world. He is self-serving, short-tempered, and devious. He would like nothing more than to possess Greer; the thing is, I can easily see the little guy is merely something he tolerates. He knows if he wishes to have Greer, he must accept Wren. My question is, once he has her within his control, what will become of the little boy who cannot survive this world alone? My issue is he may not care what will befall him, but I do.

Though in all fairness, I alone cannot claim this because Avalon not only adores him, I know if something were to happen to Greer, she would take on the responsibility of raising him. Yet I also know this is the last thing she wants, not because she does not care about him, but because she loves him and would fear for his safety if he had to travel with her.

Avalon has rightly deemed herself dangerous to be around. She alone is responsible for calling forth my brothers, making her a highly sought-after woman by my kind as much as her own.

"You look lost in thought," Avalon says as she suddenly appears next to me.

"I was merely thinking."

"About?"

"The little one."

"And what thought is plaguing you about our sweet little Renny?"

"Do you believe he intends to honor his declarations to protect them both?"

"So the crease between your eyes is more about Jay than Wren."

"He has made several assertions. I simply aspire to clarify if you believe his words as well."

"No. I think he's an asshole, and I don't put a lot of stock in people like him or anything they have to say." As self-serving as this may be for me, and yes, I realize I just admonished him for having this precise attribute, I see an opportunity I will not ignore.

"Should you not express your concerns to Greer?"

"No." Why must Avalon make every effort to thwart my plans?

"May I ask why?" My attempt to contain my frustration is for naught since my exasperation is unmistakable in my response.

"Because my jealous friend—"

"This is an emotion I am not afforded."

"Whatever you say, my green-eyed rider."

"My eyes are brown, not green… Oh, I comprehend what you were inferring, and I can tell you nothing could be further from the truth, not to mention it is not as humorous as you find it to be, little lamb."

"Hey, I'm just calling the green-eyed monster the way I see it, P."

I release an annoyed groan knowing there is no point in arguing. Avalon will only counter any objection I offer with an affirmation of her own. "As you were saying."

"I won't say anything to Greer because she's a grown woman who will make her own decisions. Unless he physically hurts her or Wren, I won't interfere. In a situation like this, it's best to let them come to their own conclusion and be there to help only when asked."

As annoying as her response is, I know she is right. Thankfully, she refrains from giving me the smug grin I was expecting.

So as Avalon does what she declared, which is to wait for Greer to choose her own path, I do what I must. I distance myself from her and Wren.

A task I am finding more difficult each day.

~ *Greer* ~

I don't know what happened. Pestilence was commanding my lips one second, kissing me like his very life depended on it, only for him to pull away almost as abruptly. Before apologizing. Apologizing! I think this was the most humiliating part. I've never had a man kiss me and then express regret. Talk about an ego buster. I don't know how else to explain it because his rejection felt precisely like this.

The worse part is he has been avoiding me ever since then. I don't know if this is because he regrets what we did, if he was afraid of liking it too much, or, god help me, I pray this isn't the reason... it repulsed him.

Too afraid to find out the real reason, I steer clear of him. Hopefully, with enough time, space, and avoidance, he'll forget all about it, and I can go back to being a nobody who admires him from afar. Better this path than the one where he tells me to get lost.

Marcelle Valentine

I can't help the side-eyed glances I keep sneaking, but I know I've monumentally failed at hiding what I'm doing when I look up to find his eyes on me. For a brief second, I think he may actually plan on coming over to talk to me, but all my hopes are dashed when Avalon approaches him.

Hope? Is this what I really wanted? Did I truly want him to come over to talk with me? I do because even if he doesn't want anything from me, I would love nothing more than to be friends. Something about Pestilence quiets the world around me. And unless you have a child whose only form of expression includes screaming, you will never understand what a luxury this is. As terrible as this is to admit, I envy my son in some ways. He has no fear. No reservation. If he sees something he wants, he is not afraid to obtain it. This means he still spends time with the rider… time I only long for.

"You ready to go?" Then there's Jay. He behaved like such an asshole over the whole Wren issue. If we didn't have to work together for the good of our community, I would tell him to go pound sand. A saying I stole from Avalon. Of course, most residents believe we are still together because Jay thinks all is forgiven. Nothing can be further from the truth, but it keeps the peace during times like this when we are assigned to work together.

Not just work together but travel over three hours away to another community. Since it will take so long to get there, we'll have to stay overnight, and then the plan is to stop at the town with the farmer's market on the way home. We'll be gone until tomorrow evening sometime. I don't particularly like leaving my son for this long, but Suki and Xander agreed to take him, which is the only reason I finally relented.

I don't know how I got assigned this duty, especially since I know Oliver was supposed to go. I guess Cole changed his mind and decided to send Ollie elsewhere. Still not sure how I translate as a replacement for Ollie; if I had to guess, my travel companion had a hand in it. And since no amount of objecting is getting me out of this... I'm stuck with Jay all day. Yay me.

"The sooner we leave, the faster we'll be back."

"Damn, when you say it like that, it sounds like you don't want to go." Even though this is an excellent chance to lay everything on the line and hold nothing back, I do what I always do: clam up while appeasing the other person.

"Not at all. I'm just worried about Wren."

"I'm sure he can live without you for one night." And I'm sure you do believe this since you also believe I'm not his mom.

We are only an hour into our trip when he starts with questions and comments I have no desire to hear or partake in.

"We should talk about what happened the other day."

"I think it's best if we don't."

"Well then, I'll talk. You listen." Okay, asshole, I'll just accept you railroading me into a conversation I already told you I don't want to have. But you go ahead and continue ignoring my request as well as my misgivings. Typical macho B.S.

"I understand how bad that sounded the other day, but I want you to know it didn't come out how I meant it. I know you took over the role of being Wren's mom—"

"No, I didn't take over any damn role. I am Wren's mom. No other way about it."

"You're right. What I meant is—"

"Jay, it might be best if you didn't try to explain any further."

"Sorry. All this sounded so much better in my head. It's that damn rider."

"How is any of this conversation Pestilence's fault?"

"It's time for him to be on his way and leave us in peace, don't ya think?"

"No, because I agree with Avalon. If he's in our community, he isn't out there annihilating humanity."

"You would rather he stay? In the same vicinity as your son?"

"I already answered your question, and my response hasn't changed in the last five seconds. Besides, I have no fear he wants to hurt Renny. He would have allowed the men who attacked us to take Wren out if he planned to do it himself. He didn't, so I don't think Wren is high on his hit list."

"But other people in our community are. I think it's time for him and Avalon to be on their way."

"And I think we've talked enough for one day." He says something else, but I've sped up my pace, which puts enough space between us and spares me from hearing his inane comments.

*****

To my utter dismay, when we arrive at our destination, it appears they are planning a community party. As much as I hope to wrap this negotiation up so I can fall into bed putting an end to this awful day, they have other plans. It seems they expect us to take part, and no amount of polite declining will dissuade them from what they have already decided. I even tried the old I don't have any clothes for a party retort only to have a perfectly lovely lady who I wish wasn't so helpful offer one of hers.

Pestilence's Judgment

The most irritating thing is the stupid grin Jay gives me.

Chapter Twenty-Three: Peek

~ Greer Late Summer 2025 ~

THE DRESS LUCY PROVIDED ME WITH is much sexier than I would like. It's a light-yellow low-cut spaghetti strap summer dress. The only thing I feel good about is the length of the skirt since it hits right around my knee, yet my excitement quickly vanishes when I put it on and realize there is a slit in it… a large one. And the darn thing reveals most of my thigh. Every time I sit down, I will have to be mindful of this, or else the entire community will get a good look at my panties. Which I can assure you is not high on my list of things to do.

I assume you can imagine my distress since Jay is already looking at me like he's ready to mount me right here in the middle of the camp, and this stupid dress isn't helping me any.

Now if I were here with a different man. A man with blonde hair, golden skin, brown eyes, and a body most women fantasize about. It might excite me to take part in this party tonight. Sadly, he's not, so I am left with an overwhelming sense of dread.

Although we are much smaller and nowhere near as secure, I would like to take the idea of festivities similar to this back to our community. There are balloons, those paper lanterns, so much food it could feed us for a week, music, and dancing. The craziest thing is the bicycle they have repurposed to generate soft low lighting. Since the arrival of Death, we have never been able to restore power. To my knowledge, every person who has tried to accomplish this gives up after failing repeatedly. And even though the lights are barely illuminated and flicker out more than they glow, people happily volunteer to take their turn on the bike to power this little piece of our previous life. The joy every person in this community displays is a sight to behold.

If I could show Pestilence one thing, this would be it. Not to rub it in his face that we figured out how to return something he and his brother had taken away from us, but more as a look at what humanity is capable of when we come together. When we stopped worrying about what we had... what we wanted... when we stopped running out to buy all the latest and greatest things, life started anew for us. We may have initially thought we lost everything; the truth is those things we once felt were so damn important just weren't. And in remembering this, most people discovered we are capable of great things, compassion, and camaraderie. This is a perfect example. Something that may sway a rider from erasing us from the history books.

"Don't you look pretty." The unexpected comment pulls me from my wide-eyed, slack-mouth amazement. When I turn around, I find one of the older leaders of this community standing behind me, holding a delicious-smelling pie. If I remember correctly, her name is Tracy.

"Thanks. Lucy lent it to me for the party tonight."

"Well, you would never know it wasn't made for you. So tell me, are you enjoying yourself?"

"I am. The lights are...." I look up at a loss for words seeing them twinkling above me as a young man works overtime to keep them glowing. I can't help the grin spreading across my face.

"Are amazing? I know. One of our community members was an engineer in their previous life. She figured out that as long as we, and I mean humans, continue to pedal, they stay illuminated. Even if we try to use the wind, it doesn't work. I'm not sure what those darn horsemen did, but whatever it was, they did a bang-up job keeping us in the dark ages." Okay, so... maybe I don't tell her about Pestilence, but there is something else I can share with her.

"We have warm running water."

"Get out. Do you know how long it's been since I have even had a tepid shower?"

"Probably as long as it's been since I saw lights."

"Touché, my dear. Touché."

"Tracy, I don't think I can hold off the pie seekers much longer," a young woman yells from a table on the other side of the makeshift dance floor.

"Coming," Tracy says with a massive grin. "Well, make sure you get a plate, and if you're daring enough, you should try some of Ed's moonshine. It burns like the dickens the first swallow you'll take, but it's mighty tasty after you get past the heat."

"Will do."

"Or if wine is more your speed, Lucy might have more blueberry or apple," Tracy says as she takes her pie to the anxious dessert connoisseurs.

After getting a plate of food and a glass of wine, because yes, I was too much of a chicken to try the moonshine, I looked for a place to sit. I claim the last chair at the only open table. A young couple who was sitting with me was as welcoming as Lucy and Tracy had been.

Until five minutes ago, I had no idea where Jay was at. It seems he has found some new friends. I can't help but notice how this small group of men and women has distanced themselves from everyone else. Are they also travelers from another community? If so, why would they not mingle with the rest of this group? Now that they have my attention, I realize they appear to be assessing the place, and the entire situation makes me uneasy.

When Jay catches me watching them, he stands, hugs the two women, slaps several men on their backs, and shakes hands with the others before weaving his way over to where I'm sitting.

"You look amazing," he tells me as he takes an empty chair to pull it next to mine.

"Thanks," I reply as I look past him to the table of people who have returned to their hushed conversation. "Are they also visiting?"

Jay looks over his shoulder. When they see his attention back on them, the woman who was sitting next to him gives him a two-finger wave. Jay returns it with a half-hearted acknowledgment.

"Yeah, most of them, except for the bigger guy. He's lived here for six months." Hoping to get more information without seeming overly eager, I push forward with what I hope is an innocent question.

"Are they close enough to us that we could add them to our list of communities to trade with?"

Jay hesitates a beat too long. "I don't think so.... They plan on moving further South."

"So they're just passing through?"

"Yeah." Something in his answer is off.

"What do you mean — yeah?"

"Nothing."

"What about the place they used to live? Are there still people there we might be able to trade with?"

"It's out west somewhere."

"You don't think it's worth looking into?"

"Care to dance with me?" Honestly? No, I don't want to dance with him, but if I do, maybe I can keep him talking about the table of men and women, not to mention their strange behavior. I know one thing, if these jackasses are planning on doing something to this community, I intend to find out.

The little guy's giggles fill the air as he runs around the camp with Suki and Avalon chasing him. He has been at this game for nearly an hour, and neither he nor the two women appear to be tiring of this activity anytime soon. If I am honest, I delight in watching them.

But this enjoyment brings thoughts I wish I could push aside, even for one afternoon.

Witnessing them like this reminds me of the task I am here to complete. It is one of the few times I despise what I am. I loathe knowing they do not deserve what Raum has started, specifically since my brothers and I, not him, are responsible for carrying it out.

For only the second time, I regret having been sent here. The first was when Greer kissed me, or truthfully when I kissed her since the moment I felt her lips upon mine, I was desperate to prolong our time together. I have never desired something as much as I do her.

The second time is right here, watching the innocence they are all capable of. They find immense pleasure in something so simple as making this special little boy laugh. His joy is infectious. I am drawn to him. His happiness is one of the few things I crave. I know our creator did not put us on this path to covet them; however, it is precisely what I do. I wish with all my being to stay with them always.

Even if I face punishment for this choice, any being who threatens them or tries to harm them will not be long in this world. This declaration also extends to the little lamb, and my proclamation no longer has anything to do with my brother's request. I do this because she has proven time and time again she is worthy of our grace. As surprising as you may find this, Suki, Xander, and Nehra are also under my protection. The little woman has threatened my existence more than once, yet

I know she only does this because she loves these people as much as I selfishly do.

I embrace the sins I break for a chance to spend one more day with them, one lingering second, because those memories will carry me through my long existence. The smiles, the laughs, the feel of her against me. These things must sustain me when I am called back to my endless sleep. Dreams of a little boy who captured my heart and the woman who holds my soul. Father, forgive me; I am no longer certain I can complete my assigned mission.

"I found you," Avalon yells as she runs around the side of the trailer. Wren's excited squeal replaced the giggles that allowed her to easily find him. Most days, the other children would join in, but today they are out doing other things, leaving Wren to enjoy this game without them. "Now I'll hide. You seek."

"Peek," he replies as he follows her.

"No. No peeking little cheater. Now you go over by Auntie Suk, cover your eyes, and wait for me to hide."

"Pook," he calls for her, which of course, brings her running. It is one of the few names he actually says.

"Come on, Renny, we have to shut our eyes if we want to play hide-n-go-seek with Auntie A."

"A, bee, see, dee—"

"No, not the alphabet, silly. Aunt Avalon needs to hide. Then we'll find her." Suki takes him over to the table, where she makes an admirable attempt to teach him how to cover his eyes. It would have worked well if not for his splayed fingers permitting him to watch the little lamb as she darts behind a bolder.

"One–two–three—"

"poor... ive... ixs... evan."

"Good job, Wren. Eight-nine—"

"N," he yells excitedly.

"Ready or not, here we come."

"Umm," he parrots as he takes her hand.

They have been playing this game with him for the last week, and each time he persuades them with a sweet smile to play longer than they did the day before. I overheard Greer saying she thinks this is beneficial to him. The repetition seems to help his speech, although it does nothing for him following the game's mechanics. I would say she has not watched him close enough because he understands what must be done and has figured out that if he watches where they hide, it will permit him to be the hider rather than the seeker much sooner. Unsurprisingly, he runs straight to where Avalon is crouched down to hide from him.

"Did you peek?" She asks with a laugh as she scoops him up, tickling him until he releases another giggle before his enthusiastic confirmation.

"Peek."

"I know you did, you little cheater." He places her free hand over her eyes, indicating it is his turn to hide. She sits him down, only for him to run to the same spot where he found her.

"No, silly. Don't hide there. I'll find you right away." He stands up, scratching his cheek before sticking his thumb in his mouth as he tilts his head. "Aunt Suki, it's your turn to close your eyes so I can help the little man find the best hiding spot." Suki sits, putting her head down on her arm as she begins counting.

Avalon takes him to a tree and places him behind it, but he immediately runs to some dead brush. "I can see you there, Renny. Hide where I can't see you." He looks around briefly before skipping back to the tree she originally put him behind. She gives him a thumbs up when he peeks around the trunk before waving for him to return to his spot as she squats behind a table. A location that offers little in the way of obscuring her from view. The instant Suki stops counting, Wren stands to come out of his spot, but Avalon waves frantically for him to return to the place he was hiding.

This round lasts longer than normal because they can't stop laughing at him peeking at them from behind the tree. When Suki jumps in front of him, declaring she found him, he runs over to Avalon, who happily tosses him into the air, followed by peppering his face with kisses.

"Okay, last time. Then Aunt Avalon and Suki need to get their bums back to work, or Uncle Xander is going to tan our hides," the little one tells him. As if this would ever happen. This man's adoration for her only rivals my growing affection for Greer and Wren.

Leaning against the wall to the pen the mortals created for my horse as if he is a normal horse who must be confined to keep him from roaming, I watch as Avalon sits him down prior to closing her eyes to count. To my utter amazement, the place he decides to hide this time is behind my legs.

"We're coming to get you." It seems both women will be the seeker for this round. For the first time since they began teaching him how to play this game, he does not poke his head out from his hiding spot to watch them. It could be because of the way I am standing with one ankle crossed over the other he has the smallest gap to look through. They start off by looking in all his usual spots. If not for him placing his hands on the side of my legs, they would not have found him so easily this time. Both women meander their way in my direction.

"Pestilence, have you seen Wren anywhere?"

"Not since he was last held by you," I reply matter-of-factly.

"Are you sure he's not hiding over here by you and Storm?"

"Neither my horse nor I can offer any assistance."

"I think we have a traitor in our midst," Suki says playfully. I believe I have grown on this one over the last weeks we have remained in their camp. Perhaps she does not find me as reprehensible as she once did.

"Oh well, I guess we'll never find him. Come on, Suk, we better get to work."

"Peek," he yells as he jumps out from behind my legs.

"Oh my gosh, we didn't see you there," Avalon tells him as she picks him up, but my heart fills when he reaches for me.

"Ess." It seems Suki is not the only name he knows now.

"Oh, you want Pestilence. Who am I to deny such a sweet little face anything his heart desires?" The lamb asks, while I waste no time obliging him, which awards me a smile from the little one.

"If you keep this up, I might actually have to admit I am starting to like you," Suki tells me over her shoulder as she walks across the yard to greet Xander.

"Perish the thought, little one."

"Heaven forbid, rider," she laughs before giving a cursory wave.

"Come on, Wren, I have to take you back to Nehra now."

"He may stay."

"With you?" I cannot tell if the raised brow, wide-eyed expression, or tone conveys her astonishment more. "Yes. Is there an issue?"

"No," she enthusiastically says while shaking her head.

"I have something for him," I explain as I move closer to where my horse is waiting. Pulling the gift from my saddlebag, I hand the object I found to him.

"Orsey."

"Yes, now you have your very own Storm."

"Orm." Avalon's grin could be in regard to me finally acknowledging the name she granted to my horse or the fact Wren has adopted the name for his stuffed animal, but if I had to guess, it has a much deeper meaning.

"What?"

"Nothing... actually, it seems like you found what I failed to show your brother."

"This being, they are worthy of our forgiveness?" Her emotions seem to affect her ability to answer, so rather than responding to my question, she confirms it with a nod, to which only one thought comes to me...

You did not fail, little lamb.

Chapter Twenty-Four: Hope and Noll

~ Greer Late Summer 2025 ~

I THINK IT SHOCKED JAY WHEN I took his hand rather than advising him to take a long walk off a short pier. Heck, I surprised myself. If it wasn't for the little voice in the back of my head nagging me something was off, I probably would have. I'm unsure if he thinks there is still a chance things between us can continue progressing. For me, it's a hard no. Pestilence may only ever be a distant dream; regardless, he changed things. The way I felt the night we kissed made me realize I was settling, which is the last thing anyone should want to do. I would never want my son to settle, so why am I?

I notice him nod his head at the men playing music for the festivities as he leads me to the center of the makeshift dance floor, and the song immediately shifts to a slow ballad. Oh my gosh, did he have this planned all along? Here I thought it was me luring him into revealing his secrets, and now I think he may have been the lurer while I'm the duped luree. Is that a word? I don't think so; maybe dupee? No, definitely not. Why the hell am I debating this now?

"You do look beautiful, Greer. I meant it when I said it earlier; hopefully, you can hear the truth in my words." I don't want to admit it to him, but it would be a lie because I can hear the truth in what he is saying. I think, in Jay's own way, he might care for me. In another life, maybe there could have been an us. In this world, there isn't. But do I really want to make the rest of this trip miserable? No. Do I think if I tell him this budding romance is done, this is precisely what will happen? Yes. Is this why I opt to hold my tongue? You bet your bottom dollar it is.

Besides, if I had to guess, there is only room for two people when he envisions our life together, leaving Renny where? Alone? Abandoned? Suki and Xander's responsibility?

"I'm glad the rain held off. It's such a lovely night for this," he says as he spins me away from him before pulling me back into his chest to dip me back. This puts me in a precarious position, with him leaning closer to kiss me, something I do not intend to allow. With one quick push, we are both upright and swaying around the dance floor again.

"They probably had a contingency plan in place if it didn't." Okay, so it seems he will let my blatant rejection of his kiss go.

"Well, even so, I'm glad it happened the way it did."

We are only out there for a few seconds before the eyes of the people at the table Jay was sitting at are on us as he glides me around the dance floor. The one I notice the most is the big bald guy who is glaring at me like I kicked his puppy or something. I've never so much as said hello to him, let alone anything to piss him off. Yet this big ape glares at me like I'm the biggest piece of shit who has ever walked this planet. I don't know what I could have done to make him so angry, but whatever the reason, his behavior gives me an opportunity to question Jay further about these people.

"I don't think your new friends care much for me."

"Huh?" he asks as he looks over in their direction. "Why would you think that? They've never met you before."

"It doesn't seem like this little nuance matters much to them. Who did you say they were?"

"Travelers from a community."

"Right. Such a shame they're not close enough to us to add as a potential trader."

"It would take us too long to get there. The community they came from is up by Waterford."

"Waterford is north of us. I thought you said they were west of our camp?"

"Did I? My mistake."

"Are you not telling me something?"

"What the hell is the deal with the third degree, Greer? What is it you think I'm hiding?"

"Whoa, no one said anything about you hiding something. I just thought maybe you didn't want us to get involved with them for some reason. I mean, you talked with them; I didn't." He spins me so I can no longer see the group of men and women.

"If you must know, I didn't get the vibes our community would mesh well with theirs."

"Okay. You don't think they'll start any trouble, do you? Because if you do, then maybe we should head back now rather than waiting for morning." I do not really want to leave at this late hour because it's unsafe to travel the roads at night. Mainly, I asked this to make sure they aren't going to cause issues for this town. The one thing I've learned about Jay is he likes me to act like the scared little rabbit to stroke his ego. Which is fine—as long as I get the information I want, I'll pretend to be whatever he needs me to be.

"They won't cause any problems. Wayne doesn't care for how these people act... like the world isn't coming to an end. He thinks they have their heads shoved up their own asses, and I can't say I disagree with him. He and his companions believe we need to be better prepared. Yet another thing I don't oppose."

"What do you mean better prepared? Better prepared for what?"

"The way the world is now."

"Which means?"

"The damn assholes who want to end us. They think we should reserve our supplies rather than throwing elaborate parties that serve no purpose other—"

"Other than to remind us of who we are."

"Come on, even you have to admit this is a bit much," he says, lifting his hand, signifying I should examine our surroundings.

"And you agree with them?"

"With regard to some things they pointed out, I have to admit I do. So my answer is yes."

"But not everything?"

"Can we not just enjoy the damn dance without arguing, Greer? It's one damn dance."

"Sorry. I was just trying to —"

"Interject yourself someplace you shouldn't. Which seems to be an ongoing theme of yours."

"I think I've had enough party for one night," I snap as I drop his hand and turn to put some much-needed distance between us before I say something I might regret.

"Greer." When I don't respond, he tries again to gain my attention. "Goddamn it, Greer, let me explain."

"Go to hell, Jay," I hiss as I continue marching over to the woman who I pray will be my saving grace in getting me the hell away from this insufferable man.

"Hi Tracy, I was hoping you could point me in the direction of my room."

"We put you in Building A, room 103, right over there. I think you and Jay will find it—"

"Wait, we're staying in the same room?"

"Yes. Is that a problem?" she asks cautiously as her eyes move from me to Jay like she already cleared this with him. Did he tell her to put us in the same room?

"No," Jay quickly says, with me interjecting just as fast.

"Yes! Are you sure there isn't anyplace else? I don't mind sleeping on a couch. Heck, even a floor would work."

"I suppose I could try to find you something. I'm really sorry about the confusion. We're just a little tight on space right now because of the other folks who are passing through." She stands up so she can have a better view of the area. Her face has become rosy red as she taps her chin. I also can't miss the nervous little cough she keeps doing. "Now let me see, maybe I could put you up in... no, that won't work. I guess—"

"It's okay. I'll stay in the room you already picked out for us."

"Are you sure, sweetie? I don't mind."

"No. It's fine." Her shoulders relax as she lets out a loud breath. My concession may have let her off the hook from having to find me a place to stay, but it does nothing to waylay her embarrassment since she won't make eye contact until I tell her goodnight and that I had a lovely time. Turning, I head in the direction of the room I have to stay in, with Jay following close behind.

"Way to make me look like a real asshole, Greer," he mumbles as he finally catches up with me.

"I don't care what I made you look like, Jay."

"What the hell is your problem?"

"Right now, you're my problem."

"Yeah, it seems to be an ongoing issue since that fucking rider showed back up."

"Pestilence? You actually still think this has anything to do with Pestilence. Because I can assure you it doesn't."

"Could have fooled me."

"Stop following me, Jay."

"No, it's time you hear what I have to say. Ever since that damn asshole showed back up, you've done nothing but treat me like a second-class citizen unworthy of your precious fucking time. If I didn't know any better, I'd say you want to fuck him." When the only response I offer is an eye roll, he throws his head back while overly exaggerating a groan. "You have got to be fucking kidding me!"

"I don't know what you think is going on, but I think he deserves just a little bit of our damn respect because he's the only reason we made it through the night we were invaded."

"Of course you do. I'm going to get a damn drink."

"You do whatever the hell you want. I'm getting my stuff and going home."

"Are you fucking insane? It'll be four in the morning before you make it back there."

"Your point?" I don't wait for him to continue as I turn on my heels and head to where we have our supplies packed up, but I only make it a couple of steps when he snatches my arm. He pulls me back to his chest a little too hard, making me lose my balance and stumble into him.

"What the hell, Jay? Get off me."

"I said you can't go back at this hour."

"And I don't give a flying fuck what you said," I snap. I admit that using a word not normally in my vocabulary feels odd, but I felt the situation warrants such an expressive adjective. Storming over to my bag, I grab a change of clothes. If I have to make this trek back with no sleep in the pitch dark, then I'm going to do it in a damn pair of jeans.

****

Much to my chagrin, Jay follows me back home. The entire time he repeatedly tried to convince me we should make camp for the night and start fresh in the morning, but I have no intention of doing any such thing. The only thing I want to do is get home, take a shower, put on some clean bedclothes, kiss my son, and fall into bed.

Had I known what was happening, I might have moved faster because the second we entered our community, the only thing I saw was my cabin... fully engulfed in flames.

I drop everything as I race to Suki's door, only to discover it cracked open. With my heart pounding hard enough to snap a rib, I barge in as I cry, "Suki, is Renny in here?"

"Greer?"

"Suk, where's Wren?"

"He's right... where did he go?" she says as she pushes the covers off. Spinning, I look at my house and see the door slightly ajar, and everything inside me breaks as the absolute certainty of where he is courses through me like poison.

Oh my god, no. No-no-no-no. "WREN!"

~ *Avalon* ~

Right after Nehra came over to retrieve Wren from Pestilence, I noticed him preparing Storm. This begs the question, where—oh where—is this rider off to? If he thinks I'm going to let him stroll out into the world so he can decimate some poor unsuspecting community, then he has another thing coming.

"Hey, P—"

He sighs dramatically. Admittedly, I love getting under his skin. "I believe we have discussed your little moniker ad nauseam."

"We did. Right around the time we discussed my nickname, and it is nauseating to have to repeat myself... soooo—moving on. Where are you going?"

"I have something I must take care of."

"Which is?"

"A task which does not involve a meddlesome little lamb."

"Are you trying to say I'm nosy?"

"If this is the word you prefer I use, then so be it.

"Well, in that case, I'm definitely coming with you."

Not waiting for him to help me, I climb the wall before hopping onto Storm's back. If I didn't know any better, I'd say his horse waited for me to board him. Ha. I think I've won over yet another of the rider's companions. He can grumble all he wants. I notice he doesn't force me to dismount Storm. Not that I would, but we could have pretended I would have if it made him feel any better.

We ride for a little longer than an hour before we round a corner, and the sight before me causes me to brace for the worst.

On the side of the road, a man who appears to be in his mid-forties and a little girl not much older than Wren is sitting next to a dilapidated cart filled with what I assume are their meager possessions. Son of a bitch, did they have to break down right here... on this day... when one of the damn riders would be passing through. I am getting ready to tell him not to hurt them when the man lifts his hand and says something I wasn't prepared for.

"Didn't expect to see you back so soon. Did the little guy like them?"

Pestilence slides off his horse, giving me a look that says I know what you were thinking. With my brows damn near disappearing into my hairline and my eyes wide, I shake my head slightly. Which is my way of asking Pesilence what the hell is going on here, without actually saying anything. My answer comes in the form of a grin. A damn grin. What the hell? This doesn't tell me shit. Flipping my leg over Storm, I drop to the ground to follow behind him.

Am I nervous he might still do something to these people that would only serve to piss me off?

No. Nope. Nah-uh. Not at all.

Well, maybe a little.

I mean, this is a rider we're talking about—and let's face it—they tend to do shit that pisses me off. Since a little girl is here, I won't take any chances. What I don't understand is why they aren't running. More perplexing is they seem to be welcoming us. This has never happened to me when I'm traveling with a rider. Is it possible he is blind and doesn't sense who has stumbled across them?

"Presswince," the little girl yells as she runs over to him, leaping into his arms. Mind. Fucking. Blown. "I fown one. Can you bewieve it?"

"Congratulations, it is a rare gift indeed."

"Oh my dosh, I wooked ebrewhere and den it was just here. Wike magic. Poof." I lean around Pestilence to get a better view. My gaped mouth displays my amazement and has my chin damn near hitting my chest. Not only are they welcoming us in, but they also fucking know him... and like him.

"I should like to see your magnificent treasure, young one."

She giggles, displaying a toothy grin. Can baby teeth be considered toothy? I don't know, but it's damn adorable. "You still talk funny."

"As do you," he says as he sits her down, allowing her to scamper over to their cart to retrieve whatever treasure she wants to show the rider.

"You brought a friend with you today?" The man says as he does a cursory half-stand.

"She insisted," he says as he looks over at me. He can pretend he's pissed all he wants. I can see the slight tip to the corners of those damn lips.

"Avalon," I announce as I step forward, offering him my hand.

"Hmmm, you don't say." Okay, what the hell is that supposed to mean?

"Oh, dis is your friend. The one who was sick. Huh, Pessy?"

Pessy? The tilt of my eyebrow informs him we will discuss this nickname in detail later; my response from him was the typical groan he gives every time he knows I'm about to irritate the shit out of him. The little girl's question seems to go unanswered when she returns with something clenched tightly in her hand. Let's hope whatever this treasure happens to be isn't some once-living creature because I'm not sure it will be when she opens her hand again. But I have to admit whatever she has piqued my interest as well.

"It is. So allow me to see," he says, dropping to one knee and putting his hand out for her. With no fear or hesitation, she gently places her treasure in the care of Pestilence.

"See. It is one, isn't it?"

"It is, little one." Pushing up on my tiptoes to see better, I almost fall over when I realize what she has. It appears to be the piece of meteorite he carries with him.

It is something I found in his saddle bag one day. I had meant to bring it up when he returned to our camp but forgot until a week later when I discovered him rolling it between his fingers during our question-and-answer session. When this was one of my inquiries, he first told me it was a memory, then after several weeks, he told me it was a piece of his realm. Something he brought to remind him of how fleeting life is.

The fact he was preparing to remove us—his father's favorite children—from history left a mark on his soul. Pestilence told me this is what he held while waiting thousands of years to be called forth to complete a task he wished he did not have to fulfill. This was when I realized the burden each of these riders must carry.

The two I have met are not wicked, evil creatures. They are beings who have an immense capacity to show compassion, strength, resolve, and love. Or maybe this last one is my hope. Their task weighed heavily on Pestilence because he knew it was his actions ending us. Did he really give this little girl the only piece of his home he had with him?

"It's a tar. Isn't it?"

"It is. A very special one at that. You should put it someplace safe so you never lose it," he tells her quietly.

"I will," she mimics his tone and volume perfectly.

He stands as she skips away to hide her treasure; however, his soulful eyes remain focused on the little girl. Was he thinking about his home? His task? Or the fact this little girl's life could have been snuffed out had they crossed paths with him sooner. I don't know if I'll ever have the answer to these questions. But right now, those answers don't seem all that important.

It seems the man's name is Noll, his daughter is Hope, and he just so happens to be the producer of the gummies Wren is so enamored by. When he pulls out a box for him, I can't help but look over at Pestilence to tease him. "From a man who did not need them, huh?"

"The ones he gifted me were no longer required by him."

"You made me think you—"

"You formed your own assumption on this, since I only advised I commandeered them from someone who no longer needed the sugary blobs."

"By force is what you said. I have a feeling Noll gave them to you. Which is kind of the opposite of by force."

"Yes… well, I had to lift his cart to permit him to fix the wheel, which is where the force came into our exchange." Noll desperately tries to hold back a grin while I look at him like he is full of shit, but when I don't say anything, he clears his throat before turning his attention back to Noll.

"You just didn't want me to know you are going all soft and gushy."

"I assure you, little lamb, this could not be further from the truth."

"So what, you just act like a cart jack in your spare time then? You know when you're not out commandeering stuffed horses or rescuing injured women."

"When I am holding my tendrils at bay. Which is something you may soon see if you continue this path."

"Uh-huh." I laugh as I clap his back before sitting next to the man Pestilence never wanted me to meet.

This man and his daughter are a rarity in this world now, and Noll continued to prove it when he invited us to stay for supper. He advised they were fortunate enough to trap three rabbits along the path they traveled, and his plan was to have a nice stew over an open fire. When the noisy growls of my stomach answered for us, Noll and Pestilence could only laugh before the rider gave a resounding yes. And I'm glad we did because it was the best thing I've had to eat in a long time.

"Is it just you and Hope?" I ask while eyeing the bowl, wondering if it would be rude to lick it clean.

"Since my wife passed, yes."

"I'm sorry about your wife. Was it after?" my focus moves over to Pestilence, who has left the campfire, opting to explore with Hope rather than converse with Noll and me.

"No, it was before. It was Hope's first birthday, and Amy was determined to make it unforgettable. I kept telling her it wouldn't matter, Hope was too little, but when my Amy set her mind to something, she was relentless. She forgot to buy candles for the cake she made, so my beautiful wife had to run out to the store to get some." Oh god, please tell me she didn't die on her daughter's birthday. "A freak mid-March snowstorm made the roads dangerous. I tried to tell her not to go, but her teasing response was, 'This was the exact reason we spent so much on our overly extravagant vehicle.' The last thing she said to me before kissing me was, 'I worried too much,' to which I responded, 'It was my job to worry about them;' I suppose I should have worried more. I knew when I saw the police car pull into our driveway after I couldn't reach her that my life was about to change forever. The officer told me she lost control on a patch of ice and went head-on into a tree."

"Noll, I'm so sorry," I say, taking his hand in mine. I don't know if this was the right thing to do, but I felt like it was. Here's hoping he isn't like me.

"Geez, I don't know why I told you all that. I haven't talked to anyone about Amy since all this started," he advises as he wipes the dampness from his eyes. "She must be on my mind since tomorrow is Hope's birthday. Though, in a way, I guess she got her wish to make Hope's first birthday a day I will never forget." We sit in silence after this. I mean, there is nothing you say to make something like this better; any attempt would only be platitudes.

We stay until the day slips away to night, and he has everything packed up to head home. He jokes his sales are never as good when Pestilence comes to call. Even with the loss of revenue or trades, I don't think Noll minds.

"Shall we?" Pestilence asks, lifting his hand in the direction of Storm.

"Anything you say, Pessy." His growls make me laugh, which is the opposite of what he hoped to accomplish. "Hey, you had to know I wasn't letting that one go."

"One can dream."

"Good one. Sadly, not going to happen—"

The scream of a little girl cuts me off. Pestilence leaps onto Storm before pulling me up behind him as we rush in the direction the sound is coming from. When we round the corner, we find a gang of men attacking Noll as another is carting Hope off into the woods. I know I can't take on ten men, but I can sure as shit handle one. Jumping off of Storm, I sprinted in the direction the asshole disappeared.

"Avalon, no!" Pestilence yells as he releases the first arrow from his bow. The sound of it finding its mark is the only answer he'll get because I have a little girl to save. Thankfully, Hope's muffled cries confirm they are not far, and the shouts of the dying men tell me Pestilence is dealing with what I left behind.

When I come around a blind spot, I crash straight into the asshole who took Hope. The issue is I'm flat-out running and on top of them before I can halt my momentum, which sends me flying over them. I have a split second to decide what I'm going to do. Go for Hope, or go for the asshole. The asshole is who I choose, and his long-ass greasy hair will work perfectly for me to have a handhold. I have enough time to twist my fingers through his mop as I try to lock my legs around him but only get one hooked before we slam against the ground. The impact knocks the breath out of me.

With as much force as I can put behind it as I attempt to suck in any air possible, I yell, "Run, Hope!"

Our time together today must have made her trust me, so she did as I instructed and disappeared in the direction they came from. The next couple of seconds is a blur of tangled limbs, dirt, leaves, and him wrestling to get his hair out of my grasp without me rendering him a patchy bald dumbass.

"I'm going to wring your fucking neck, bitch." He screams. If the smell of his sour breath isn't bad enough, the spit dropping from his gaped mouth on my face almost makes me vomit. "And no one will be able to save you."

I think someone upstairs likes me because the asshole no sooner gets the upper hand when Pestilence is there ripping him off me. If I wasn't desperately trying to suck in lungs full of oxygen, I would have jumped up and yelled... Hell, yeah. Now, what bitch? I have a rider of the fucking apocalypse in my corner.

Would this have been childish? Yeah. Would it have made me feel better? Hell yeah.

"Little lamb, next time I say no—"

"Yeah-yeah, I got it."

"But you won't listen."

Shaking my head, I vehemently exclaim, "No."

Which gains me a head shake from him. Does he want me to lie to him? Probably not. Besides, Pestilence needs to learn I can—at least most of the time—take care of myself. When we get back to where he left Noll, I discover the men who had attacked him sat nicely on the side of the road.

It almost looks like they just plopped down for a rest. I imagine Pestilence did this for Hope's benefit since she made it back and is currently cradled in her dad's arms. Noll does his best to soothe her, including softly stroking her hair as he assures her she's safe. Pestilence's way of confirming they got home safely was to follow behind them.

Half the trip, he doesn't say a word to me, pissed that I 'so carelessly risk my own safety for no reason,' his words, not mine. When I tried to argue that I did it to save Hope, the pissy rider huffed he had it under control. I figured rather than arguing with him, especially since he had to rescue my sorry ass, I apologize. I don't know who was more surprised by this, him or me, but at least it gets him talking to me again.

When we arrive at their house, we help him unload his cart while he carries a sleeping Hope inside. Once done, he shakes Pestilence's hand, hugs me, and tells us he will never forget what we did for him tonight. We wait on the porch until he locks the door before I ask him something I have wanted to ask all day.

"Did you give Hope the stone?"

"Yes."

"Why? I know how much it meant to you."

"It meant more to her. Besides, if one of my kind ever comes across her, they will sense it and leave her in peace."

"So you gave her immunity to all this?"

"Not only her, but any who are in her vicinity, providing they are not attempting to harm her." Without a second thought, I march to where he stands to kiss his cheek.

"What was that for?" he asks me cautiously.

"A thank you for caring enough about one of us to do something like that."

"She is not the only one I care for, little lamb. She is merely the furthest one from my protection," he says as he runs his hand down my arm. When I feel my eyes misting over, I walk away, not wanting him to see how much his action affects me, but I don't miss his quiet response. "Thank you for believing in us."

Once we are both on Storm, he decides to address my short flight to save Hope rescue mission.

"Please don't take off like that again."

"You weren't moving fast enough."

"Regardless, I must request that you do not venture off after men like the ones we met today by yourself again."

"I can't promise that."

"Then I cannot promise I will not tie you to my horse."

"You sound a lot like your brother right now. You know that, right?"

"Having spent this much time with you, I would be astonished if Thanatos didn't chain you up."

"He did."

"This I should like to hear."

"Really? Cause I almost killed him." He looks over his shoulder, his one brow raised, proving he's — at the very least — skeptical of my proclamation.

"What? It's true I almost killed him. Here, let me tell you what happened there, Mr. Cynical. After I tried to ditch him, he found me again. Or actually, Ghost found me, and Thanatos tracked Ghost. He tied me up after returning me to my cabin but neglected to check my bags. Because of this oversight, he awoke with a knife to his throat."

"I assure you, little lamb, Thanatos was not sleeping."

"Yeah, I kind of figured that out when he called me out as soon as I had the knife to his throat. But it could have been lights out for a rider if I hadn't hesitated."

"You know this is not possible. Correct?"

"Doesn't mean I couldn't try." I will spare him the details about the time we spent at our house on the hill. And we replaced the ropes with scarves. Scarves we used for an entirely different reason than stopping me from running.

It's been a long day. Truthfully, two days since the sun is already cresting in the eastern sky as we get closer to home. I can't wait to fall into bed and sleep until tomorrow morning, but all my exhaustion melts away when the smell of burnt wood carries to us with the wind while visible smoke looms just over the tree line.

"Pestilence is that—"

"Camp?"

"Yeah." His response comes by way of Storm racing in the direction of where our home used to be.

Chapter Twenty-Five: Loss

~ Greer Late Summer 2025 ~

HE CAN'T BE IN THERE. HE can't be in there. It's the only thing keeping me from falling apart as my body switches to autopilot and sprints toward my house. I'm almost there when someone tackles me from behind.

"Get off me!" I scream.

"No," Jay snaps. Of goddamn course, it's Jay. He never wanted Wren in the equation to begin with, which makes this the perfect opportunity to remove him. Remove my fucking son.

"Get. The. FUCK. Off. Me!" I scream as I struggle in his arms. How is it possible Xander is one of the few people out here trying to find a way inside? He begins to kick the door in, but when the flames erupt through the shattered window, he is left with little option other than to back away or risk severe burns.

Suki is running from one cabin to the next, yelling Wren's name. She is praying he isn't in there as much as the rest of us are, or at least most of us are. While I'm stuck on the fucking ground because Jay won't get the fuck off me. With as much effort as I can manage, I slam my elbow up, catching him in the nose. He howls from the impact at the same time as he rolls off me. This is the opportunity I need to get my son out of the damn burning cabin.

The entire community is out of their homes now. Some people are running to get water while others are helping Xander. I am almost to the door when Jay grabs me from behind and pulls me back as the first wave of heat from the flame licks over my skin.

"Greer, you can't go in there. Stay here. Let us find a way into him." Fuck that. Wren is my son. I will be goddamn go to hell if I stand here and let everyone else risk their lives to save him. If it worked once, it should work again; my mind screams as I raise my elbow. It seems the problem is Jay is prepared for it this time and easily avoids my assault as he drags me further away from my son.

"WREN!" my strangled sobs as I scream his name fills the space surrounding us. Seeing the house is nearly destroyed, I know if he's in there, he can't survive. I failed him. I fucking failed my son. I should have been here with him, not fucking dancing and eating and fucking laughing. The scream rumbling through me will live inside me for the rest of my days. It will be the sound I hear whenever I think of my son or believe I see him.

Xander turns to look at me, and the heartbreak I find in his eyes confirms there is nothing they can do.

"Get your fucking hands off her." Avalon? Pestilence and Avalon are back. Where were they? If they had been here, maybe my son would still be alive.

"What the hell happened here?" Avalon shouts. "And where's Wren?" I can't answer her as another wave of sobs wracks my body. With my hand shaking uncontrollably, I lift it, pointing at the cabin now nearly completely engulfed in flames.

"Wren's in the house," Avalon screams as she dashes for the cabin, only to be stopped by Xander.

"A, we tried to get in, but we can't," his voice breaks as his emotions overtake him. The only thing left for me is a life without my Renny. It's the only thought repeating as my body crashes to the ground crying for my lost son. Avalon and Suki rush over to me, but my heart soars when I see Pestilence storm toward the house and kick open the door like it was nothing before rushing inside. If anyone can save him, it's the rider. I know he can. He has to.

But all hope evaporates when he comes out carrying my son's lifeless body.

~ Pestilence~

When the lamb and I arrive back in camp, Greer's house is on fire; the asshole is on top of her while Xander and the other men are attempting to... what? Extinguish the flames? Surely these men realize this is a moot point. It is not until Greer indicates Wren is still inside I understand what they are doing. They are trying to rescue him.

The current state of the cabin leaves little doubt if he's in there; he has not survived, yet I still must try. I will not merely stand by and witness this atrocity. As I barge through the first wave of flames, the smoke clouds my vision, making it infinitely more difficult to find his tiny frame. My skin sizzles as the fire looks for a new target to destroy. With the knob searing my flesh, I check the bathroom but find nothing. Could Greer be mistaken? Did he get out without them realizing it? The first piece of the roof caves in, dropping to the space I just occupied. Seeing only one viable option left, I open the door to the closet. This is where I find him. Slumped on the ground, the stuffed horse I gave him clenched to his chest, face stained from the tears he surely cried.

Not breathing.

Unmoving.

I waste no time grabbing his tiny body, hoping there is still time left to save him, but as I have previously stated, I do not give life; I take it. If he is to survive, it will have to be by one of the sons of Adam or daughters of Eve within this community.

It comes as no surprise the instant I am clear of the burning cabin, Avalon is there, yanking him from my arms as she lays him on the ground. She frantically begins pumping his chest as Greer forces air into his lungs. They do this until the first rays of the sun cast a long shadow across the ground. The mortals in this realm would see it as nothing more than the sun rising, but when it stops on Wren, I know what it signifies... his soul is being called home.

"Greer, he's gone," Xander tells her softly; however, it's not until he places his hand on her shoulder she looks up at me.

"I can't—can't lose him, Pestilence. Please, I won't survive without him. You have to save him."

"I cannot."

"Please," she begs, as tears stream down her cheeks.

"I bring disease, Greer. Not life."

"You're a rider," she whispers.

"I am."

"You're special... not like us... please. They can take me instead. Please save my son."

"Greer," I breathe as I run my thumb over her face to wipe away the tears, an act which does nothing to help her breaking heart. Avalon has now also realized her attempts are futile. So I do the only thing I can....

I pick him up and ferry him to my brother.

*****

I am unaccustomed to the swell of emotion overwhelming me. I never thought I would long to listen while Wren sang his song with the animal sounds, but now that it is gone, it is the only thing I wish to hear.

"Brother?"

"I know what you seek, Pestilence, but I cannot."

"He is but a child, Thanatos."

"Children die every day. We have been the reason some of those young ones are gone." He's right of course. When I destroy entire communities, I am not naïve enough to believe children are not among the victims. Yet it was not until this child showed me the magic only these little ones possess did I understand how special they are. A child's capacity to love so unconditionally and without expectation of anything in return is something we thought they did not possess.

"It would not be the first time we have broken the rules."

"As much as you want me to do this, I cannot. You know it is forbidden."

"Thanatos."

"It's time, brother. You need to let him go. Allow him to rest now."

"I am unsure I can do as you ask." Thanatos comes to where I stand, looking down at his little face still covered in ash and soot. "He is everything that was right within their world."

Thanatos's remorseful smile confirms as much as he also believes the words I say are true. He is right. He cannot change what has come to pass. My brother has already broken too many rules; if he does this, they will surely force him into chains. By asking him for this, I would be sentencing him to an eternity of torment. How could I expect him to do this? He has never met this child. He has never heard him sing his song or held him in his arms. Thanatos has never... loved him.

"Pestilence?" My eyes slip closed as I know this will be the last time I ever look upon his face, and my heart aches in a way I never dreamed possible. Reaching up, I wipe the ash from his cheek.

"He did not like his face or hands to be dirty."

"I will cleanse him," Thanatos says as he reaches out, but he does not take him from me. He waits for me to release him.

This is it. There are so many things I wish I had said or shown Wren. I despise how much time was wasted away from him... away from Greer. If I had only admitted my feelings to her, perhaps he may still be alive. This is as much my fault as the flames that claimed him.

With no hope left, I lean over, doing something my heart wishes had been done long ago. I kiss the child who taught me they are worthy of our forgiveness.

"You will stay with him?"

"Until he crosses." He promises as he gently accepts the tiny boy from my arms. Thanatos places his hand on my shoulder. "I am sorry, brother."

Unable to answer—it seems my voice has been stolen from me—I nod. Thanatos turns to take him away, but after ten steps, he quietly asks, "What was his name?"

"Wren, but the people who love him called him Renny." He begins walking again. Each step he takes is another step closer to purgatory, where he will wait to carry Wren's soul to his next life. It is a task I would not wish on anyone, yet Thanatos has been made to do it for his entire existence.

Four steps. Orse says, nay... nay... nay.

Three steps. Tank you. My heart squeezes tighter.

Two steps. Orm. Orsey. Yes, little one Storm is a horse. He is my horse, my companion on this journey.

One step. Oh-tay. What do you want? You, little one... I desire only to have *you* back.

"Do you love them, brother?"

"I... I—"

"Because you know what this means if I do this."

"I understand."

"And you are prepared for it?"

"I am," I say, taking a cautious step toward them.

"So be it." Thanatos runs his fingers along Wren's cheeks, still white from soot, across his hair, singed and damaged from the flames. His wings extend fully out from his sides.

"You are sure you are prepared for the consequences?" I ask because this choice affects me but, more importantly, has ramifications for my brother.

"If it were Apple, it would never have been a question."

"But this is not her."

"Yet I believe he is your version of her."

"He and his mother, yes."

"Then do what I could not. Protect them always."

"Thank you."

"We must hurry before they arrive." As he bends down, his eyes come up to meet mine. With one nod, I lay my hand on Wren's chest and close my eyes. I can feel my brother's breath rolling over his face as life flows back into his tiny frame. My heart stills as I wait for his to take its first beat; every second it doesn't is a lifetime of living in limbo. When I feel the first flutter, Thanatos quietly says, "Now is not your time, Wren. You must wake now, little one."

My heart fills with more love than I thought possible as I watch him take his first breath as my son.

Holding him to my chest, my softly whispered promises to him that I will protect him always is but the first oath I make. When I turn to take him back to Greer, Thanatos quietly asks, "Is she doing well?"

"She is doing as one might expect, longing for a love she knows will never return."

"Keep her safe, brother."

"You needn't ask."

*****

When I arrive back in their community, every soul feels the effect of this loss, but I do not stop to allow them this reunion, for there is only one who needs it. Opening Suki's door, I discover her on the floor sobbing uncontrollably as Avalon, Suki, and Nehra try to offer any comfort they can.

Avalon is the first to look up; with her sharp inhale, everyone else does the same. All but the one person who needs to see.

"Greer," I whisper.

"I can't, Pestilence. Can't live without him."

"Greer," I repeat, but when my words and their encouragement do nothing to make her lift her head. His words do.

"Peas. Tank you." Greer's body bolts upright, her head swinging wildly around the room. When her eyes find me standing there with Wren alive and well in my arms, she jumps up and rushes over, pulling him into her arms.

"Is it true? It's my Wren?"

"Yes."

"Thank you—thank you—thank you."

"It was not my actions that saved him."

"If not for you, he wouldn't be here."

"I merely carried him to the one who could spare him."

"I don't care. My son is alive. My Renny is back."

"You should care, Greer, because it came at a steep price. One someone else must pay."

"Who?" Avalon asks cautiously. She may be inquiring about who I am referring to, but her eyes inform me she already knows my answer.

"My brother."

"Thanatos?" Avalon asks as she slowly stands. "Thanatos will be punished for saving Wren?" My grief-filled expression causes her to sink to the ground. I may have saved Greer from a lifetime of anguish, but I did it at my brother's expense as much as.... Avalon's.

Chapter Twenty-Six: Run

~ *Greer Fall 2025* ~

HIS SWEET LAUGHTER FILLS THE AIR, and I thank God every day for it. Although I suppose the one I should thank is Death. I can't believe a being known for taking life spared Renny's. I asked Pestilence a couple times what price his brother must pay for his role in saving my son, but his response was always the same. A price he knew would be expected but one he opted to pay for Wren.

They are still investigating what caused the fire that came so close to claiming Wren's life and destroying our community. Some tried to claim it was his fault. He must have attempted to light the lantern when he entered, knocking it over in the process. I know better than this. Wren knew he wasn't allowed to touch it nor the matches required to light the wick. Hell, I'm not even sure he would know how to strike the matchstick, let alone reach where I had them placed.

Suki and Xander felt awful about him sneaking out, but I told them they had nothing to feel bad about since he had also managed to give me the slip a couple of times. One thing about my Renny is if he sets his mind to something, he'll find a way to accomplish his goal. I will admit after such a close call, I am not so keen to let anyone else keep him overnight. Oh, who am I kidding? I don't plan to let him out of my sight for the foreseeable future.

Since there were no other unoccupied cottages, Jay offered to give us his place. I declined initially, as the thought of sharing space with him wasn't high on my priority list, but he assured me he would bunk with Cole until they could find other accommodations for Wren and me.

This arrangement usually works; the only issue is that Jay thinks showing up day or night unannounced and uninvited is acceptable. Here's my problem. I can't say anything about him doing this because it is his darn cottage. All the same, I wish he wouldn't show up every time I have just put Renny to bed. I offered to stay with Avalon, but he adamantly opposed this, saying Wren needed his own space. But the truth is, Jay doesn't like the idea of me being around Pestilence. He doesn't even try to hide his growing disdain for the rider. Here's the thing, Pestilence seems to dislike him almost as much.

Pestilence.

Pestilence is another issue altogether. I was always attracted to him, but the attraction grew from merely fantasizing about him in bed to fantasizing about life together after he brought Wren back to me. It's embarrassing how often he catches me staring at him. The worst part is I get flustered and babble like some love-sick teenager whenever I try to talk to him.

Then there is Avalon, who does a great job acting like nothing has changed until she's alone. When she thinks no one is watching or it's just her and Pestilence. This is when she drops the mask showing the worry brewing just under the surface, the only time her fears and concerns slip out. I have also heard her whispering to the sky. I imagine whatever she says is meant for Death or Thanatos, as she and Pestilence call him. I don't know what happened between them, but if forced to venture a guess, I would have to say I'm not the only person attracted to a rider.

"Hey Greer."

"Hi, A. What time are you and Pestilence heading out?" They are supposed to travel to one of the furthest communities we trade with. They sent word they have medicine but are short on grain, which works since we have more than enough grain and are short on medicine.

"Not sure."

"Is everything okay?" As one of her friends, I hate seeing her like this. Everyone who cares about her can see how upset she has been since learning Death has to pay the price of sparing Wren. Which makes her even more protective of him. Most people would step back if they found out someone they care for is being punished for someone else, but not her because, honestly, I think it made Avalon love Wren more.

"I'm just not in the mood for a run today."

"So don't go. I'm sure Pestilence won't mind."

"No."

"Why not? I get how protective he was when you both returned, but I think he'd be okay with you staying behind today."

"I don't go with him because he's worried about me. I go so he isn't tempted to...." She looks at me, waiting for me to catch up with what she's saying, and when it hits me, it does so like a ton of bricks.

"Ohhh."

"Yeah."

"Is he still..." I pause because I'm not sure what word to use here. Saying the words *killing off us humans* isn't a term I want to use when it comes to a man I have fantasized about having a life with. "following his path?"

"No, not since... the night." Meaning the night of the fire. "At least, I don't think so."

"Can't anyone else take your place? You deserve a break, and you should take it." When she raises her eyebrows and smiles, the reality I just stuck my foot in my mouth comes to mind. "Oh, no. Not me."

"Why not?"

"Cause I need to be here with Wren."

"You deserve a break, and Aunt A deserves a day with her favorite little man."

"I don't... I'm not... its-its—"

"Are you trying to say you don't trust me with him?"

"Of course I do."

"Then I'm not seeing the problem. You go with Pestilence, so I know he isn't out there using his killing mojo shit, and I'll stay with the little man so you learn you can trust us again."

"I don't know if I'm ready."

"Well, there's only one way to find out." Before I can argue further, Avalon takes it out of my hands. "Hey, Pessy, change in plans."

The head shake he gives her in response as he continues to saddle his horse can mean so many things. Either he's pissed she changed up their plans, he's angry she called him Pessy—which, by the way, what's up with that—or Pestilence is irritated because he knows she wants me to take her place. I don't think I want to find out which it might be.

"Avalon, I don't think he wants me—"

"Nonsense. Pessy won't care. Will you, Pessy?"

"Little lamb, we have discussed this moniker—"

"So many damn times one would think you would have figured out I don't plan on changing it." She smiles while batting her eyelashes at him.

"If you continue annoying me, I will leave you here."

"Okay."

"Okay? You are never this willing to let me out of here without your company. What are you playing at, little lamb?"

"Nothing. I'm staying here today."

"Is this a trick?"

"Nope. I'm staying. Greer's going in my place."

"Excuse me?"

"Are you asking me to excuse you because you farted?"

"No, I most assuredly did not expel air from my rectum."

"Then what are you wanting me to excuse you for?" His exasperated sigh as he rakes his hand down his face tells me I'm stepping into something he doesn't want, and I don't reckon Avalon laughing is helping his mood any.

"I don't have to go—"

"Nonsense. Pessy would love to have you along for the day. Isn't that right, rider?"

"If it will give me a moment's peace from your constant nagging." He growls, to which Avalon responds with another round of laughter. I mean, who the hell would laugh at one of the damn riders? Well, apart from a crazy person. I never thought Avalon would fall into this designation, but now I'm questioning it.

"I do not require a... what do you call them?"

"Babysitters?"

"Yes! One of those. I believe I can handle a run on my own."

"Bullshit."

"Avalon, I don't think he wants me—" Without letting me finish, she immediately cuts in and continues with her plan to send me with the rider. Any doubts about whether or not he would want me along for the ride have been answered thoroughly. He definitely does not wish to have me tagging along with him.

"Don't consider it a babysitter then," she taps the side of her face several times before blurting. "Consider yourself a tour guide. Greer's personal tour guide of the countryside. Pessy." Oh god, has his face ever turned that color before? If I didn't know any better, I would have to say he's ready to have a meltdown. A full-on... end-all... nuclear meltdown. Did she have to add that last part?

"Let's go," Pestilence snaps, and I don't know if he is talking to Avalon, his horse, or me, but he doesn't leave me questioning this long when he looks at me and continues. "We have a long ride. We should be on the road soon if we wish to return before Wren retires for the evening."

"Um, just let me check on Wren and grab a bottle of water. Okay?"

"I shall await you by my horse." Without another word, he spins and lumbers over to where Storm waits patiently.

"Avalon, I don't think he wants me to go," I mumble, and the last thing I want to do is piss him off or ruin his day, especially since my preference would be to remain with my son.

"Greer, I see the way you look at him."

"I don't—" she lifts her hand to silence my objection.

"Take today to find out if your growing attraction has any basis. You never know what may come." She says with a slight knowing smile as if what she is telling me to do is a road she has already traveled. I plan to ask, but when my mouth opens, something else tumbles out.

"And what if it doesn't?" I want to smack myself for asking this even more when her knowing smile turns into a full-on 'gotcha' grin.

"Then nothing. You get a day out. Wren gets to play with his aunts all day, and tomorrow you'll know."

"Know what?" Once again, my only answer is a telling grin. Oh shit, know-know, as in, know if anything is happening between us. Oh hell, I'm not sure if I'm ready for this.

"Hi, ladies," Jay says in his typical annoying way while he strolls up next to us as I stand to retrieve my stuff.

"Hi, Jay. I'll be right back." Rushing to grab a light jacket just in case it gets chilly on our return trip. I can't imagine an already irritated rider will want to deal with a shivering woman behind him the entire ride home. I also grab a bottle of water before gently kissing Wren. He's napping on the couch, courtesy of another one of Jay's late-night visits. By the time I return to the table Avalon is sitting at, Jay is storming away, but from the brief glance I got of him as he left, she must have said something to piss him off.

"Avalon, what happened?"

"Nothing."

"That didn't look like nothing."

"I may have told your stalker you wouldn't be able to hang with him today—by the way, you're welcome—because you have plans."

"Oh god, did you tell him I was —"

"Going with Pestilence? Yeah," she says with a wicked grin. "I may be many things, but a liar isn't one of them."

"Avalon!"

"You better get going before you have to deal with a moody rider all day," she says as she strolls towards the cottage holding my Wren.

"You won't fall asleep, will you?"

"Go, Greer. Wren will be fine." Having nothing else to argue about, I slowly look at the rider rubbing his horse's snout. His fitted shirt pulls across his sculpted back showing every well-defined muscle, and I realize this will be my view for the next couple of hours.

Lord, give me strength.

He senses my approach without me saying anything. Walking to the side of his horse, he hoists himself up. Oh damn, okay, so this part never occurred to me. How the hell am I supposed to get up on this mammoth beast? While I'm standing here debating how to get on top of a horse darn near as tall as I am, he rides up next to me before offering me his hand.

"Oh, thanks." Okay, I could have said this with slightly more confidence. How his grip on my hand is so gentle since he lifts me with so little effort is shocking.

"Ready?" he asks as he glances over his shoulder. Not knowing where else to hold on, I wrap my arms around his waist, taking extreme caution not to put them too high or too low.

"Yeah." Without another word, he clicks his tongue and rides us out of our community.

This day is starting out swell.

~ *Pestilence* ~

Her unease is palpable. She's nervous, although why wouldn't she be with how I acted back at their camp. She must believe I despised the thought of her coming along. Quite the opposite. I have wanted to spend time with her since the night we shared the kiss but did not know how to go about it. I simply loathe that, once again, the little lamb did what I could not.

"Um, I'm sorry about this." And there it is. She is afraid I don't want her here.

"You needn't apologize."

"Still, Avalon kind of sprung this on both of us, and I get the feeling you would have preferred her—"

"No. I'm glad you are here. Avalon can be... difficult to deal with at times. I like the quiet you offer."

"Oh, sorry."

"For what?" I ask as I glance over my shoulder. Her eyes are focused on my back, which I would have said is only because of my size versus hers, but when she realizes I witnessed where her concentration was, her face turns a bright red.

Approximately two months after we began traveling together, Avalon explained this phenomenon to me. Back then, I often caught Greer looking at me, and each time my eyes would find hers, the color of her face shifted. Avalon told me it was because she was embarrassed I had caught her. When I inquired why she did this, the lamb said to me matter-of-factly, 'She likes you.' As if this is something that would happen on any given day. The fact I was a rider didn't seem to matter, as Avalon told me, 'You're kind of a hottie.' I was unsure what this meant, but one conversation with Xander clarified it.

"For interrupting your quiet."

"I did not mean to imply you shouldn't talk. I rather like the sound of your voice."

"You—you do?" she asks timidly after attempting to swallow down her mounting trepidation.

"Do I make you nervous, Greer?" I asked after slowing my horse down to give her my full attention. He doesn't require my focus to be on the road we travel. Storm could navigate without me ever looking, but her grip around my waist would suggest her unease atop him. I have noticed each time my horse changes his speed or direction, her hands squeeze slightly tighter.

"At times, yes."

"May I ask why?"

"Um... well... you're a bit intimidating, and honestly, I don't know how to read you."

"Read me?" I was unaware that I am akin to one of the books Avalon occupies much of her time with most days.

"Figure you out?" Is she asking me if this is what she meant, or is Greer too afraid to tell me her true feelings? The latter is possible, especially after everything she has experienced since I rode into her life.

The rest of the ride is something I am unaccustomed to any longer... we ride in silence. I have grown used to traveling with Avalon, who never goes long without saying something. I never thought I would utter this from my lips, but I miss her ceaseless chatter. Yet there is something to be said about having Greer with me because I quite enjoy the feel of her hands on my body.

When we arrive at the community we will trade with, she hops off Storm. The only issue is she doesn't land on her feet; it is her backside smashing against the ground. Greer's face transforms from her normal golden hue to scarlet.

"Are you injured?" I ask, moving over to assist her, but she leaps up almost as swiftly as she fell.

"Yep, must have slipped in a hole or something." The color on her face is now creeping down her neck as her eyes scan her surroundings. I am unsure if she is checking to see if others witnessed her fall or if she does not want to meet my gaze. The fact I do not see a hole confirms her story is fabricated, but I imagine it is only due to the heat coloring her features. Whenever she believes I am not watching, she rubs her backside while mouthing her discomfort with a simple....

"Ow."

Greer completes the negotiation while I unload the grain we brought for them. Twenty minutes after our arrival, the transaction was complete, and she was gathering her belongings to return to camp, but I may have other plans.

Since we finished faster than anticipated, I opted to share something with her, something discovered during my journeys with the lamb.

"Would you be opposed to me showing you something?"

"No," she says with a small smile. When I lead her over to my horse, her reluctance is visible. "Oh, on Storm?"

"Yes."

"I guess I thought it was something... around here," she declares as she lifts her hands, indicating the community with less to offer than the one she resides in.

"No, but it is not far."

"Well then why don't we walk?"

"It is too far to walk," I advise, swinging my leg over my horse before offering her my hand. She looks around for a second before accepting my offer to help her. With Greer seated behind me, I turn Storm towards the hidden gem I wish to share with her.

Chapter Twenty-Seven: Bliss

~ *Greer Fall 2025* ~

WHEN PESTILENCE ASKED IF HE COULD show me something, I quickly agreed because my butt still hurts like hell. Misjudging the distance and falling in front of him while he was watching was humiliating. I bet Avalon doesn't tumble off his horse. Geez-Louise, how embarrassing. My butt was sore just from riding here, and now I have to climb my aching ass up there and pretend everything is okay because there is no damn way I can tell him how uncomfortable this is.

Thankfully, he was right. It only takes us fifteen minutes to get there, although I have no damn idea where there is because we're in the middle of nowhere. There are trees to the left, more trees to the right, and a lot of empty road in front of us.

This time when Pestilence swings his leg over and drops to the ground, my eyes are glued to how he does it. With any luck, I won't end up on my ass this time. Honestly, my butt couldn't handle another fall from Storm so soon. I wonder if sliding down his side on my belly is an option rather than trying to stick the landing. But it seems all my debating is for nothing when Pestilence turns and reaches up to help me get down. Okay, now I'm unsure if it's more humiliating needing to be lifted off his horse like a child or falling off his horse like a dumbass.

Following him through the tree line, he leads me down an overgrown path. You can tell it was a highly traveled route at one time, but this must have been pre-horsemen because the brush had overtaken it. As we go further into the wooded area, the faint sound of running water carries to me from somewhere ahead of us. When Pestilence pulls back a canopy of low-hanging branches, I am stunned by what I find.

It's a pool of water surrounded by a rock face with water coming over the highest ledge. It's like a lagoon you would expect to find on some tropical island.

"Do you like it?"

"It's beautiful." Actually, the word beautiful doesn't come close to doing it justice. It's stunning. Like a hidden oasis locked away from the world except for a few lucky souls who happen across it. "How did you know this was here?"

"Avalon and I discovered it during our travels." The way the sun filters through the trees and hits the water's surface makes it look like diamonds. It's not crystal clear but not murky like most of the ponds I'm used to seeing around here. The best word to describe this water is inviting, and this place is paradise. My every thought keeps returning to stripping out of these clothes and swimming in this hidden utopia. It's a hot, muggy day, so what would be better than cooling off in this amazing place?

"What are you thinking?"

"Honestly?"

"I would not have asked if I did not wish to hear the truth."

"Swimming."

"Swimming?"

"It looks so refreshing. The only thing I can think about is diving in."

"What are you waiting for?"

"Oh. No, I...." Looking from Pestilence back over to the water. I watch as the ripples from the cascading waterfall fan out to lap at the rocks along the shoreline.

"You wish to swim. The day is warm. You have a pool of water before you. I do not understand why you hesitate."

"We should head back soon."

"We have time."

"I don't have a swimsuit."

"This is required to enjoy the water?"

"No."

"Then I'll ask again. Why do you hesitate?" Letting my eyes go back to the pond, I wipe my brow with the back of my hand. Damn, this is one of the few times I wish I could channel Suki's throw-caution-to-the-wind attitude, but just as I look at him to tell him no, I find him pulling his boots off. His shirt is already tossed aside, and my chin damn near hits the ground when he drops his jeans. It would have been fine if he wore underwear, but I quickly learned this horseman doesn't believe in them.

And sweet baby Jesus, I can't pull my eyes away from him. His perfect body isn't restricted to the upper half. Here's the thing. He doesn't realize he's the reason I can't close my mouth.

Oblivious.

He is utterly clueless about the effect he holds over me. He apparently doesn't realize how long it's been since I have enjoyed the touch of a man. Especially a fine-ass specimen like this man. I can tell you... entirely too damn long. And here he is, strutting in front of me, showing me everything I have only fantasized about.

He dives into the water, and when he resurfaces, it doesn't help my soaring libido because now his back isn't just rippling with every movement; it's glistening. He's a rippling, glistening, golden God.

"Will you be joining me?" Okay, decision time. I can either stand here watching him like some damn creep or woman up and do what Avalon encouraged me to do. Which includes finding out what's happening between us.

The only ridiculous thought in my brain now is... thank God I wore the only matching set of panties and bra I own. Because, of course, this is what the horseman will judge me on if my bra matches the boyshorts I'm wearing. I know one thing if I don't do this, I imagine it will be one of those things I regret later in life. Well... if I have a later in life, that is.

This is when I decide not to let the logical part of my brain get in the way. I kick my shoes off before quickly and awkwardly moving onto my clothes. On the upside, Pestilence has submerged himself again, so he doesn't get to see me stumbling around like I just got home from an all-night booze fest. I suddenly have a newfound respect for any woman who can remove their clothes while making the act look erotic and sensual.

As I slowly enter the oasis, Pestilence breaks the water's surface, and again my eyes are pulled to him as he lifts his hands to push his hair away from his face. The way each muscle in his upper back, shoulders, and arms flex and bulge when he does this makes it hard for me to concentrate on anything else. As a result, I slip and fall face-first into the water. Thank god he didn't witness this mortifying display. And as luck would have it, I can play it off as though I dove into the pond rather than face-planting while gawking at the living Adonis.

I surface right in front of where he is standing. Okay, I so didn't plan it this way, but I'm not complaining.

"You came in."

"Yeah, I guess I couldn't resist."

"It pleases me you did. The water is, as you said, refreshing?"

"Yes, it is." Why is it that whenever I'm around him, I get so flustered that my responses sound ridiculous? Because he makes me nervous and aroused and flustered. So what options does this leave a tongue-tied, semi-clumsy, salacious mortal with an infatuation for the man before me?

Simple. Put some much-needed space between his naked body and me before I do something crazy like run my tongue over his abdomen's well-defined ridges. So I dive back under the surface to swim closer to the water flowing over the rocks.

Without stopping to think about the lack of clothes currently covering my body, I climb out to stand under the waterfall. The pressure is only slightly stronger than what you get in a fantastic shower, and since one of those hasn't been available in years, I love this. It occurs to me that standing here like this closely resembles every bikini-clad woman posing for a men's magazine.

When I turn back to face the rider, his focus is on me, but he dives under the water before I can overanalyze this whole interaction. Here's the thing. Right before he disappeared, I would swear he was checking me out, which makes me feel slightly better that I wasn't the only one doing it.

When the rider does not surface after several minutes, I wonder if something happened to him. Did he dive down and hit his head? Did he get out, and I didn't see him? Concern creeps in on me the longer I stand here, thinking about everything that could have gone wrong.

"Pestilence," I yell, but the unease transforms into alarm when I receive no response.

"Pestilence, can you hear me?" Deciding I have waited long enough, I slip into the water. I don't know how deep this pool is, but this doesn't matter because I need to find him if he's down there.

On my first dive, I easily find the bottom but no horseman. The second time I stayed down until my lungs burned, which left me with no other option but to surface for air. Each time I come up and find no rider, my heart rate ramps higher.

"Pestilence!"

"Greer?" I spin in the water to find him directly behind me. Without thinking, I throw my arms around him.

"Oh my god, you scared the shit out of me. Where were you? You were under the water for so long." The response I receive from him is not what I expect because rather than pulling away, he wraps me in a comforting embrace.

"My intention was not to frighten you. I apologize." His tone is soft and soothing as he rubs small circles on my back.

"Don't do that again. I thought something happened to you," I murmur as I pull him tighter against me.

"Greer." He attempts to move away from me, but I'm not ready to let him go. Not yet. Not when I thought the worse had happened to the man who gave me back my world.

"Greer." This time, when he pulls away, I let him. "You do comprehend, since I am a rider, there was no danger to me?"

"I do now," I mumble my response as I turn to swim back to shore. I think I've had enough of swimming and humiliating myself in front of him for one day. Besides, the day is quickly slipping away to evening, and if we don't get moving soon, I won't make it home in time to tuck Wren in for the night. I know he is still talking, but I can't seem to make myself care right now. I suppose the trip gave me one thing... answers. And the resounding one is there is nothing between us.

Once back on shore where I left my clothes, I realized it was pointless taking them off because I don't have anything to dry off with, so they're going to be soaked anyway. Yet another thing I didn't think through today.

"Shit!" My irritation trickles through with my grumbled reaction to this crappy situation.

"Did I do something to upset you?"

"Nope, you didn't do a thing."

"Yet I can sense your frustration. I believe it has to do with my response."

"Not at all. It's getting late, and I'm ready to go home," I tell Pestilence, forcing a smile as I make myself turn to face him. This is my issue to deal with, not his. The bottom line is we — and by we, I mean Avalon and I — were wrong, and this little infatuation seems more one-sided than mutual. Which is fine. I suppose it is better to know than to wonder.

Not waiting for him to lead, I take the route I know will take me back toward where we left Storm. My issue is we spent so much time here it's getting dark, making the path impossible to see. So I've only gone a few yards into the tree line before I have to step aside to let him lead me out. I guess we can add super vision, night vision, or some damn kind of vision I don't possess to his list of attributes and my list of shit I don't know about a rider. As much as he may believe I'm upset at him, he's wrong. It's me I'm mad at. Pissed that I let myself buy into a fantasy.

Once we are back on Storm heading home, I realize how poorly I behaved after he was kind enough to show me such a beautiful spot. In fact, it knocks me in the head, and I end up feeling like a real jackass. Which is the reason why I decided to metaphorically put on my big girl panties and woman the hell up.

"Thanks for today. I really enjoyed myself."

"Until I caused you concern."

"No. Sorry, I overreacted. Of course, I knew you would be fine; I just wasn't thinking."

"I'm glad to hear it. I also enjoyed myself today."

"You did?"

"Yes, Greer, I did," he tells me with a smile. Of course, I only saw a piece of the grin since he was looking at me over his shoulder.

*****

We are an hour into our return trip when the weather turns foul. The skies have opened up to release a deluge of water on us. With the addition of the wind, it doesn't take long before my teeth start chattering, and my body is shivering violently. Fortunately, I only have to endure this for a couple of hours. I can handle a little discomfort. Hell, after everything that happened today, what're a few more measly ticks of the clock gonna do. Just a few short hours, I tell myself while willing my body to stop shaking. The issue is that it refuses to listen, and it doesn't take long before Pestilence realizes how cold I am.

I immediately question him when he veers off the main road because any side trips now will only prolong this misery.

"Where—where r—are we go—going?"

"We need to find shelter until this storm passes."

"We should key—keep going."

"No, it would be best for you if we stop until it passes."

"I—I'll b—be fine. We can key—keep going."

"You're shivering body and chattering teeth would seem to suggest otherwise. We will find someplace to stay until this passes, and then we will be on our way again. I apologize you are upset you will not be home to kiss Wren before bed."

"Real—really, I c-c-can keep go—going," I stutter.

He pulls the reins, forcing Storm to stop, which is the opposite of what I want him to do. I realize there are yet hours between me, a warm cottage, and dry clothes, and these delays only add to this time. I am shocked when he takes my hand in his, partly because I didn't expect him to do this and partly because his hand is so warm it only proves how damn cold I am.

"I do not believe this color is something you typically associate with mortals." Yeah, okay, he's got me there because my fingers are pruney from being exposed so long to the rain, and they have taken on a bluish hue. I could have lived without the mortal comment. I suppose it's just another way for him to remind me we are leagues apart in how we view one another. Knowing there isn't a chance in hell I'm going to be able to convince him to keep going now, I give in and nod my agreement.

Within fifteen minutes, we come across a row of houses. Thankfully, they appear to be abandoned. Here's hoping appearances aren't deceiving. He selects one that sits slightly further off the road than the others. I don't have any objection when he reaches up to help me down this time because I know my shaking legs would never hold me upright if I tried to climb down without his assistance. At this point, they scarcely keep me upright while I stand here and wait for him to grab supplies from Storm's saddle bags.

"Wha—what are you do—doing?"

"Grabbing this," Pestilence tells me, holding up a bag as another shudder causes my legs to shake violently. If he hadn't grabbed me, I would be on my ass in the mud right now. He ascends the steps to a covered porch, and being out of the rain is a welcome relief. I figured he would plop me down on my feet the second we were out of the storm, but he continued to hold me as he shoved the door open.

"But what about...."

"About what?" he asks as he looks at the empty road behind us.

"Storm?"

"Greer, are you talking about the weather or my horse?"

"Your horse. We can't leave him out there."

"I will tell you as I have told the lamb, my horse is unaffected by the weather."

"Still, it's not right. Besides, what if some band of roving assholes comes by? Isn't leaving him out there only inviting trouble?"

"Are you worried about — as you put it — the roving assholes or my horse remaining in the elements?" he asks as he gently sits me on the couch before dropping to one knee to keep his face in line with mine.

"Roving assholes?" I know it came out more question than a statement, so here's hoping he can't detect the lie since I could give a shit less about roving assholes, but Storm standing outside in a... well, a storm isn't high on my priority list. And he can compare me to Avalon or call me soft-hearted all he wants; it won't change how I feel.

"So bringing him inside to avoid attracting the attention of rabble will ease your troubled mind?" he asks as he gently pushes the wet strands of my hair from my face.

"Uh-huh," I mumble while slowly nodding. Without another word, he stands, taking with him the delicious warmth his hand provided so he could retrieve his horse. It's a damn good thing too, because as hard as I thought it was raining the instant he closed the door, the already hellish storm kicks up a notch bordering on nothing short of a monsoon.

Even though we are protected from the pouring rain and driving winds, I still can't stop my teeth from chattering, which may have something to do with the soaking wet clothes clinging to every curve. Pestilence's heavy footsteps inform me he is going upstairs. I assume he is doing this to ensure we are alone in here — which, right now — I don't care if we are or not. The only thing I do care about is getting my blood circulating to my extremities again and getting my damn shaking body under control.

The sounds of Pestilence opening and closing something upstairs filter down as I shuffle around this level on wobbly legs looking for anything I can use to dry off. A blanket would be ideal, but honestly, I would settle for a damn paper towel right now.

The sound of him returning to this level carries to me as I continue searching through kitchen drawers. Once I get my legs under control, I'll venture upstairs to search for something better.

"Here," he says when he enters the kitchen. And I could kiss him, seeing him holding a towel out for me, not only a towel but a blanket too. "I found these as well. They appear clean and are among the only items I believe will fit you."

Taking the clothes he found for me, I hold up the shirt and immediately start giggling, "Ah… thanks, Pestilence… But I don't think I'll be wearing this?"

"It's dry."

"It is."

"And it is clean?"

"It is laundered, yes. But clean is one thing it's not."

"I don't understand."

"Let's just say this is something a man would wear."

"Regardless of whether it was intended for a son of Adam or daughter of Eve, it is clean, dry, and will assist so you do not continue shivering." I guess I can put it on until my clothes dry, especially since he doesn't know what it implies.

Sighing heavily, I roll my eyes before leaving the kitchen to change my clothes. The jeans he found are a bit too big, but if I roll them down, it helps keep them from sliding off my hips. I can't help but shake my head at the shirt as I look at myself in the mirror. With my clothes tossed over the side of the shower drying, I return to the main floor to find him plating the food.

"Is that what you had in the bag?"

"It was evident we would be gone all day. I figured it would be best to bring sustenance with me to prevent the noises made by your body when you have not eaten. I presume your body reacts much the same way as the lamb's stomach does when she has not received proper nutrition."

"Are you talking about when our stomachs growl?"

"I have heard many different kinds of growls throughout my long existence, and never have I feared as I did when I heard this sound coming from the little lamb." I laugh as I bite into the sandwich he placed on an actual plate for me.

For the first time since arriving at the oasis, our conversation doesn't feel strained. It's relaxed... easy, and I find myself laughing more than I have in a long time. He's funnier than I originally thought, or he even knows. Many of his comments are humorous, but I don't think he meant it this way.

We spend the next hour asking or answering questions posed by the other, but it's not until his next comment that my mouth falls open.

"So tell me, Greer, have you ever partaken in the comment penned across your shirt?"

"Wha—what?" I stammer.

"Free mustache rides. Have you partaken?"

"Um... uh... Do you even know what this means?"

"I may not be mortal, but I do understand the concept of procreation."

"Wait, you knew what this meant the entire time, and you had me wear it anyway?"

"I deduced the meaning. It is not as clever as the mortal who penned it believed it to be."

"And you let me continue wearing it?"

"It was this or no shirt."

"Ah... not true. I have a shirt upstairs—"

"One I would not permit you to wear since you would have been uncomfortable."

"Um — what?" before I can react, he stands and moves directly in front of me, invading my space before he answers my question.

"I did not want you to wear it until it had ample time to dry since you would be cold and uncomfortable. In case you have not figured this out yet, I desire only to comfort you."

My damn swallow is entirely too loud, and the slight tipping of his lips as he tries to hide his grin confirms he heard it too. "You do?"

"Yes, and you have not yet answered my question."

"Wha—what question?" I stammer while clearing my throat. When he runs his fingers over the letters on the shirt, my heart — which has picked up its pace since this conversation began — ramps to frantic levels.

By the time he's done, my nipples are rock hard. There is a pounding ache within my core, and if I had to guess, the panties that were dry five minutes ago are wet again for an entirely different reason. His finger under my chin forces my gaze from the letters he has been tracing on the shirt to his eyes. We both remain perfectly still. Neither of us moves or speaks. Hell, right now, I'm not even sure if I'm breathing. His eyes follow the lines of my face, but when they land on my lips, followed by his thumb, I am done waiting. Tilting my head back as I lift myself out of the chair, my mind is made up. He is worth any risk this might bring as my mouth seeks his. The second our lips meet, all of my fears and doubts over the last weeks vanish, and I feel like I'm right where I was always meant to be.

His hands slowly snake around my waist to lift me onto the table. A low moan escapes me, making his hand find my face so he can tilt my head, giving him a better angle to ravage my lips. I don't know what excites me more: his mouth on mine, his hands on my hips pulling me closer, or the dominance of his tongue as he sweeps it across mine.

"Since the night of our kiss, I have thought of little else outside of these lips or the feel of your body against mine." His whispered confession is almost as sensual as his touch. Without taking time to overthink this, I slide his shirt over his head, assuring my fingers glide along his skin as I do it, which causes an immediate response from my rider.

His reply is to pull my legs around his waist, anchoring my body to his so he can carry me upstairs. The amazing part is he managed to navigate us up the steps, down a hall, through a door, and onto a bed without his lips ever leaving mine or falling. Coming from a self-proclaimed klutz, this is an accomplishment in its own right.

Once Pestilence has me placed on the bed, he moves to the end, where he can grab the bottom of the jeans he provided. With little effort, he yanks, and just like that, the jeans I wore are gone before my brain fully registers he removed them.

"Now let us explore the meaning of these words," he tells me, running his finger along my leg. Holy Mother Mary. Who was the asshole who said fantasies cannot become a reality? His finger stops short of touching me where I am desperate to feel his caress. Instead, he begins slowly — and I mean inch by painful inch — sliding the shirt that started this entire interaction up my body. I will never understand how he accomplished this without letting his fingers so much as graze the flesh underneath. The one thing I do comprehend is that I might lose my damn mind if he doesn't touch me soon.

"So, now that I have you back to the clothing you wore this afternoon while you tempted a rider. Enticing me to sample the flesh you allowed me to marvel at all afternoon... let us begin," he purrs against the hand pressed to his lips before adding. "For this is merely but one of the many things I plan to rectify immediately."

"I did... what?" I ask with a stutter because, let's face it, my lust-fueled mind is incapable of little else.

"The sight of you today was so inviting; I had to fight my every urge to allow my fingers to reach out and caress this soft skin. Was my desire not obvious to you?"

"Ah, nope. I'm pretty sure I had no damn clue."

"Regardless ... what am I to do with you now?"

"Um... is this like a rhetorical question? Because if it's not, I'm happy to explain." He leans over, bringing his mouth against my ear before answering me.

"Very rhetorical, la meva bella temptació."

"I'm not sure what you just said. Would you like to clue in the clueless mortal?" But before he answers my half-hearted question, Pestilence climbs onto the bed, placing a massive thigh on either side of my waist.

"I can tell you or show you. The choice is yours."

"Show. Definitely show," I pant as I paw at him, hoping to return his lips to mine. But rather than kissing me, his lips find my neck, one of only three spots that makes me melt. His fingers skim down my chest catching on to the bra still covering my breast.

"Alguna cosa haurem de fer al respecte, la meva bella temptació."

"Again, I'm going with huh," I say in a breathy whisper, which only makes him laugh.

"I said," he flicks his fingers over the bra, popping it open like it was made to do this, "we shall have to do something about this, my beautiful temptation."

"Yes, please," there's no point in hiding what I want any longer. The gravelly tone I respond with would only give away the desire my rider evokes. He moves his kisses from my neck down my chest settling for the space between my breasts. Which I can assure you is not my first, second, or third choice of where I want his lips and tongue right now.

He turns his head only far enough to bite into the tender flesh of my breast. My initial reaction is to pull away, but as his tongue slides over the abused skin, soothing the pain he evoked, I twist, hoping he will do it again, only this time to the nipple, eager for his attention. I go for a more direct approach when he doesn't take my subtle hints.

I twist, turn and struggle to move him over to the pebbled nipple I want him to lick, taste, touch, but he refuses to give in. Refuses to move where I need him. He has his own agenda, and it seems, in part, he desires nothing short of seeing how much he can make me squirm. I'm not even sure I can be angry with him since I don't know if this is his lack of sexual experience or expert knowledge on bringing a quote-unquote mortal to their knees.

"I plan to enjoy every second you are willing to gift me," he says as he slides lower. My sex is now pressed against his chest, and I am not ashamed to admit I grind against him. "Your scent drives me senseless with my desire to claim you."

"Fuck," I moan. My hands have taken on a mind of their own as they grasp his hair.

He readjusts again, and now he is centered squarely between my legs, and suddenly I miss the feel of his chest against me, especially since he has refused to touch me where I want him to. His finger teases along my panties.

"So if I understand the meaning of the shirt you wore, the premise includes this part of your anatomy pressed against this part of my face." His finger sweeps along the cotton, separating his touch from my body, but it's enough to send me from panting to begging.

"Yes-yes-yes. Please."

"Please, what?"

"Pestilence," I moan. He presses his mouth against me, and the contact has me grasping the blankets. "Oh, my — my... fucking... oh, damn." My cries are met with him grinning against my thigh. He hasn't even gotten to the part that I am willing to beg him for, and I'm fucking begging him.

"I believe I like this side of you, my beautiful temptation."

"What? A foul-mouthed horn dog?"

"A beautiful temptress who writhes under my touch." He tells me, sliding the cotton panties away that are now thoroughly soaked with my arousal.

"You are magnificent."

"I am far from it," I pant as I lift my hips hoping he will grant me my wish.

"To me, you are everything great this world has to offer. You and Wren," He whispers against my thigh as his tongue runs the length before finally sweeping across my clit.

"Don't stop," I beg, and with this final plea, he gives me his full attention. By full attention, I mean his tongue sliding along my slit, wet with anticipation. The feeling sends me reeling as I damn near come off the bed, but his hand on my chest stops me from moving away from his blissful ministrations. If I prayed, it would be at the altar of Pestilence because... right here... right now... he is my salvation.

His tongue dips, probes, and licks until I am ready to scream from the maddening pace he continues to tease. I am so close, but because he refuses to increase his tempo, he leaves me stuck on the brink of the euphoria he provides and falling over the cliff of the climax I am chasing. I don't just want to fall; I want to crash and shatter into a million pieces while his tongue licks away the evidence of my orgasm, only to have him do it again and again until the thought of uttering his name is a distant memory.

He grabs my hips pulling me against him hard. The combination of his tongue chasing and the moan rumbling from him is the last piece I require to lose myself completely and come harder than ever before meeting this man and the magic of the mustache-free ride he provided.

"Mm. I have never experienced something so delectable, so delicious in my existence." He tells me as he continues to lick my clit.

Okay, so I certainly enjoyed his attention, but is this where it will end? I mean, I may have found my release once, but I would not be opposed to doing it again only while he's filling me full with the glorious cock I got to see today. But is sex in the normal sense possible? Would he even want to go any further? When he sits up, the evidence of how our encounter affected him is obvious from the hard erection begging for release, and all my concerns melt away.

When he hesitates, I decide it's time for me to take control. Pushing him down on the bed, I carefully unbutton the jeans concealing my goal. Once this pesky little nuisance is out of the way, I pull them from his body before I straddle him. The second my hand grasps his cock, the hiss he gives me confirms he will enjoy this activity as much as I will. Thank god he granted this horseman normal human functionality and sensation. Functionality I fully plan on taking advantage of.

With my hand lining him up at my entrance, I slide down his immense length, and this time he doesn't hiss; he growls as I throw my head back on a breathy moan.

"Why did I deny myself such pleasure this entire time?"

"A question I would love to hear the answer to as well." I pant while circling my hips, grinding his cock further inside me. He grabs me, pulling my breasts down to his mouth, where his skilled tongue begins a different kind of assault on my senses. He starts by circling his tongue around my nipple until he moves to bite the flesh around it before he sucks the abused breast deep into his mouth. I can feel his tongue still circling the nipple he holds firmly between his teeth.

"Rest assured, it was a grievous mistake and one I have no plans of perpetuating."

"Thank god," I moan as I circle my hips again. I was unprepared for his hands on my hips so he could flip me under him. I was enjoying being in control, but he took it back in one fell swoop.

"My beautiful temptress, I believe the soul you should be thanking is me, not my creator."

"Fuck I would thank Santa if it only means you keep fucking me like this." my response is more purr than spoken as I press my lips to his.

"Provided no other man is permitted to slide within you as I am now, you may thank whomever you wish, because this is my desire as well. Apart from one minor detail."

"Which is?" I pant as his hips hammer into me at a punishing rate, pushing me ever closer to reaching the peak of the heavenly, blissful, oh-my-fucking-god Mount Orgasm once again.

"To live within you until time and space erase everything around us except you and Wren." With his confession made, I not only reached the peak, I fell head fucking first off it.

And the fall is utter bliss.

A utopia provided only by my horseman... a horseman named... Pestilence.

Chapter Twenty-Eight: Choices

~ Greer Fall 2025 ~

AS CONSCIOUSNESS SLOWLY OVERTAKES ME, MY eyes flutter while my mind tries to piece together where I am. The light rain outside the window registers first. The body next to me comes second, and the lack of clothing brings everything back in a flash.

I had sex with a rider.

A horseman who was sent here to destroy us, and as much as I know, I should be ashamed of what I did. I'm not. In fact, if he wakes up and is willing to do it again, I will have no issues wrapping my legs around him the same way I did three times last night. Once my rider had a taste, he seemed insatiable, but I was only too happy to offer my body as he attempted to quench his thirst.

He even kissed my other cheeks when he realized the fall from Storm produced more than the scarlet face he witnessed immediately after. It seems the ones I landed on were colored an ugly bluish-black from the damage inflicted on them. But I would fall a million times over if the healing balm was his lips pressed against them.

I would stay here until time ends or Avalon cracks another seal if only my Renny was with us. Never having to return or face the fallout I know will come from Jay when I tell him things are really and truly over is something I am not looking forward to. But it didn't matter because the man holding me stole every single piece of my heart, and I could not deny it even if I wanted to.

Especially after he confessed how happy he was when he discovered I would be coming instead of Avalon. Even more, when he told me the reason he submerged himself in our private oasis was in part because the only thing he could think about was pressing me against the rocks as he slowly removed the clothes I had neglected to discard. So he could allow his eyes to admire what he called sheer perfection. Perfection only I could provide for him. Before the cheeky bastard whispered,

"Much like your eyes followed me." But he made my face turn scarlet when he added. "I enjoyed watching you torture this lip as you marveled at what has always belonged to you."

Which resulted in me slapping his chest next to where my head was resting before telling him he was full of shit. His response was to flip me over as he trailed kisses from one breast to the other.

"We should head home to our Renny soon," Pestilence murmurs, and if I wasn't already infatuated with this man, his sentiment would have me going weak in the knees. To have a man who is as concerned about my son as I am is something I have not experienced since taking on the role of his mom. "But only after I hear you scream my name once more."

Before I can respond, he has me under him with my legs positioned against his hips so he can run the length of his growing erection against my wet core pulsing with anticipation. And if I wasn't already willing to let him use me however he saw fit, I sure as shit would after his thumb began circling my clit.

With his lips devouring me and his tongue swirling mine, he slowly pushes inside, and the delicious torture it results in is both pleasure and agony. Because the size of his cock and skills he learned from only god-knows-where results in every nerve within my body firing at once, overwhelming my senses with the sweetest fucking rapture. I want to tell him how wonderful it feels, how I have never experienced such delicious pleasure before, how he is the best lover I have ever known, but when I open my mouth, only one word comes tumbling out. A word I have never said as much as I have in the last five hours. "Fuck!"

"This word you keep repeating. What does it mean?"

"Depends on when and how it's used."

"So, explain what it means when uttered from these lips," he demands as he brushes his lips over mine.

"It means I like what you're doing. It feels good. It makes me feel good all over. It's also the act itself."

"The act itself?" he asks as his lips find the spot on my neck that turns me into a gooey mess.

"You sliding inside me."

"I thought this was referred to as consummating."

"Also known as sex, making love, or when you're feeling dirty," he shifts, hitting me in all the right spots and making the last word more moan than anything else. "Fucking."

"Dirty?"

"Yes, my inquisitive horseman... Dirty."

"So it is not something I should routinely use?"

"Not if you don't want people looking at you like you have ten heads," I say with a giggle as his fingers trail along my side.

"Most mortals already do this."

"Well, let's just say it would be worse if they heard you yelling it. Oh, and the most important thing is to never use it in front of Wren." The last part is said as a groan since he has flipped us around, so I'm straddling him. Which allows him unobstructed access to the breasts and nipples he is lavishing his full attention on.

"I like that my actions illicit such a dirty word from these beautifully innocent lips," he informs me while dragging my face down to claim the mouth he speaks of.

"Not as much as I do," I whisper, still holding my lips against his.

"Well, shall we see how many times I can make you scream them before leaving for home?"

And scream, I did. I lost count after ten. He had me begging with it as his tongue provided the first orgasm. He made me moan it when he took me from behind with his fingers circling my clit. He made me groan it when he put me on top but took control of my movements. He made me growl it when he pinned me against the wall. And this time....

"Fuck, Pestilence!" he made me scream it.

"The pleasure you provide is unlike anything I knew possible," he groans as he thrusts into me. Each pivot of his hips, every movement, prolongs the climax while building me up for another. "If my kind knew of the rapture you can give, we would have come long ago. Not to remove but to claim... just as I have claimed you."

"You have."

"Tell me you are mine."

"I'm yours... always."

"As I am yours, Greer. My beautiful temptation, my perfect blessing." His words are spoken with conviction and given as a promise. For the first time in my life, I understand how someone can claim they love one another after only a short time together. Because I swear, as he pledges himself to me, I am fully prepared to do the same.

His fingers entwine with mine as his hips move faster to confirm his pledge and seal our bond, and as he roars his release, I realize there is no point denying what I have felt for a long time, so I return the promise he gave me.

"Forever."

*****

The ride back to camp was much more pleasant since I was no longer worried he didn't want me there. He even put me in front of him. He claimed it was to teach me how to ride, but his lips were against my neck more than he provided guidance. Although, in truth, I don't think Storm requires directives aside from the one command issued by his rider.

"Wren."

Something tells me he would take me straight to my son even if I tried to steer him off track. He is a loyal companion to his rider, which makes me finally understand a comment that Avalon made once. Their horses are an extension of the man.

"So, Pestilence."

"Yes, a meva bella temptació." I don't know why hearing him call me his beautiful temptation is alluring, but every time he does, my toes curl.

"When we get back to camp, I'll have to tell Jay we're done." A low growl rumbles through his chest. I also don't miss how the hand he wrapped around my waist tightens and pulls me closer against him possessively.

"I do not trust this mortal."

"Are you worried about me, Rider?"

"As I told you earlier, you are mine, as I am yours. Of course, I worry about you."

Twisting to look at him, I place my palm against his cheek, "And as sweet as that is, you don't have to because Jay may be capable of many things, but he would never hurt me. Especially in the middle of the camp." With his expression still revealing his doubt, I try again. "With everyone around us. Where he knows my friends will not tolerate him hurting me or anyone else."

His eyes flick to mine, but they still showcase his disbelief. "When he knows they would expel him from our home. He may be a hothead, but he's not a stupid hothead."

"Fine." His matter-of-fact tone — coupled with his one-word response — is surprising, but it doesn't feel finished, so my answer isn't as resolute as his.

"Okay?"

"Together." And that's why he gave in so easily.

"Pestilence."

"Together, Greer. I have already proclaimed I do not trust this mortal, nor am I willing to risk the safety of the gift I have only just been granted."

"But you can trust me, my sweet rider," I tell him as I place my hand against his cheek. I don't know if it was from the contact or my words of endearment, but one of them finally has him glancing at me as his face softens. "Having you there will only cause more issues, so I'm asking you to let me talk to him."

His forced exhale confirms he's unhappy with my request, but I know I've won when his eyes meet mine. He dips his head, which is a good thing because I don't imagine the next thing I plan on saying will be as well received.

"I also think we shouldn't flaunt this—"

"This?"

"Us."

"I do not understand the word flaunt," he says.

"Um, I don't think we should kiss—"

He pulls the reins to stop Storm. His brows lower as his mouth drops open like he wants to say something but can't. His expression is pained. I think I hurt him, which I never intended to do. "You no longer wish me to touch you?"

"What? No! Of course, I want you to touch me. I can't imagine living without your touch now that I have experienced it. I only meant that we should keep our relationship to ourselves for now. At least until Jay has time to adapt to everything. There's no point in making camp life uncomfortable."

"I care little for his comfort."

"Pestilence, please try to understand—" his finger against my lips silences the rest of my plea so he can give me his response.

"But I do care for yours, Wrens, and the lambs. So I will do this for you and them."

"Thank you."

"You shouldn't thank me yet, a meva bella temptació, because I plan to make up for the lost time when no one is around to see us," he informs as he kisses me before clicking his tongue to get Storm moving again. Leaving me wishing we could find another house to stop at.

*****

When we arrive at camp, the only thing I want to do is see Wren and give my sweet boy a kiss.

Thankfully, the sun had not yet risen, so no one was awake to see our arrival. Pestilence must sense my need to check on Renny because the second he lifts me off Storm, he pulls me close, kissing me passionately. A kiss that leaves me breathless and ready to throw every request I made about keeping this quiet out the damn window or, in my case, the damn camp. Seeing the reaction he obviously was attempting to provoke achieved causes a grin to slip across his face. He kisses my nose and pats my ass before telling me he will see me later. Leaving me missing his touch already.

"How soon," I whisper, which causes him to laugh as he leads Storm over to his corral.

Sneaking into Avalon's cabin, I don't take my first breath until I see him sleeping soundly. Avalon was kind enough to give him her bed while she opted to sleep on the loveseat. Careful not to wake either Avalon or Wren, I tiptoe to the bed to gently kiss his head before sitting on the side so I can watch him sleep.

"When did you get back?" Avalon whispers as she rubs her eyes.

"Not long ago."

"Huh, it took you longer than normal. By like eight hours," Avalon says teasingly.

"Um... well... yeah."

"Those are a whole lot of words that don't say anything."

"We stopped at a house when we got caught in the rain."

"And?"

"And he took me to the waterfall you two found."

"He did, did he?"

"Yeah, I hope you don't mind."

"Not at all. Did the trip give you the answers you sought?"

"Um... well..."

"I take that as a yes. Since you can't wipe the damn beaming grin off your face," she knowingly informs.

"Go back to sleep," I tell her while tossing the stuffed bear Wren no longer sleeps with since receiving the horse from Pestilence at her. Curling next to my son, I can't help but smile as my thoughts drift back to the rider who declared he belonged to me. A declaration I would never have received if not for the insistence of the woman chuckling behind me, which prompts me to look over my shoulder and say, "Thanks. For everything."

"You're welcome," she quietly replies.

*****

"Greer." I am only vaguely aware of someone shaking me. The long day and lack of sleep courtesy of mind-blowing sex have taken a toll on me.

"Greer."

"Hmm?" is my sleepy response.

"Wake up, sweetheart."

"Five more minutes, Pestilence," I mumble, snuggling my head further into the pillow.

"I'll assume you said his name because you spent the entire goddamn day yesterday traipsing around the county with that fucking prick." Fuck, definitely not Pestilence. Jay. And gauging by his tone, he's not happy with me calling him the wrong name, one he seems to despise. Bolting upright causes my bruised butt to ache from the sudden movement.

"Ow," I groan as I rub it.

"What's your problem? Too much riding with the prick you never should have been with?"

"No!" I snap, hearing him call my rider a prick yet again. If he doesn't knock this shit off soon, he won't like how I inform him of how things will be from now on because it ends with my lips pressed to the quote-unquote prick's lips while Jay receives my middle finger. "Remnants from falling yesterday."

"You fell?"

"Yeah, in case you haven't figured this out yet, I'm a bit of a klutz."

"When did you get back?"

"A while ago," I tell him as I rub the sleep from my eyes.

"What took you so long? I waited for you."

"Why would you do that? I don't need a babysitter, Jay. And I certainly don't remember asking you to do it."

"Regardless, I did because I wanted to make sure you made it back safely."

"Safely? I'm pretty sure no one would mess with me since I was accompanied by a rider." His upper lip twists into a snarl, hearing me defend Pestilence.

"What took you so long? Did he do something to you?" he asks again as he gnashes his teeth together.

Boy did he ever. Over and over and over again, and I damn well loved every blissful second of it. This thought almost slips out, but decorum wins over the snarky response I want to give him. "Relax, Jay. We just got stuck in a storm and had to wait for it to pass."

"So why not come back to my cabin to sleep?"

"Because I wanted to see—" When I look down, I realize Wren is no longer in bed with me. "Where's Wren?"

"Suki has him."

"What time is it?"

"Close to lunch. And I'm still waiting for an answer."

"And I already gave you one." He gives me a side-eyed glance, pissing me off further, but I decide to let this go. "Why did everyone let me sleep so late?"

"Apparently, they felt you needed the rest, and since I didn't know you were back, I couldn't really wake you up. Now could I?"

"I guess not," I mumble while climbing out of bed, stretching my back to work out the kinks from being on Storm all day yesterday. "Are you doing anything right now?"

"Besides waking you? No."

"Could we... maybe go to your cabin and talk?" My preference would have been to remain in Avalon's cabin, but I opt to go back to his place because if he throws a fit—which is not out of the realm of possibility with him—and decides to break shit, I want it to be his crap, not Avalon's stuff. He steps closer, pulling me against him as he does it. His lips on my neck informed me he misunderstood the meaning of my request. Shit, he thinks I want him alone to have sex with him. Shit-shit-shit. Maybe I should rethink this whole going to his cabin idea.

"I thought you'd never ask. It's the reason I waited for you all night."

"Ah... well... I mean, talk-talk. Like with actual words."

"Fine, talk first, but after...." he tells me, taking my hand to lead me out of Avalon's cabin. Something tells me this isn't going to go as smoothly as I had hoped. Perhaps I should reconsider the whole not having Pestilence present for this conversation with Jay thing.

~ Avalon ~

Since waking this morning, I have had this weird feeling hanging over me like that damn proverbial shoe is getting ready to drop. The issue is I can't put my finger on why. When Jay entered my cabin, I thought about following him. But Greer is a big girl. If she needs us, she'll yell, which is something Jay doesn't want since it will bring one pissed-off rider raining down on him.... Wait, where the hell is Pestilence and Storm? I think to myself as I look toward the spot we can normally find them.

"Hey Xander, have you seen Pestilence?"

"He rode out shortly after dawn. Said something about checking on Hope?"

"Did he say if anything was wrong?" I ask as the weird feeling turns to dread. Dread that promptly crawls up my spine.

"It didn't seem like anything was wrong. He told me he would be gone for a few hours and that I should watch over Greer and Wren. Not sure why he felt they needed it, but I promised him I would." My eyes scan the field for Wren. He and the other kids have been playing for nearly an hour and show no signs of coming in soon.

The door to my cabin flies open, and I fully expect to see Jay storming out, but rather than just him, I find him and Greer both exiting. My eyes follow their path as Jay pulls Greer toward his cabin. She doesn't seem scared or hesitant, so I won't interfere. I suppose this is Greer giving him the old heave-ho since I know the man she wants is not the one currently holding her hand.

"Should we do anything about that?" Suki asks, flicking her finger in the direction Jay and Greer travel.

"Not yet." I may be willing to give her time to tell him in whatever manner she feels she needs to dump his sorry ass, but it doesn't mean I'm not listening for any sounds or signs of a struggle. The prick must be taking the news better than I thought he would since the only sounds coming from his cabin is nice, calm talking. No screaming or furniture breaking. All good signs. Right?

"Avalon, Xander," Nehra pants as she runs up to where we are sitting. "I need you to come with me right now." The distress in her voice sets off alarms with us as Suki, Xander, and I all come to our feet.

"Is everything alright?" Xander asks.

"No. I need you to come. Right. Now."

"Suki, stay here."

"No damn way."

"Suki, sweetheart, one of us needs to stay with the kids."

"Fine, just hurry up," she huffs while Xander and I follow Nehra. She sprints through the tree line straight toward our lookout tower. The mad dash feels like it took an eternity when it was probably closer to five minutes. I really need to work on my damn cardio and endurance. My breath is escaping me in wheezing ragged pants when we finally burst through the tree line. The minute we round the corner of the watch tower, we find Ollie looming over Cole, who is on his knees with his hands behind his head.

"What the hell is going on here?" Xander asks between sucking in heavy breaths. It seems he is just as confused by what we discovered as I am.

"Tell them," Nehra yells.

"Fuck you, bitch."

Oliver slams his foot into the back of Cole's head, knocking him over. What the hell is going on here? Since when do we attack one of our own? I know Ollie, and whatever his reason, it has to be bigger than Cole simply calling Nehra a bitch. "Show some fucking respect, you piece of shit, and tell them what you fucking told us. What you fucking did."

"Fuck. Off!" Cole snarls as his eyes land on me.

"He set the damn fire."

"What?" I yell as I step closer to him with my hands clenching into tight fists.

"It needed to be done."

"Needed to be done? You almost killed Wren, you fucking bastard."

"Why the hell would you do it?" Xander growls.

"To teach Greer a lesson before...."

"Before what?" I yell, advancing another step.

"Before she could become someone like you," he snarls, looking directly at me.

"Like me? What the hell is that supposed to mean?"

"Tell me you didn't know Renny was in there when you set the damn fire," Xander snaps, stepping in front of me.

"He wasn't supposed to be in the damn cabin, but honestly, I could give a shit if the brat was in there or—"

"What the fuck did you just say!?" The roar this time didn't come from Xander or me. Nope, this came from one very furious rider. The same one who is storming toward the man who will soon regret his choices.

"You are the reason Wren was injured? You are why my brother now faces punishment!" Pestilence growls as he grabs Cole yanking him off his knees. I have witnessed the riders pissed before, but I have never seen one on the verge of losing all control. When I see the first black mist swirling around him, I grab Xander and Nehra to pull them away and motion for Ollie to do the same.

"Are you all really going to let this abomination kill me?" he screams as his eyes widen.

"You better start talking," I yell.

"Jay! Jay paid me to do it so Greer would have to move into his cabin. He said if he could keep her away from you...." his eyes flick over to me. "and him," he jerks his head in Pestilence's direction. "then he might be able to stop her from becoming another horseman whore until he could...."

"Could what?" I snarl, furious he could be so cavalier about almost taking a child's life.

"Take her away from here. Someplace with like-minded people."

"Like-minded people? What the fuck does that mean?" Xander may have posed the question to Cole, but Pestilence replies.

"Mortals who believe they can stand against my brothers and me."

"They aren't just thinking about it. They are preparing to do it. Jay plans on joining them, but he refuses to go without Greer. He had some fantasy they were destined to be together. The problem was he knew she didn't want to leave here. She thought Wren was safer here with him than out on the road. Jay figured he could convince her to go if he had enough time with her; if not, he planned to force her to leave. The kid wasn't supposed to be in there. Even so, Jay wasn't torn up over the idea of Wren no longer being a factor for Greer to consider. That's it. That's everything, so you'll let me go?"

"No." Pestilence calmly declares.

"I told you everything."

"I am aware."

"But I thought you were going to let me go."

"Yet another mistake you won't make again." With this declaration, the mist shifts faster as it takes form. The last thing we hear before his plague swallows them is Cole's terrified shrieks and Pestilence's furious growls.

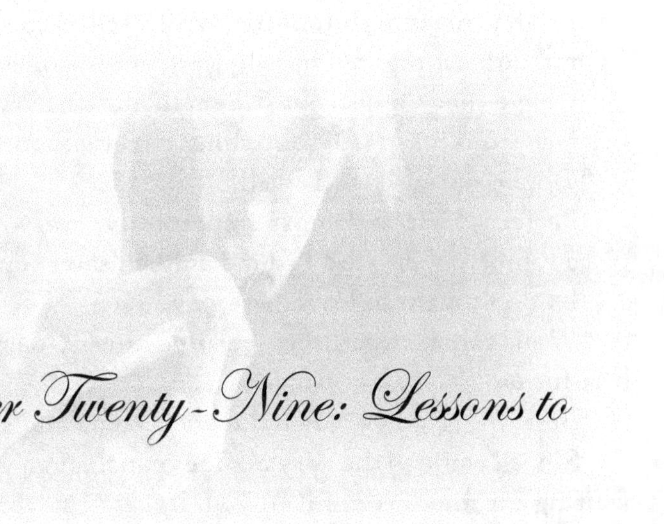

Chapter Twenty-Nine: Lessons to Learn

~ *Greer Fall 2025* ~

THE PACE HE PULLED ME ACROSS the yard between Avalon's cabin and his was nothing short of brisk. My preference would have been to remain outside in the common area, but he insisted we needed to speak in private. At the very least, I owe him the courtesy of not revealing my intentions publicly. People will figure it out soon enough, but there is no point in embarrassing him in the process. In fact, discretion and decorum would be best in diffusing what I imagine can rapidly become volatile.

The second he shuts the door, his hands are on my face as he smashes his mouth to mine, which only reinforces what I figured out last night. These lips are not the ones I desire.

"I have made a decision," he tells me as I try to dislodge my face from his grasp, something he refuses to allow.

"Oh, because I have as well."

"Perfect. First and most importantly, we will leave this place tomorrow because I found a much safer community."

"I-I don't want to leave here, Jay."

"Well, sorry, sweetheart, but I've already decided what is best for us."

"Best for us? Since when did we become an us?"

"Since I came to the very obvious conclusion, you were just waiting for me to commit to you. I guess I never understood how important a promise could be to someone like you. So there you go, sweetheart. You have my promise to always take care of you."

"Take care of me?"

"Yeah, babe, I promise I'll always take care of you."

"Just me?"

"And Wren of course."

"But of course," I grumble. Does Jay really think this is why I was so damn hesitant with him? Because I wanted an oath of his allegiance. Surely, he cannot be this damn blind. It has now become clear I will have to be direct with him, but logic tells me I should put some space between us before I begin, so I pull out of his grasp and back towards the couch, dominating the room.

"You need to pack light because it will take us a few days to get there, and I'm no damn pack horse, so whatever shit you plan on taking has to fit in your backpack."

"I'm not leaving—"

"Don't worry, babe, we'll replace anything you have to leave behind once we get there," he tells me as he grabs his pack to shove his shit inside.

"No, you're not listening, Jay. I'm not leaving. Period. I'm not going with you because there is no us."

His stance turns rigid before he slowly turns to face me. The look covering his face results in me taking a cautious but prudent step away from him. His eyebrows are pulled together, resulting in his eyes narrowing to little more than thin slits, but even with much of his eyes hidden from view, I do not miss the malice staring back at me from within them. His nostrils are flared, and his jaw is clenched so tight his lips have all but disappeared.

"What did you say?" he snaps as he removes the space I deliberately put between us. Okay, now I'm regretting the whole 'letting him retain his dignity' thought because I wish we were anywhere other than behind closed doors. But regardless, the cat is out of the bag, so I might as well rip the bandaid off while I'm at it.

"I said there is no us. There never was, nor will there ever be, because I have also come to a decision."

"Which is," he snarls.

"Which is whatever you thought there was between us is done. I don't want to be with you like that, and if you want to leave, you'll be doing it alone because Renny and I are staying right here."

"And when did you come to this conclusion?"

"It's something I've been contemplating for a while, but I made my mind up yesterday—"

"While you were with him. Because of him. A fucking rider who wants to kill us."

"No! Not because of him. Pestilence had nothing to do with my decision. I came to this conclusion all on my own," I retorted, crossing my arms over my chest. I realize this act appears to have been done to show my determination which in a way it was, but I did it more to keep my hands which have begun to tremble, out of view. The last thing I want him to see is that he is scaring me right now.

"You mean to tell me after spending the entire day with the asshole, you damn near spread your fucking legs for every time you look in his direction, had nothing to do with this sudden change of heart!?"

"I don't know what the hell you're talking about! Because there was nothing sudden about it, and there sure as shit was never a change in heart since I never promised you shit."

Jay takes the last tiny bit of space separating us and obliterates it. The biggest issue is there is no place left for me to retreat since my legs are now backed against the couch; if I even so much as lean back to put more distance between us, I will have no choice but to look up at him from my spot on the couch. A position I sure as shit don't want to be in.

"I don't fucking believe you."

"I don't care what you believe. Even if Pestilence partly played into my consideration, it's none of your goddamn business."

"You cannot love a fucking horseman of the apocalypse. I won't fucking allow it."

"You won't allow it?" I shriek. Okay, now he's pissed me off. In what damn world does this asshole think he has a say in what I do because I can assure him he doesn't.

"What part of my statement are you having problems understanding, Greer?"

"All of it because last I checked, you don't own me, so there is no allowing or not allowing in this fucking lifetime."

"If you think I will stand by and permit you to become another horsemen whore like Avalon, you are sadly fucking mistaken."

"Horseman whore?"

"Don't think for one second I don't know you wouldn't spread your legs and let that thing fuck you if you had the opportunity. I'm not going to stand by and allow it to happen. One whore is all this world needs."

"Well, I hate to break it to you, Jay... Too. Fucking. Late."

"What did you say?" he growls while his fist twists the material of my shirt to yank me directly in front of him.

"I said I already did, and he was the best fucking lay I ever had." I was prepared for whatever reaction he wanted to give me, except the one he gave, because the last thing I saw was his fist coming at me.

Then everything went dark.

~ Pestilence ~

The death I granted him was only a piece of the agony and fear I believe Wren experienced. I'll admit the petty satisfaction I felt, as he choked on the tendrils of the disease I shoved further down his throat each time he attempted to scream, is small in comparison to the terror I imagine Wren experienced as he was engulfed by the suffocating smoke and searing flames that ended his precious life. His wide-eyed, terrified expression will never be seen by anyone except me. He was not worthy of any soul's sympathy. Therefore, I continued to force more of my disease into his mouth, which was gaped open in a silent scream. The more I provide, the faster he deteriorates until nothing is left but a mummified version of the man who so carelessly tried to remove one of the few bright spots this world has to offer.

By the time the world came back into view, I had released his desiccated remains, allowing them to crumble to the earth, where he will remain for the rest of his days. Even if his soul attempts to ascend, Thanatos will be there to block him. My brother's retribution will be far worse than mine.

With my breathing coming in short ragged pants as I attempt to contain the fury I experienced as I listened to his confession, my eyes come up to find Avalon's worried expression.

"Are you... okay, Pestilence?" she asks while taking a tentative step toward me. I lift my hand, indicating she should not advance, and thankfully she understands and halts her progression. I draw in several more deep breaths. I almost have my racing emotions under control when Avalon's face turns ashen before she spins and sprints back toward the community. I am only vaguely aware of Xander's question, but when I hear Avalon's response, everything clicks back into place as I race after her.

"What are you doing, A?"

"We left Greer alone with that fucking bastard."

I arrived at the camp much quicker than the rest of the party who witnessed Cole's demise, and my first instinct was to search in the last place I left her. Avalon's cabin. When I discover it empty, the fury I am only beginning to reel in returns in a flash. The door of the next place I search does not stand a chance as my heavy booted foot smashes it open. But like Avalon's cabin, I discovered Jay's just as deserted.

"Suki." Xander must have been the first of the party to arrive back, and like me, he is frantically searching for the woman he loves.

"Did you find her?" Avalon pants with her hands on her knees as she tries to catch her breath.

"Where were they?"

"In there," she informs, pointing at the cabin I just left.

Xander bursts through his door, only to be followed by a string of obscenities. "What the fuck? Who the hell did this to you?"

I am there before the last syllable is uttered, only to find the little one bound, gagged, and struggling to escape. As he rips the gag from Suki's mouth, the one word she yells has me racing back out the door.

"Kids!"

This was the first time since returning I realized how deserted the community is. The only sounds come from the four mortals who witnessed my response to Cole.

"Horse!" my command brings him running as I throw my leg over his back. "Find Wren."

He races toward the field they often play in but continues through it directly toward the thickest part of the woods surrounding this area. When he rears up on his hind legs, I know I am near where I will discover my son.

"Wren!" I receive nothing. Silence is my only response for several pain-filled seconds until a muffled reply is finally given.

"Orse says nay-nay-nay."

"Shhh, Renny, you have to be quiet, little buddy." It seems I have found not only my son but the other children as well.

"You no longer need to hide children. You can come out; you are safe," I yell, hoping they will trust I am not here to harm them.

"Pestilence?" is the child's tentative question.

"Yes." With my confirmation, the first child reveals himself. He is one of the older boys, and it seems he is the one who spoke to Wren since he has him held protectively in his arms. "Are the other people gone?"

"What other people are you speaking of?" I ask as I take a squirming Wren from him.

"The men who were talking to Jay."

"There were men here?"

"Yeah, they tied up Suki, and I think they took Wren's mommy."

"Is this why you hid?"

"I saw what was happening and told the kids to follow me. Wren didn't understand, so I had to tell him we were playing hide-n-go-seek so he would stay quiet."

"You did well, young one. Come, permit me to return you to your homes." I expect we will find the rest of the adults in much the same condition we discovered the little one in, and as much as I want to rush out to find Greer, I need to ensure my son will be safe first.

Once the children have all been returned and their parents liberated from their bonds, I return to Suki for the answers I suspect she can provide.

"What happened?'

"I don't know. One minute, I was watching the kids, and the next, several men were overrunning the camp. They immediately attacked any guy they came across before tying up the women. The last thing I saw before they threw me into our room was Jay coming out of his cabin with Greer flung over his shoulder." A low growl rumbles through me, knowing he has her.

"I think they were looking for you, A."

"What? Why?"

"I don't know, but I don't think it was for anything good."

"How do you know?"

"They kept calling you the... the...."

"Suki, it's okay," Avalon tells the little one as she sits beside her on the bench, placing an arm around her shoulder to further reinforce that she can handle whatever Suki overheard.

"They called you a horseman whore." The last part is whispered. Avalon's eyes shoot to mine, fully aware that if they called her this, they must view Greer as the same, and if these men do, there is no telling what they have planned for her.

"I can assume you do not know in what direction they traveled?"

"Sorry, Pestilence, I didn't have time to see. They had already taken me in there." She says as tears brim brightly in her sad eyes.

"You do not need to apologize. The men who took her and hurt the members of this community are another matter," I inform her as I place a hand on her shoulder. I know, like the lamb, this one will blame herself for Greer. I hope to remove this thought. I wait until she nods before I hand my son to Avalon.

"What are you doing?" the lamb's question is filled with concern. She knows I will allow no one to harm Greer, so she must understand I plan to retrieve her. "Pestilence!"

"I need you to watch after Wren while I reclaim my… his mom." I almost said something I am unsure if Greer is ready to reveal. And even though I figure the little lamb knows, it is not my place to take this decision away from my girl.

"No. No fucking way! Absolutely not," Avalon yells as she hands Wren to Suki.

"This is not open for debate, little lamb."

"You're damn straight it isn't because if you think I'm letting you do this alone, you don't know me very well."

"I do not have the time to argue this point."

"So don't."

"You are not coming."

"And once you're gone, who the hell do you think will stop me? So the way I see it," she informs as she swings her leg over my horse before sliding back to make room for me. "You can get your ass up on Storm so we can bring Greer home now, or you can hunt for me while I hunt for them. Your damn choice, Rider."

"Avalon!"

"Pestilence!" she growls with the same conviction I did. Knowing that every minute I waste debating this with the lamb is another mile they put between us, I give in and take my place in front of her.

"Wait," Xander yells as he sprints into his house before returning with a bow, a quiver full of arrows, and a dagger he hands to Avalon. "Be careful and bring her home." He says, shaking my hand before patting Avalon's leg.

"Take care of Renny," Avalon directs, which is better than me telling them to take care of my son since none of them are aware of this fact yet.

I turn my horse and head in the direction of the trampled grass.

"What's the plan here?" Avalon asks as she conceals the dagger inside her boot after settling the quiver and bow across her back.

"Simple, I am going to kill them."

"Pestilence."

"Yes, little lamb."

"All of them. We kill all of them. Every last fucker who thought they could invade our world and wreck it."

"You needn't ask."

Clicking my tongue, we race toward the men who have claimed the one being holding my wrath at bay. Unfortunately for these few, they will not receive her grace. A mistake they will learn the hard way.

Chapter Thirty: Two Fights

~ *Death Fall 2025* ~

WHAT IN ALL THE REALMS OF hell is my brother doing allowing Avalon to travel with him? He knows how dangerous this undertaking is. I understand his need to retrieve the soul Pestilence has declared is their salvation, for I would do the same if it were Apple. What he shouldn't do is risk the life of the woman I have deemed as such. Especially since he does not yet understand the full extent of the forces he is sprinting towards.

It seems the mortals of their plane are willing to risk their lives rising up to oppose my brother. A grievous mistake if done in small groups, but if faced with their full force, my brother... not they, will be quickly overwhelmed. If this should come to pass, what will they do with a woman they see as the reason we were called to their world? I'll tell you... they will kill her only after they torture her.

Something I will never allow.

This is why I now strap the baldric across my back as I prepare to rebuff every command they have decreed so I can return to their realm and assure her survival. My only hope is my brother can move fast enough to catch up with the small group currently traveling with his chosen. If he does, this group poses a negligible risk to him and, as such, little risk to Avalon.

And if my brother wishes to reclaim her before the son of Adam decides he is done waiting for her to consent, he better move fast. Ghost's front hoof slams the ground fervently.

"I don't think you should come this time, old friend. This is not sanctioned, so I face even greater punishment when they catch up with me." His snorted response tells me he disagrees with my request and is unwilling to be left behind.

"Correction, we have discovered you," Gabriel announces as he storms into the room I have not been to since restoring the life stolen from the child.

"You go too far this time, Reaper."

"And tell me, Michael, where is the line I crossed?"

"The line where your role was ignored." Michael snaps as he pulls his blade.

"Since when is it your decision what my role is?" I demand, following his lead and reaching for the sword on my back.

"Since you decided to restore a soul you should have been ferrying to his next life," Michael advises as he circles left while Gabriel moves right. "An act you knew you would face punishment for since you went into hiding after committing it."

"I never hid."

"You remained within Purgatory."

"As I said, I never hid since you knew where I was the entire time."

"A place I do not enter."

"Are you fearful it was your soul I would retrieve if you ventured there?" His lips curl in scathing contempt and frustration. He knows this is the reason he does not follow me there. Besides, if our creator truly wished for my punishment, he simply needed to call me home because he knows I will always heed his call. Yet it was something he did not deem necessary.

"Lay down your blade, bend thy knee, and prepare for thy judgment, wretch," Gabriel commands.

"If you desire to separate me from my blade, you must first remove it from me."

"If you wish to learn the full extent of my might, I am happy to reveal it to you."

"I await your show of power, Michael." With my challenge issued, Michael attacks from one side as Gabriel charges from the other. Blocking Michael's blade, I shove him back before twisting to parry Gabriel's.

While my focus is on Gabriel, his brother takes advantage of this, slashing his blade across my back before landing a blow that snaps my head to the side. Faster than he can react, I bring my blade up, inflicting a long slice across his chest.

This continues with them attacking and then desperately scampering out of range as I block... parry... and lash out with an assault of my own. The problem they face is they did not account for the ferocity I now fight with because Avalon's very life may hinge on the outcome of this battle.

They fall back, assessing their strategy. Their retreat gives me a momentary reprieve; my eyes scan the room to plan my next move. Their eyes reveal the instant they have decided to begin their next advance. I block the first blade, spin away from the second, dive over the third, and duck under the fourth.

"My turn," I growl as my wings erupt behind me. The first slash runs the length of Gabriel's arm. The second pierces Michael's right thigh, the third blocks another attempt by Gabriel, and the fourth ends with Michael on the ground looking up at me.

"Enough!" Dropping to my knee, I place the blade on the ground before bowing my head as Michael and Gabriel follow suit. The only being who could save these angels—our father—has issued his command, and as expected, we immediately obey.

"I instructed you to retrieve him, Michael, not remove him."

"He refused to comply, father."

"Did you give him a choice? Or did you merely attack?" His shoulders tense, but he is smart enough to remain silent.

"And what of you, Gabriel? Why have you interjected yourself into this?"

"I was only trying to help my brethren fulfill your request, father."

"So you both show up armed and wonder why he refused to come?"

"Father," they say in unison.

"As for you, my son, why would you do it?"

"I did not feel it was his time. I merely restored a life stolen."

"And your brother's supplications had no bearing?" I remain silent. There is no need to confirm what he already knows. "How am I to bring my children of their world to behest when I cannot do it with the ones who have pledged their souls to me?" Our father asks, but when he receives no response from any of the beings within the room, he turns and issues his next command.

"Chain him." Michael's head jerks up, realizing our father's intention is not to remove me.

"Father, surely you do not plan to permit him leniency?"

"You believe being chained is compassion?"

"Forgive my insolence," Michael responds as he dips his head again.

"How long do you intend for me to remain this way?"

"Until the lamb has broken your seal or until time and space have removed her from your thoughts."

After our creator has left, Michael grabs my arm, pleased he is the one who will carry out my sentence. It is not the realization I will remain in chains for the rest of my days that bothers me. It is the knowledge I have failed her that is plaguing my soul.

~ Greer~

I don't know how long I've been out, but my pounding head and foggy thoughts tell me it's been a while. The other thing is I don't recognize the room I'm in or most of the muffled voices filtering through the door to me.

"I told you we're not ready for an all-out goddamn war with one of them."

"And I told you I wasn't leaving her behind." But I do know this one. Jay.

I try to sit up, but my hands and legs are tied with a length of rope and secured to the bed I'm lying on. Okay, so escape doesn't seem to be an option.

"It doesn't damn well matter anymore. If he's coming, he's coming. We'll deal with it then. So knock it off, both of you." This voice is familiar, but I am having difficulty placing it.

Hoping to get a better look at my surroundings, I push myself upright, only to have my head swirl as a wave of nausea threatens to expose I am no longer passed out. I remember Jay hit me, but this feeling isn't coming from that. If I had to guess, they drugged me. I suppose this makes sense, especially if you want to cover a lot of ground without an unwilling traveler giving away your location every two seconds. Rendering them unconscious would be the easiest way to accomplish it.

Based on the skyline, height, and shape of the room, I would have to say I'm being held in a building of some kind. A tall one most likely converted from offices to flop houses. It certainly isn't a proper home because the bed looks ready to fall apart. Even though yellowed with time, the walls at one point appear to have been stark white, and aside from one large whiteboard, nothing else is hanging in here. The other issue is that aside from this stupid decrepit bed, they have stripped the room of anything I could use as a weapon. Not to mention there sure as shit isn't any place I can hide. So, in a nutshell... I'm screwed and not in the fun, toe-curling Pestilence sort of way.

"So, what's the game plan here?"

"What do you mean the plan hasn't changed?"

"Don't you think having a damn angry horseman chasing after his bitch—"

"Don't call her that, and don't ever claim she belongs to him," Jay hisses. How noble of the asshole to defend my honor after he had no problem punching me. A real damn gentleman this jackass turned out to be.

"Alright then, how do you feel about this? Your damn girlfriend is going to bring hell raining down on us."

"Technically, not hell. The being who created us is the same one responsible for their existence. The same one you pray to." The one I recognize but can't place corrects the talkative one.

"Bullshit."

"Perhaps if you read the damn book you insist on carrying, you might learn a thing or two because, trust me, they are biblical, not demonic." Well, at least one of them has a semblance of intellect. Regardless if one of them has an IQ in the double digits, I have no intention of waiting around to see what they or—better yet—Jay has planned for me. To accomplish this, I need to get out of these damn restraints. "The plan is we continue to our destination. Once we arrive, there is nothing one damn rider can do to us. Now get some rest because we leave in five minutes. Oh, and dose your girl again."

Shit. Is he talking about me? If he is, I may use this to my advantage by pretending I'm still out of it. Perhaps the amount they give me will be reduced, and if so, I may wake up long before they plan for it to happen. Lying back on the bed and pretending I'm not awake while they inject me with god knows what is one of the hardest things I've ever had to do, but if it gets me back to my son, then pretending is precisely what I'm going to do.

*****

The next time I come to, my surroundings are different, confirming they did drug me, and it wasn't with the half dose I was hoping for.

"About time you woke up. I was beginning to wonder if they overdosed you."

"Where am I, Jay?"

"On your way to your new life."

"I don't want a new life."

"Too bad we took the choice from you."

"I just want to go home to my son."

"He's not your son. He's some kid you got saddled with because his own mom didn't want him."

"Fuck you, Jay."

"Maybe if you had made better choices than the ones you did, you wouldn't be in this situation right now."

"I'm not ashamed of any decision I've made, and I can sure as shit handle making my own choices when it comes to my life."

"I'm not so sure you can based on some of the shit ones you made lately."

"Like letting you think I ever wanted anything to do with you?"

"Like fucking a being who isn't even mortal. Hell, he probably doesn't even have a cock."

"Trust me, he doesn't lack in that department. I could describe it in great detail if you want me to." Because there is one damn thing for certain. The image of him walking into the water and lying underneath me is forever burned into my brain. Ninety years from now, if asked, I will still be able to describe every facet of his abundantly beautiful cock, and how fast he learned how to make me beg for it. Wisely I opt to keep the last part to myself. Especially when the color on his face informs me it would have been a huge mistake.

"Stop saying that," he screams as he leaps to his feet. Okay, too far, and if I don't want this asshole hitting me again, I need to learn some humility pretty damn quick.

"Sorry," I mumble as I avert my eyes.

"You're testing my fucking patience."

"I won't do it again. I promise," is the soft, mumbled response I give him while raising my hands submissively.

"Better." He snaps, and the tension in the air dissipates when he stops advancing.

"What are we doing, Jay? Why are you doing this?" I ask, lifting my bound hands.

"We are joining up with a group of like-minded men and women. People who don't care for the fuckers who believe they are in charge of our destiny. We plan on regaining our independence; if the other assholes of this world want to follow their rules, fine. We simply don't intend to do this any longer. In short, Greer, I'm taking back what those fuckers took from me. A life, a woman to service my every whim, need and desire, and most importantly, claim fucking power to rule over sheep like Avalon."

"Something tells me you didn't have any of these things prior to their arrival." This comment may have pushed him a little too far because he is out of the chair he returned to and is storming over to where I am lying on the floor.

"If you doubt me so much, then I'll just have to prove how wrong you are," he snarls as he yanks me flat.

"Don't do this, Jay," I scream as I twist and turn, trying to break free from his grasp.

"Scream for your horseman now, Greer. Let's see if he rides in to save you." And screaming is exactly what I do. Not only do I scream… I buck wildly, hoping to break his hold on me and — if I'm lucky — possibly his dick.

His hand slams down on my neck, pinning me to the floor and cutting off much of my airway. He yanks my jeans. The button flies up, hitting the wall over my head, and the sound of the zipper ripping apart confirms it is now as useless as the button spinning next to my face. With my pants down past my knees, he quickly pulls out his flaccid dick to stroke it to prepare for what he has planned for me.

When he slams his mouth against mine, I take the opportunity to latch down on his lips and bite as hard as I can. His screams echo around the empty space as he yanks his bloody mouth away from mine.

"You like it fucking rough," he howls before hitting me several times. The flashes of blinding white lights burst across my vision as pain explodes across my face. "I'm going to make you forget all about that fucking rider."

Before I can stop him, he flips me over and presses my head against the floor as he yanks my ass up. Once done, he forces his way inside me with a groan. Horror fills every atom when I register what's happening to me.

"You want a fucking kid, then I'll give you one. Scream for me whore. Scream for the man who is claiming you. Feels fucking good, doesn't it?" he grunts as he thrusts inside me brutally.

No, no-no-no. My mind shrieks as the world spins around me. His weight forces me down against the floor as he continues his assault from behind.

Do-something-do-something-do-something.

My brain somehow believes these jumbled words are spoken, but his weight on my back and the hand clamped around my throat know these words live only within my head.

Twisting my hips as hard as I can, I somehow dislodge him, which allows me to flip to my back. Once there, my feet kick out, landing directly against the dick he used to attack me. The second he falls away from me, cradling his cock in his hand, I do the only thing I pray will save me....

"Pestilence!" I scream for my rider.

Chapter Thirty-One: Déjà vu

~ Pestilence Fall 2025 ~

WE HAVE BEEN TRACKING THEM THE entire day. Each time I believe we are close, we come up short, and the fear of what she is enduring mounts. Only Avalon's quiet assurance we will get to her in time keeps me from losing control. As much as I did not wish her to come, I'm glad to have her with me. In my moments of need, she is there to comfort me. I hope I do the same for her. The little lamb who called me here is truly a remarkable woman.

We have been searching nonstop for hours now, and even though Avalon has never so much as uttered a complaint, I know she needs a break. Pulling on my horse's reins halts our progression to provide her with the human minute I imagine she requires.

"What are you doing?"

"You require a break."

"I'm fine. We should keep going."

"No, little lamb, take a break." When she refuses to disembark, I reach up and gently remove her from Storm. "Fifteen minutes, lamb. We can spare fifteen minutes."

"But what if she—"

"No, don't do that. Please." I cannot bear the thought of anything my beautiful temptation may be suffering. "Take a couple minutes, get some water, and we will head back out after you have done as I requested." Reluctantly she agreed as she wonders into the thicker brush to relieve herself before returning to find the food and water I have sitting out for her.

"I'm not hungry."

"I will require you at full strength when we locate her."

"I will be—"

"Please eat, little lamb."

"You can be a hard-nosed pain in my ass. You know that, right?"

"And will stay this way for as long as I am present on this plane. Now if you please." I say as I sit down. Her shoulders slump, and much of the determination she has melts away. I am unsure what I could have said to result in this reaction, but whatever it was, I hope it does not happen again.

She quietly picks at her sandwich for several minutes until the silence feels like an oppressive weight against us.

"What is troubling you, little lamb?"

"Are you going to leave us also?"

"Someday. I imagine my creator will call me home someday, but not soon."

"So you'll leave Greer and Wren? Like Thanatos left me." This is when I realize why she has grown quiet. She fears her friend will suffer the same way she does. A sentiment she does not wish to perpetuate and one she will take responsibility for since I am sure she encouraged Greer to explore her growing attraction for me. Something I will forever be thankful she did.

"Not for a very long time, little lamb. If I have it my way, it will be after Wren is returned to the earth. I plan to remain with them as long as they permit me to stay."

"They?"

"Greer and Wren," I confirm. At least, this is what I believe she was inquiring about.

"How do you know? How do you know you'll be able to stay?"

"Because I have a task."

Her humorless little laugh is equal part disbelief, and how could I forget before saying, "What if your creator changes his mind? What if six months from now, he beckons you home?"

"Then, for the first time in my existence, I will be forced to refuse my father's request."

"You can do that?"

"I will."

"How?"

"Because my heart is here. It belongs to a few special souls living within this realm, and I will not leave them."

"So it's a choice you'll make. A choice to stay?"

"Yes."

"Oh," she quietly replies as she looks away. Her chest rises and falls faster than normal, and she refuses to meet my gaze.

"Did I say something wrong?"

"No. I'm glad you'll pick them over your duty."

"Yet you seem upset." Not only upset, but as she lifts her hand to swipe at her eyes, I believe I have made her cry. Is she relieved knowing I will always be here for her since Thanatos... Oh... damn... Thanatos. She is upset because she believes he chose our father when he could have chosen her. How could I be so insensitive? "Avalon, you have to believe he would have stayed if he could."

"If he could?"

"When he was sent, it was not to reap. It was to judge. He believed by going back, he could prevent us from coming. He could protect humanity. Protect... you. If there would have been any way for him to remain, I believe he would be here still."

"I used to think the same thing. I think I somehow managed to convince myself of it, but I'm not so sure anymore."

"He asks about you."

"My elderly neighbors used to ask about me when they didn't see me for a while. It didn't mean they couldn't live without me. That the thought of never seeing me again hurt them in a way they never knew was possible. They never felt like they couldn't breathe without me."

"Avalon—"

"I think we should just go." I am preparing to tell her my belief Thanatos loves her every bit as much as I love Wren and Greer, but a single scream in the night stops me dead in my tracks as all thoughts except one disappear. The scream belonged to Greer...

And she just screamed for me to help her.

*****

It seems grace and a little luck are on my side since Avalon also heard her shriek when it pierced the air because she sprinted toward Storm almost as fast as I did. Throwing my hand down to her while Storm rushes by; she snatches ahold as I flip her behind me. She has traveled with us long enough I don't have to tell her to hold on as she wraps her arms around my waist. Once I know she is securely held in place, I spur my horse to race in the direction of the woman I love.

The closer we get to the area where I believe she is being held, Avalon's grip tightens around my waist. High-rise buildings dot the landscape as the first sign of a sprawling metropolis comes into view.

"Pestilence, wait."

"She is here. I can sense her, little lamb."

"Regardless, we could be racing straight into a trap. Maybe this is all just a set-up to get you here. One orchestrated by the people who took her. We already know neither of us is high on their list of people they want to share space with."

"I am clearly not mortal, little lamb," I say, addressing her use of the word 'people' when speaking about us, which she clearly comprehends without my abrupt response.

"You know what I meant." And I do. Just as I know when Thanatos pushed my horse headlong into danger when Avalon needed help, I am preparing to do the same, but just as I had to be the voice of reason for him then, she has become mine now.

As hard as this is, I yank on his reins, forcing Storm to stop. Only because of the silence surrounding us can I hear the faint shouts announcing my arrival. This allows me to call upon the tendrils I will use to shield us.

"Um, Pestilence." Avalon's concern weighs heavily in her words when she realizes the death swirling around her becomes evident, but the little lamb has nothing to fear from my plague. The ones who took her are a different story.

"Fear not, little lamb, for I am the white rider. The bringer of scourge and disease. The embodiment of the black death. My plague seeks the weak, never the strong. As such, you will always be protected."

"Stop right there, Rider."

"Return what you took from me or face my wrath."

"Turn around, vacate this city, or prepare for your eminent death."

"You do not possess the ability to kill me. Yet I possess more than one way to end you." with my warning delivered, I release much of my plague. The tendrils race out, seeking any who oppose me. Like a missile homing in on its target, death is upon them before they utter their first screams.

As my feet slam against the ground, the vibration sends a wave toppling the mortals on the street. Avalon leaps from Storm before I can object or direct him to remove her from the battle. Pulling her behind me, I call forth more of my disease. The thick black tendrils curl around us, shielding us as they fire volley upon volley of arrows in our direction.

Once the last arrow falls, I can return the kind gesture they showed us. Such a gracious welcome should never go unreciprocated. Nocking the first of three projectiles. I remove the man from the roof. The woman who hides behind the truck and the man on the balcony. Avalon takes care of the man to my left. The one I did not see.

Again, they prepare for their assault, and I call forth my disease once more. The black death moves faster as it desires only one thing... release to claim its next victim. Once we have made it safely behind a van, I push the little lamb against it and remove victims four, five, and six. While my black death claims seven, eight, nine, and ten. This was when I noticed a man who seemed to be protected above all others. A band of men surround him as they escort him away from where the battle is underway.

"Little lamb, I must ask you for a favor. One I fear may place you in harm's way."

"Find Greer and get her safely out of here?"

"Yes. I will draw their attention and fire here." Her answer comes by way of her sliding her jacket off as she nocks another arrow. Her eyes seek mine as she waits for me to give her a clear path to the building we both believe they hold Greer in. With their focus on me, Avalon quietly slips away.

~ Avalon ~

Sneaking around the side of the building, I'm not afraid to admit my heart is pounding wildly in my chest. Greer is here. I know she is... Pestilence knows it... and the assholes who fight us know we know it.

Their first mistake was in taking something he holds sacred. It's not just an assumption I have come to. It is evident with every glance he stole of her, every time he says her name, the way he loves Wren. He somehow talked Thanatos into forgoing all else to bring him back, something I don't think I will ever be able to thank either of them enough for.

To have one of the riders depending on me for his every happiness is a task I don't take lightly, nor is it something I intend to fail. I slip through a door just as several men rush by, which sends my already racing heart into overdrive.

"Fuck-fuck-fuck-fuck!" I quietly repeat as I ascend the stairs to the second level. Unfortunately, the instant I step through the door, I am met with the cold dead stare of one of the first victims who fell by Pestilence's bow. My hand flies to my mouth as my ass hits the ground. Death is something I don't think I will ever grow used to seeing. At least, I hope it isn't because the day this becomes commonplace is when I'll have to face the fact that I have become everything I fought against.

This is when I decide to see how he is faring in this battle which is why I poke my head up only to see some bitch preparing to shoot him from behind as he gets ready to take out some asshole running away. With an arrow already nocked, I take aim and release the shot. The projectile barely misses its mark but alerts the bitch of my whereabouts. The problem is this doesn't stop her from returning fire, which she does. I move just as the arrow whizzes by my head, impaling the wall behind me.

"You bitch, you fucking shot at me," I yell as I decide turnabout is fair play, yanking the bow back up to return the damn favor.

I fire a second shot as some guy busts through the door and grabs me from behind. Reaching out, I snatch the bottle the dead man was drinking from and bash it into his head, knocking this asshole away from me. As he staggers back, I realize there is not enough time to prepare the bow, so with all the might I can manage, I slam the arrow through his chest. He stumbles back several feet, looking from me to the arrow buried in his body. His eyes come up to mine as his hand reaches to dislodge it, but this isn't the right choice since the second he pulls the arrow out, the color in his eyes fades before he collapses. A shuddering breath is the last sound he releases before death claims him.

Panting heavily, I spin to see if my body count includes two lives or just the one. Unfortunately, it looks like when the man grabbed me from behind, my arrow went wide, and while it may not have landed, it was enough to send the bitch scurrying away as Pestilence's tendrils prepared for their next attack. Since it appears he has this under control, not to mention I don't have any more arrows, I drop the bow and pull the dagger from my boot.

Three doors down, I hear what sounds like a struggle. I don't know if I'll find her inside this room or not. One thing is for certain, I sure as shit will not find Greer standing on the balcony like some wanna-be fucking Rapunzel waiting to let down her hair.

Caution is the key word here as I quietly slip through the door. The first room is vacant, but this isn't where the sounds originated. They're coming from the next room, and since I have no idea what I am walking into with the door closed, I am left debating if fast or slow is the better option. Here's hoping I won't be the next one to scream his name.

With one last deep breath, I open the door, and what I see snatches the damn oxygen from the room almost as fast as I can inhale the shit.

I am faced with Greer with her pants yanked down below her knees, with Jay on top of her. Greer's hands are restrained over her head. Jay's hand is knotted in her hair, preventing her from moving. The entire scene sends me back to when Calvin was still alive. When I was a powerless kid unable to stop him. And for the briefest of seconds, my legs refuse to move. My heart ceases to beat, my brain refuses to think, and my lungs refuse to work. I am reduced to that scared fucking little girl who prayed my mom and dad would come back to pull me out of the hell they dumped me in.

But I'm not that terrified little girl any longer. And my parents certainly aren't going to save the fucking day now any more than they did then. No. The simple truth is that if I want to protect my friend, it will have to be by my hand.

So, with my mind made up, I rush forward, grab him around the throat, and plunge the blade into his chest several times. If I had taken the extra time, I may have landed the blow where it would have dropped this fucker, but rather than striking vital organs, it was delivered to the left side of his chest.

Jay rips the blade out much as arrow boy did outside, a stupid rooky mistake because that blade was the only thing stemming the rush of blood now flowing from the damage I caused.

Two things happen next. First, I put myself between my injured friend and the fucker who hurt her, and second, he realizes if I'm here, then Pestilence isn't far behind. And if he catches him in here with a brutalized Greer, nothing in this world will save him from his vengeance. Which sends him rushing out of the room.

"Come on, Greer, we have to go," I tell her as I help her redress as much as her tattered clothes will allow.

With her leaning against me, I drag her out the door onto the balcony hallway just in time to see Pestilence's eyes settle on the man who started this entire interaction. Jay understands his mistake seconds before it's too late, causing his eyes to grow wide. He realizes any fight would be futile because you cannot fight what you cannot see or stop what has no form. In contrast, the rage filling the rider's eyes as his tendrils lash out to knock Jay from his feet confirms this man's life won't last as long as it takes me to descend the stairs. The only problem is Pestilence has left the safety the van provided, so they are now firing arrow after arrow at him, and most are finding their mark.

"I need you to move faster, Greer. I have to get you out of here so I can help Pestilence."

"Pestilence. He's here?" she cries.

"Yes."

"He came."

"Of course, he came, but a lot of people are fighting him, so please try to hurry," I plead as I pull her through the door and down the stairs. When we exit the door on the ground floor, I promptly whistle, praying Storm will hear me and heed my call.

As I continue to help her move further away from where they are fighting, Storm runs up behind me. With the last of my waning strength, I push Greer on Storm before climbing in front of her. I just need to ensure some distance between her and the fight before I return to his side. Here's hoping he can hold out until then.

The instant I believe I have her at a safe distance from the worst of it, I slide off Storm but provide him with specific instructions.

"Take her to safety, Storm. I'm going back for your rider. Greer, don't get off this horse no matter what happens."

Storm immediately complies as he dashes further away from the fight while I turn and sprint back into it. If Thanatos is watching, I imagine he has a sense of déjà vu and is likely calling me a dumbass. Right now, I can't say I disagree with this sentiment.

The closer I get to where the main battle occurred, the icy fingers of dread slither up my spine because of the familiarity this brings back from the time I crept through the streets of Charleston to rescue another rider... my rider. Not to mention all the sounds that previously filled the air are gone, replaced by an eerie silence.

Since losing my only weapons, I nearly do a jig when I find some poor sap with an arrow through his eye. It's not his death I want to celebrate — well, not entirely his death — it's the bow and quiver full of arrows I am ecstatic about. I may not be the best shot, but it's better than sashaying my ass in there with no weapons at all and no way of defending myself or, if the worse has come to pass, an injured Pestilence.

When I arrive at the last place I saw him, I take a second to steady my hands, arm the bow, and calm my racing heart before I bring the bow up and step around the corner. And the person who greets me is the last motherfucker I ever thought I would find.

"Jared!"

Chapter Thirty-Two: Reunion

But each person is tempted when he is lured and enticed by his own desire. James 1:14.

~ Avalon Fall 2025 ~

HIS LAUGH FILLS THE AIR AS I take in the scene around me. Most of the men and women who opposed us are dead. I can't say whose hand they fell by. Pestilence or the bastard who tricked me into breaking the first seal.

As startling as it is to see all these people scattered around him, it's finding Pestilence on his knees with a dagger pressed to his chest, directly next to an arrow that pierced his heart. Something I am quickly learning is like the rider's own form of kryptonite. If not for the handful of hair Jared has fisted, Pestilence's head would be slumped forward.

I'm not the only one to hear the creaking of the strings as I pull the arrow further back into position.

"I wouldn't do that, little lamb, and my name is not Jared. It's Raum. But I think you already know that."

"I don't give a fuck. Now let him go."

Jared… or Raum… or whatever his fucking name is, clicks his tongue several times as a wicked grin covers his face. "Then what leverage would I have throughout this negotiation?"

"I don't negotiate with fucking birdmen."

"Cute, yet just as incorrect as the name. What I am is an immensely powerful demon who has the ability to change into a raven."

"And again, I don't give a fuck."

"I see your vast vocabulary has diminished since last we traveled together."

"What do you want, asshole?"

"You—or, in reality—your hands are the only things I require. Such a shame they must still be functioning and attached to you for what I need them to do."

"Me? You think either me or my hands are going anywhere with you?"

"No. I am under no illusion of your willingness to work with me. Hence, I tempted these mortals until they provided me with a boon I knew you would want. Of course, a rider wasn't my first choice. The woman was, but one should never look a gift rider in the mouth. I believe this is an accurate saying. Is it not?"

"It's a gift horse, fucker."

"You say it your way. I'll say it mine."

"So what is it you really want?" I ask as I pull the string tighter.

"I believe it is time for the next seal to be broken. Don't you?"

"I'm not breaking another seal."

"It is... of course, your right as the lamb to refuse your path."

"Glad we agree on something." The first drop of blood falls from my fingers because of the pressure from the bowstrings poised to fire the arrow I still hold nocked there. Let's face it, I'm not even entirely sure if I'm doing this correctly. No one ever thought to teach me how to fire one of these things, but it makes sense now why pre-horsemen archers wore gloves when shooting a bow.

"Then you leave me with no option but to take this rider's life."

"What?" He plunges the blade into his chest rather than answering me. "Stop! Wait!" I scream.

"Mere millimeters separate his heart from my blade. I promise you the next one will not miss."

"I don't even have the damn second seal."

"Fortunately for you, I do," he counters before tossing the paper at my feet.

"Don't do it, little lamb," Pestilence mutters. Raum's response is to shift the blade, which has Pestilence howling in pain.

"Now hold your tongue, rider, as I negotiate with the lamb."

"You have to know if I call another rider, they will never let you get away with this."

"I have a very distinct feeling the rider will be busy annihilating humanity," he says slowly, enunciating each word dramatically before finishing in a rush. "So I'll take my chances."

"I will not break the seal."

"So be it. Just remember, his blood is on your hands."

I release the arrow, and I can't believe how still he stands, only moving his head at the last second to avoid the projectile while I quickly nock another one. The blood flowing from my fingers made the task more difficult than necessary. "Take the fucking blade out of his chest."

"As you wish," he smirks, ripping the blade from the wound. Pestilence screams again from the interaction. "What is it to be, young one? Will you save the rider who protected you and the ones you hold dear, or will you allow him to perish? All to prevent his brother from arriving."

"You can't kill one of the riders," I snarl as I close one eye, hoping to sight my target better this time.

"Tsk-tsk-tsk. Are you certain of this? I suppose the better question is, are you willing to bet his life on it because I think you are aware by now I am no mere man."

"Yeah, asshole, I kind of figured that out when you turned into a fucking bird."

"Not a bird. A raven. A raven whose job is to carry the souls shunned by their father to live the rest of their days in torment and torture within my realm. Forgotten souls cast aside from their creator. Such a sad... sad tale."

"You mean to hell."

"You mortals have such a limited understanding of the worlds around you. *But...*" The way he says this word with his overly dramatic emphasis is infuriating. He actually thinks he's better than the rider and certainly better than me. Self-righteous little prick. "If it makes things easier for your simple mind and helps this conversation progress, then yes, young soul... to hell."

"Release him first."

He clicks his tongue while tilting his head. "I am many things, but trusting of your kind is not one of them. You will break the seal, and you will do it now, or I will end this rider."

"Don't do it, little lamb," Pestilence mutters through violent coughs. The amount of blood covering his shirt is alarming.

"You should know when I take his life, he will not return to his realm. I will carry him to mine. Where the beings he has fought so hard to hold at bay will shred his soul over and over again until he begs for his end. But no end will be granted. He will remain my minion... my plaything until time ceases to exist."

"Look at me, little lamb. Avalon, I am not afraid." His jaw is set, his eyes determined, but I cannot stop the trembling of my hands.

"Four."

"Avalon, no."

"Three."

"Humanity is worth saving."

"Two." I need to think. I need one fucking second to think... to decide what the right course of action is here. Fuck-fuck-fuck. If it was me kneeling there, would he let me die? Would he let my soul be carried to hell?

"Consider the camp, Avalon. Think of Greer and Wren," he begs, and his frantic pleas tear my heart to pieces as I continue to battle with what my heart wants and my head is demanding.

"I don't know what to do, Pestilence," I cry. This rider doesn't deserve what Raum will do to him, but what am I sentencing humanity to if I do as this asshole demands from me?

"One.

"It's okay, little lamb, don't cry for me." My vision blurs from the tears filling them as I look from Raum to Pestilence to the sky above.

"Prepare for an existence of pain, Rider." Raum laughs as he brings the knife up to plunge into Pestilence's chest. In this instant, I see Wren and the devastation of losing the man he views as his dad. An honor and name the rider never got to hear him say.

"I'm sorry, Pestilence, please forgive me," I quietly plead.

"I can't—can't...." My eyes slip closed, knowing the hell I have chosen.

"...let them lose you." As I snap the second seal.

Pestilence's Judgment

Coming Soon,

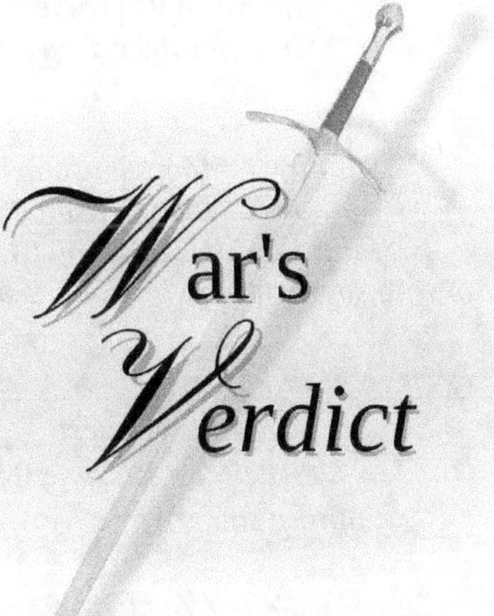

Also by *Marcelle Valentine*

Scarred by Fate Series

Ritual Nightmare
Breaking Purgatory
Fate's Ritual
Opposing Tartarus
Sacrificial Endings

The Ash Rock Series

Shadow's Moon Season One
Shadow's Moon Season Two
Shadow's Moon Season Three
Coming soon Shadow's Moon Season Four

Arrival of the Four Horsemen Series

Death's Inquest
Pestilence's Judgment
Coming soon War's Verdict

Kindle Vella

Shadow's Moon Season One through Four
Seized by Sin
Coming soon Silverwood Throne

Teaser

What could be worse than a pack that hates you? Having a mate who does not want you.

Grab your copy of Shadow's Moon to follow Shay story as she navigates the world alone

Acknowledgments

One more rider down, two more to meet. I hope you enjoyed reading Pestilence, Greer, and Wren's story. Up next is War, and he is nothing like his other brothers. While we will meet new characters in his book, the ones you have already grown to love will have cameos. The rebellion rising against our riders should prepare themselves.

As always, my deepest heartfelt thanks go out to every reader who took a chance on my books. If you love one series, I hope you might try the others, and if you like them, perhaps you'll let other readers know.

I could not have completed this series without those who supported me, including my beta readers, my niece Ashley, my mom, and my daughter Melanie. But most importantly, I want to thank my grandson, who was the inspiration for Wren. Every challenge Wren faced when trying to communicate with the world around him is something my sweet boy experiences daily. He is a bright spot in this world and has touched my life in a very profound way.

I have several projects in progress. Book three in the Horsemen series is in the final stages of publishing. I also have a Vella underway about a certain fae prince, which readers of my Ash Rock series may recognize. My standalone serial killer novella will be coming to Kindle and Kindle Unlimited later this year, and readers of my other series may find an Easter egg about the next series I have planned within the pages of this book.

Thank you to my husband and family, who have been my biggest cheerleaders. I love every one of you.

And finally, to every author that has ever put pen to paper, fingers to keyboard, whose work only inspired me more to follow this dream, I hope I do not disappoint.

Thank you
Marcelle

Newsletter

Consider visiting my website and signing up for my newsletter to receive updates on this series and all my future projects.

https://www.marcellevalentine.com

Please consider leaving a review if you enjoyed the book. Any thoughts are appreciated and will only help me improve the story. Reviews also provide new readers with a way to find my books.

You can also follow me on social media

Facebook
Goodreads
Instagram
TikTok

About the Author

Marcelle Valentine has long been an admirer of creating worlds where people can get lost. From a young age, her active imagination took her on epic journeys to faraway places where troubles and friendships abound. After discovering the intriguing world of Paranormal/Fantasy Romance, which stirred up memories of all those distant places and friends, her desire to write returned. She invites you to travel with her during these journeys and get lost in a world with friends, enemies, and lovers, all firmly rooted in the supernatural realm. Marcelle is the author of the Scarred by Fate Series and the episodic series Shadow's Moon. She lives in Ohio with her husband. She has two children, three grandchildren, and one lovable, lazy Great Dane.

Marcellevalentine. com

Facebook

Goodreads

Instagram

TikTok

www.ingramcontent.com/pod-product-compliance
Lightning Source LLC
Chambersburg PA
CBHW051329020726
47501CB00007B/1981
* 9 7 8 1 9 5 8 1 5 4 2 6 7 *